Anthony Gilbert and The Murder Room

>>> This title is part of The Murder Room, our series dedicated to making available out-of-print or hard-to-find titles by classic crime writers.

Crime fiction has always held up a mirror to society. The Victorians were fascinated by sensational murder and the emerging science of detection; now we are obsessed with the forensic detail of violent death. And no other genre has so captivated and enthralled readers.

Vast troves of classic crime writing have for a long time been unavailable to all but the most dedicated frequenters of second-hand bookshops. The advent of digital publishing means that we are now able to bring you the backlists of a huge range of titles by classic and contemporary crime writers, some of which have been out of print for decades.

From the genteel amateur private eyes of the Golden Age and the femmes fatales of pulp fiction, to the morally ambiguous hard-boiled detectives of mid twentieth-century America and their descendants who walk our twenty-first century streets, The Murder Room has it all. **>>>**

The Murder Room
Where Criminal Minds Meet

themurderroom.com

Anthony Gilbert (1899–1973)

Anthony Gilbert was the pen name of Lucy Beatrice Malleson. Born in London, she spent all her life there, and her affection for the city is clear from the strong sense of character and place in evidence in her work. She published 69 crime novels, 51 of which featured her best known character, Arthur Crook, a vulgar London lawyer totally (and deliberately) unlike the aristocratic detectives, such as Lord Peter Wimsey, who dominated the mystery field at the time. She also wrote more than 25 radio plays, which were broadcast in Great Britain and overseas. Her thriller *The Woman in Red* (1941) was broadcast in the United States by CBS and made into a film in 1945 under the title *My Name is Julia Ross*. She was an early member of the British Detection Club, which, along with Dorothy L. Sayers, she prevented from disintegrating during World War II. Malleson published her autobiography, *Three-a-Penny*, in 1940, and wrote numerous short stories, which were published in several anthologies and in such periodicals as *Ellery Queen's Mystery Magazine* and *The Saint*. The short story 'You Can't Hang Twice' received a Queens award in 1946. She never married, and evidence of her feminism is elegantly expressed in much of her work.

By Anthony Gilbert

Scott Egerton series

Tragedy at Freyne (1927)

The Murder of Mrs
  Davenport (1928)

Death at Four Corners (1929)

The Mystery of the Open
  Window (1929)

The Night of the Fog (1930)

The Body on the Beam (1932)

The Long Shadow (1932)

The Musical Comedy
  Crime (1933)

An Old Lady Dies (1934)

The Man Who Was Too
  Clever (1935)

**Mr Crook Murder
  Mystery series**

Murder by Experts (1936)

The Man Who Wasn't
  There (1937)

Murder Has No Tongue (1937)

Treason in My Breast (1938)

The Bell of Death (1939)

Dear Dead Woman (1940)
  aka *Death Takes a Redhead*

The Vanishing Corpse (1941)
  aka *She Vanished in the Dawn*

The Woman in Red (1941)
  aka *The Mystery of the
  Woman in Red*

Death in the Blackout (1942)
  aka *The Case of the Tea-
  Cosy's Aunt*

Something Nasty in the
  Woodshed (1942)
  aka *Mystery in the Woodshed*

The Mouse Who Wouldn't
  Play Ball (1943)
  aka *30 Days to Live*

He Came by Night (1944)
  aka *Death at the Door*

The Scarlet Button (1944)
  aka *Murder Is Cheap*

A Spy for Mr Crook (1944)

The Black Stage (1945)
  aka *Murder Cheats the Bride*

Don't Open the Door (1945)
  aka *Death Lifts the Latch*

Lift Up the Lid (1945)
  aka *The Innocent Bottle*

The Spinster's Secret (1946)
  aka *By Hook or by Crook*

Death in the Wrong Room
  (1947)

Die in the Dark (1947)
  aka *The Missing Widow*

Death Knocks Three Times
  (1949)

Murder Comes Home (1950)

A Nice Cup of Tea (1950)
  aka *The Wrong Body*

Lady-Killer (1951)

Miss Pinnegar Disappears (1952)
aka *A Case for Mr Crook*

Footsteps Behind Me (1953)
aka *Black Death*

Snake in the Grass (1954)
aka *Death Won't Wait*

Is She Dead Too? (1955)
aka *A Question of Murder*

And Death Came Too (1956)

Riddle of a Lady (1956)

Give Death a Name (1957)

Death Against the Clock (1958)

Death Takes a Wife (1959)
aka *Death Casts a Long Shadow*

Third Crime Lucky (1959)
aka *Prelude to Murder*

Out for the Kill (1960)

She Shall Die (1961)
aka *After the Verdict*

Uncertain Death (1961)

No Dust in the Attic (1962)

Ring for a Noose (1963)

The Fingerprint (1964)

The Voice (1964)
aka *Knock, Knock! Who's There?*

Passenger to Nowhere (1965)

The Looking Glass Murder (1966)

The Visitor (1967)

Night Encounter (1968)
aka *Murder Anonymous*

Missing from Her Home (1969)

Death Wears a Mask (1970)
aka *Mr Crook Lifts the Mask*

Murder is a Waiting Game (1972)

Tenant for the Tomb (1971)

A Nice Little Killing (1974)

Standalone Novels

The Case Against Andrew Fane (1931)

Death in Fancy Dress (1933)

The Man in Button Boots (1934)

Courtier to Death (1936)
aka *The Dover Train Mystery*

The Clock in the Hatbox (1939)

Missing from Her Home

Anthony Gilbert

An Orion book

Copyright © Lucy Beatrice Malleson 1969

The right of Lucy Beatrice Malleson to be identified as the author of this work has been asserted in accordance with the Copyright, Designs and Patents Act 1988.

This edition published by
The Orion Publishing Group Ltd
Orion House
5 Upper St Martin's Lane
London WC2H 9EA

An Hachette UK company
A CIP catalogue record for this book is available from the British Library

ISBN 978 1 4719 1034 0

www.orionbooks.co.uk

THE CHILD WAS REPORTED MISSING at 7:35 on Friday, the fourteenth. Her description, supplied by her mother, read: Nine years and ten months, tall for her age, gray eyes, fair complexion, nose small, mouth somewhat large (but shaped like an angel's, insisted Mrs. Toni), long brown hair fastened with an ornamental clip, wearing a pale blue dress and a dark blue blazer, knee-length white stockings, brown shoes. No distinguishing marks, no scars.

"Can't be above half a million kids in the Greater London area alone answering to that description," observed Sergeant Garrick, who happened to be the duty officer when the distraught mother descended like a whirlwind on the orderly station. "According to her, no boy friends. Yes, I know she's young, but Mumma Toni comes from Italy, wherever Angela's father came from, and they mature early there."

Everyone who knew Angela Toni agreed that she was pretty, lively, well mannered and docile within reasonable limits. True, she seemed rather more devoted to Mumma than was normal, but then she was a foreigner. Teachers praised her in a conservative way, never likely to set the Thames on fire, they said, but, as Arthur Crook was to observe later, plenty of people prefer London's river the way it is. A pleasure to have in the class, got on all right with everyone. Only some of her schoolmates appeared to have reservations. She was a funny kid, they said, meaning there was a quality of remoteness from themselves and their interests, but they always came back to the fact that Mumma was a foreigner, which could explain anything.

But if young Angela was just another kid to the neighbor-

1

hood, everyone knew the mother and no one wanted to come up against her twice. Her forebears had presumably carried daggers in their stockings. Mumma carried hers in her voice. People who had come up against her had actually been known to turn off a main road into a side turning sooner than encounter her again. Short and stolid, always dressed in black: black skirt, black jumper, black shawl, eyes and hair to match and teeth as white as newly erected tombstones—if there were many like her about we could start queuing up for the dole, one of the dental registrars at St. Richards had been heard to remark. Anyone else in that getup would have suggested a funeral, but not Mumma. It came of being a wop, they agreed. The dark clothes only emphasized the vividness of her personality.

She was an indefatigable worker—if there ever had been a Puppa Toni no one knew anything about him, and it would be surprising if the Saxon child had had an Italian father, so Mumma had to provide for both of them—one of her jobs was to take the morning papers around the wards of St. Richards, the local general hospital. In she would come, as soon as breakfast was over, bowed down by the bundle of daily papers so that sometimes she actually seemed to waddle across the floor. But it would have been a fast duck that could have kept pace with her. Someone in Men's Surgical had once called out, "This way, duck," and the name stuck. "Here comes Mumma Duck," they said.

She had her own ritual for delivering the papers. At the first bed in Women's General she would pause to beam at the young mother anxiously affixing her eyelashes for the day. "And what for you?" Mumma would demand, rolling her little black eyes till sometimes it seemed she must roll them out of their sockets. "A nice dish of macaroni—ha!" And she would produce the *Record* and the *Daily News*. The next bed held a gaunt patient recently retired from a lifetime of teaching. Here Mumma changed her tactics. "For you," she would say in reverential tones, "the spaghetti Bolognese," and she would whip out a copy of the *Times*, like a conjurer whipping a rabbit out of a hat. It was believed that Miss Adams was the only patient on the ward who had ever asked for the *Times*.

Now and again Mumma would shake her head. "No spaghetti on the market this morning," she would declare. "No spaghetti for you." Her arms waved like trees in a wind; her voice would have done her credit at the Wailing Wall. Then, with a brisk change of tone, "You take the *Post* instead?"

So she would proceed from bed to bed. This job accomplished, she would scuttle back to the confectioner and news agent for whom she worked and put in the rest of the morning there. In the afternoon she lent a hand at the newly opened betting shop in the High Street.

"In my country," she would boast, "we have the lottery every day, every day."

As for Signor Toni, the mention of his name made Mumma shout with laughter; her whole sturdy frame quivered. "You know what he does?" she would demand. "He collect the rubbish, the garbage, and one day they carry him away with the rest. And good riddance." She would clap her hands and grin. No one dared question her about Angela's father. Everyone knows that these Eyties use a stiletto as you or I would use a pair of eyebrow tweezers.

Her daughter Angela was the center of her world. They lived in a couple of rooms in Derwent Street, where they played the radio loudly, too loudly to please some of the other tenants, who would bang indignantly on the wall. "Can't you keep this radio down?" the landlady would implore. And Mumma, genuinely scandalized, would demand, "But if we cannot be happy when the sun shines, when may we be happy?" "If it was only when the sun shone," retorted the harassed landlady, "it wouldn't matter. But that thing of yours goes on every blessed minute you're in the house."

Because they secretly feared her or were compassionate and knew that foreigners can't help being what they are, no one pressed his objections to the limit, though one acid spinster who occupied a downstairs room for some time remarked that a murder could take place and you'd never hear the victim's dying screams.

Mumma roared with laughter when she heard that. "I do you a favor—yes?" It was no good trying to get the better of Mumma, you might as well save your breath and call it a day.

On Friday evening Mumma worked late helping to clean out the betting shop. Every Friday at midday she would nip around the corner and leave money and a note for Angel to buy two portions of rock salmon and three of chips, always the same. Others might prefer skate, but for Mumma it had to be rock salmon or nothing. Don Billing, who kept

3

the fish shop, always saved her a double portion; he said it was as much as his life was worth not to. On Friday, the fourteenth, she followed her normal routine, but when she came back to Derwent Street the rooms were dark, there was no sign of Angel, though money and note had disappeared. Mumma fell into transports of alarm. It was her secret fear that one day some appalling fate would overtake her darling, who had, as most people correctly surmised, been born without the blessing of her Church, though mother and daughter invariably attended the ten o'clock Mass at Our Lady of the Redemption, after which, if the weather was propitious, they would go out for the day. If it was wet they stayed at home and the radio did overtime.

When she found no trace of her darling, Mumma bustled around to the fish shop, where there was still an appreciable queue. As she thrust past them without ceremony, a newcomer to the neighborhood caught her by the arm. "Here, that's the end of the queue," he said, and muttered something to his neighbor about these wops not knowing their place. But before Mumma could explode, Don leaned forward to call out, "What is it, Mumma?"

"My daughter, my Angel, she has been here?"

"That's right. About an hour ago. Bit later than usual, but being such a wet night she might have waited for the rain to blow over."

"Some hopes," muttered someone else impatiently.

"Two of rock salmon, three of chips, same as always. What's up, Mumma?"

"She is not there," cried Mumma. "My Angel is not there."

A woman who had just been served, and who had strong views about the invasion of her precious country by anyone not in possession of a British passport and a white skin, sniggered and said, "Keeping herself warm somewhere else, maybe."

A sort of hiss of warning ran through the waiting line, all of whom knew Mumma by reputation, if not in person. Without an instant's hesitation Mumma snatched the woman's packet of hot chips from her hands and flung it full in the sneering, insinuating face. The woman jumped back with a scream of pain. "You're mad, you should be locked up," she spluttered.

"So now I am mad—I am mad and my daughter is a bad girl. I tell you . . ." Here she employed an epithet that

4

would have made even Arthur Crook blanch, if he'd been bilingual—and if no one in the crowd could translate it accurately either, most of them could make a pretty good guess.

"Best be getting home, lady," Billing advised the outraged customer.

"Here, what about my chips?" the woman whined.

"You and your chips," screamed Mumma. "They are all there, isn't it? Answer me—have I taken one, even one?"

"They're all dirty," the woman protested. "They've been on the floor, you can't expect me to eat them."

"Why not?" Mumma demanded. "You spew the dirt out of your mouth, you can also take it in."

"They were red-hot, you—you madwoman."

"So now you accuse Mr. Billing because he does not sell you cold chips."

Someone touched the woman's arm. "Take my tip and get out while you're all in one piece," she was advised.

Don Billing looked worried. "There's one thing, Mumma. She was brought here in a car."

"My Angel in a car? Never. Never in this world would she do such a thing. She has been warned . . ."

"Well," said Don, looking as if he expected a packet of flaming chips in his own troubled face, "just thought I'd mention it. I mean, it was late for her, six-thirty, and then I happened to look up and there she was, getting out of a car."

"And perhaps you see her getting back into the car?" suggested Mumma scornfully.

"Well, no, but then the chap wouldn't be allowed to park here, there's a double yellow line."

"You and your yellow lines. Next time you will tell me she descended in a chariot of fire." Without waiting for a reply she turned on her heel and marched out of the shop.

Sergeant Garrick was the duty sergeant that evening. He recognized Mumma at once—well, everyone knew her, but not this dynamo of a woman who looked as though she had never smiled in her life.

A young constable came forward, but she brushed him aside. "Give me the sergeant," she declared, "and if there is anyone bigger than the sergeant, then I see him. I want," she reiterated, "every damn copper on the station."

"Tell me what's wrong, Mrs. Toni," the sergeant urged. He was a married man himself, with two daughters, one of them no older than Angela. He knew that nothing except concern for her beloved child could have wrought this change in Mumma. "It's not Angela, is it?"

Up came her head, brown leathery skin, black darting eyes like stones. "Why you say that? What you know?"

"You're never in this sort of a stew just on your own account," the sergeant said shrewdly.

"You have news," she accused him furiously. "You know and you tell me nothing."

"How can we know till you tell us? There hasn't been an accident?"

"An accident? You should tell me. My Angel, she went for the fish to Mr. Billing as always, and—she is gone."

"Disappeared, you mean? Now, Mumma, calm down. We can't help you unless we have your story. If you won't tell us we'll have to guess, and the odds are we could guess wrong. What time was this when she went to Billing's?"

"He says half past six, though always my Angel go before six o'clock. Half past five they unlock the door and my Angel is waiting. But today he tells me half past six."

"There could be a reason for that. It's a wet night."

"It was not wet at half past five when she go to the shop, the rain start at six. Do you take me for a fool? I am a citizen, you are here to protect me and mine, so—find my Angel for me." She looked as though she expected him to wave a wand and produce the missing child from thin air.

"You mean, she bought the fish and didn't bring it home."

Mumma looked as if she were about to blow up. "I say it—I say it—I say it. She bought the fish, she did not come home."

"She could have gone to see a friend. That does happen."

"She would be home when her Mumma comes in. Like a clock is my Angel. I leave my work, I take off my apron, I exchange my shoes—" She went through a vigorous mime of untying an apron, kicking off a pair of shoes, donning another pair. "I come back, and what do I find? No light, no Angel, no fish. And you speak to me of an accident."

"It's not likely, Mrs. Toni, I mean in that case we should have been notified. Everyone round here knows Angela. You're sure she didn't leave you a note?"

"It is a fine thing when a girl leaves a note for her Mumma. If she has something to say she say it to her face."

6

"I'm sure she does," Sergeant Garrick agreed, thinking chaps in Vietnam must feel something like this, never knowing where the next bomb's going to burst. "But say, just for the sake of argument, she went round to a friend . . ."

The bomb exploded, nearly blowing him off his feet. "On a Friday? My Angel? On another night perhaps, but never Friday. Friday is pay night. Friday is like the Jewish Sabbath, Friday is for the family. Fridays my Angel fetches the fish, afterwards perhaps we go to the pictures or later I tell the cards—oh no, my Angel would never visit a friend on a Friday."

Rum lot these wops, thought the constable, who was listening with all his ears. The Virgin Mary on the one hand and the cards on the other. Wouldn't like her on my back, he thought.

"But there is more," Mumma was insisting. She caught the young constable's eye. "So you have nothing to do but listen to what does not concern you? I pay from my rates to support a—a young bull . . ."

"Get back to those reports, Constable," said Sergeant Garrick hurriedly, hoping the super wouldn't take it into his head to visit the nick this evening. In her present mood Mumma was perfectly capable of giving him a black eye if she didn't like his attitude. "Now, Mrs. Toni, we want to do everything we can for you, but you must help us, that's the only way we can help Angela. You say there is something else?"

"It is a lie," vociferated Mumma scornfully. "My Angel—she is not that kind of a girl."

"What have you been hearing?"

"They say she is seen coming out of a car."

Garrick stiffened. Up till now he had been prepared to regard the girl's absence as a prank; the mention of the car changed all that.

"Whose car?"

"How should I know? It is only what that Billing says. Ask him."

"I will. But—is there anyone you can think of who might have given her a lift—because it was a wet night, I mean?" He stroked his chin nervously, wondering if twenty seconds hence he'd have a chin left to stroke.

"My Angel is a good girl—she was named for the Blessed

Virgin. Angela Mary—she does not go around riding in strange cars."

"Now, don't fly off the handle, Mumma," Garrick besought her. "It's the way I told you, we can't help you if we don't know as much as you do. Now, so far as you know, has Angel ever accepted a lift before?"

"Never. Never she would. It is some other girl . . ."

"There aren't many girls like your Angela about, and Don Billing—well, there's not much point him saying he saw her get out of a car if it's not true. Maybe someone gave her a lift, seeing it was so wet . . ." Only that didn't make sense and he knew it. Chaps who intended harm to little girls didn't meekly drive them where they wanted to go and then wait around chancing recognition. Unless it was someone a bit more skilled than most who was out to win her confidence. But even so, it seemed to him unlikely. She might come out of the shop with someone she knew. And clearly he hadn't given her a lift and then waited to run her home.

"I'll have another word with Don Billing," he promised Mumma. "Could be there's something he didn't remember right off."

"I come with you," declared Mumma instantly.

"You get right home, Mumma, and you wait. You don't want your girl to come back and find the place in darkness. You went to the hospital?"

"Hospitals?" sneered Mumma. "You think I let them have my Angela . . ."

"Well, she could have slipped and sprained her ankle or hit her head and—you don't have a phone, Mumma?" He put the question delicately. You never could be sure with these adoring Mums, they could turn into hellcats under your very eyes, and he only had two, like most people, and wanted to keep the use of them as long as possible.

"A stranger in my home?" cried Mumma indignantly. "A machine to call me, like a doorbell, come here, go there, answer me, now listen. We are private people, Mr. Garrick . . ."

"What I'm driving at," explained the sergeant patiently, aware that the typewriter behind him was moving with incredible slowness, and knowing that young coppers are no different from any other young chaps who don't mind seeing a stripe torn off a superior, "is, it might be she couldn't let you know."

"If someone has her in care they have feet—no? They can bring a message, they have hands, they can write a letter. If they don't know the address they know their way to the NICK"—she invested the word with more venom than the ancient fathers employed when describing hell—"they have bowels, do they not?"

"It's to be hoped so," murmured the sergeant faintly.

"They know how a mother would feel . . ." Even though they are Protestants, her voice implied. She might be a foreigner and sojourner on British soil, and her morals might be impugned behind her back, though never, unless the speaker was hungry for the churchyard, in her presence, but she never disguised the fact that she considered she lived in a heathen land.

"Forrester," said the sergeant, "get Mrs. Toni a cup of tea. You come and sit down for a minute, Mumma, I'll just get in touch with the hospital. You see, if she was hurt, she might not be able to explain right away who she was— a knock on the head gets you muddled, it's only an idea, but . . ."

Mumma collapsed like a pricked balloon. "Not my Angel," she whispered.

"Well, I don't suppose so. I said it was only an idea. If she was there, either you'd have heard or we should. Everyone knows Angela"—that wasn't altogether true; what he meant was that everyone knew Angela's mother and most of them would sooner have faced the atom bomb than run up against her in one of her moods—"but we mustn't leave any stone unturned. Here's your tea, Mumma. Now you drink that . . ." No one brought him tea at that rate, he reflected.

"Sugar's in the saucer," murmured the young constable.

But the hospital couldn't help. No little girl, conscious or unconscious, had been brought in that evening as the result of an accident. He even made them ring Casualty, but with the same result.

When Mrs. Toni had finished her tea, he said they'd run her home in a car, a nasty wet night, and she must be tired, but Mumma shook her solid dark head. "You want for that Mrs. Leonard to see me come back with a policeman?

9

Never have we had any shame. And it is not I who cannot walk or speak."

On the way back to Derwent Street, Mumma stopped at a florist's shop and yelled for the proprietor. He came, heady with indignation, till he saw who his visitor was. Mumma, not deigning to explain her situation, bought a bunch of anemones, purple and rose and white with black beseeching hearts. When she reached home she dumped them into a vase that she set in front of the statue of the Blessed Virgin, who was as much an inmate of the home as herself and her daughter. Kneeling down she recited a few decades of the rosary at top speed.

"You remember," she harangued the plaster figure, scrambling to her feet, "you not the only one to be worried over your Child." But when she went to cut bread and pour a glass of wine she felt more reassured than before. The police might be a worthy body of men and even, on occasion, compassionate, but when all was said and done they weren't mothers.

"It's enough to make you a bachelor for life," young Forrester commented when Mumma had marched out like an avenging army. "Imagine having her for your mother-in-law."

"Personally, if I was in a jam," was his sergeant's unsympathetic rejoinder, "I'd sooner have Mumma on my side than the Lord Chief Justice."

 2

DON BILLING WAS STILL dishing out fish-and-chips when the police arrived. He had been thinking about Angela Toni, so was less surprised than he might have been, though no one wants the rozzers turning up on his premises, particularly during working hours. Afterwards it occurred to him that it hadn't once gone through his mind that they were here to buy their suppers.

"Couldn't have chosen a more convenient time, I suppose?" he suggested when they'd made their errand clear.

"We're like time and tide, we wait for no man." That was Detective-Constable Dace, a small dark uncomfortable chap. "It's about this kid who's gone missing."

"Angel Toni?"

"You're not suggesting there could be more than one? Well, are you dead sure?"

"That it was Mumma Toni's girl? Take my Bible oath. I've had Mumma round, you know."

"So's the sergeant." They both grinned. "Probably put in for a couple of days' sick leave."

"Nothing unusual about her tonight?" said the other officer. "The kid, I mean."

"Same as always. Two of rock salmon, three of chips. Bit later than usual, though. Lucky I'd put the rock salmon under the counter or it 'ud have gone."

"Dead sure about the car?"

"Dead sure."

"Didn't happen to see if she got back into it, I suppose."

"Listen, mate. No driver 'ud park outside without one of your lot giving him a parking ticket instanter." It was funny how much Don felt he was involved. Another kid— well, they were up to all sorts of tricks, but this one was different. "Double yellow line," he amplified to the police. "He'd have to park round the corner in Partridge Street, if he could find room. Friday's a bad night—don't ask me why. All roads, he couldn't stop here."

Dace nodded. "Fair enough. Didn't happen to notice the car?"

"Well, not really. I'll tell you one thing, though, it stopped almost under a light, it was a bright green. I remember thinking it looked like some sort of huge beetle."

"Not so big, then?"

"Well, no. But bigger than a Mini. Could have been a Tiger-Moth, I suppose." He brooded. "I wouldn't stake my Aunt Fanny on it, though."

"Didn't see the number?" Dace answered his own question. "No, of course not."

"I stopped taking car numbers when I was a kid," Don

assured him. "Well, I didn't know I was going to be asked questions, did I?"

"Did you see if the driver was a man or a woman?"

"Oh, it was a chap, I did see that much. Youngish sort of chap, I'd say, but if you're going to ask me if I'd recognize him again, the answer's no."

"Don't know much about it if you think anyone 'ud accept identification on no more than that," said Dace heartily.

"And anyhow I was pretty busy. Maggie, that's the wife, she wasn't there, got a cold and I told her to stop away, and the girl I've got to help—with the chips, see—well, she hardly knows her arse from her elbow."

"Shouldn't have thought that mattered much, not here."

"Mind if I get back before my clientele starts breaking up the place?" suggested Don politely. "What folks did before they could buy fish fried, search me."

"I didn't really expect anything different," the sergeant acknowledged when he heard the report. "Wonder who her special pals are? Goes to school at Fair Street, I expect. That's Miss Benson." He glanced at his wristwatch. "Might be at home; anyway, see what you can find out. Might have noticed her going off with a chum or the girl might have said something . . ."

"Catching at straws, aren't you, Sarge?"

"You should read your Bible, my lad. The Israelites made bricks with straw. Bricks are what you use to build houses with, in case you didn't know."

"They should give us danger money," Davis confided to his mate as they left the station.

"Look on the bright side," Dace advised him. "Fancy having Mumma for your station sergeant. It's coming, you know, women bossing the nick. You should hear my wife on the subject. She was in the force herself before we were wed."

Miss Benson was at home, listening to a concert on B.B.C. 4, and not too pleased to find the law on her doorstep. It couldn't be anything to do with her car, it hadn't been out all day. When she heard what they'd come about, she reacted like everyone else.

"Not Angela? You're sure? There could be two children with the same name."

"There couldn't be two mothers like Mrs. Toni."

12

"That's true. Let me think. Angela was never one of our problem children. Some of these girls hang on to one another like limpets; keep one in and the other stops in, too, always going around together. Angela got on well enough with everyone, but with her it was always Mrs. Toni first. It worried me sometimes. I like a girl to be her mother's confidante up to a point, but this one's only nine years old, and there's no escaping the fact that it's not normal for the two generations to be too intimate. Mrs. Toni lives for that girl . . ."

"If we don't find her soon, someone else is likely to die for her, and the odds are it'll be someone in uniform," contributed Davis glumly.

"The two most likely girls are Mary Hersey and Hilda Webb. They *might* be able to help you." Her brow wrinkled. She wasn't a young woman, and she had the authority to which they were accustomed, plus a manner that implied they also belonged to the human race, an attitude often sadly lacking in the upper reaches of the police force. "I suppose it's inevitable this story will spread. Mind you, we've had trouble of a similar kind before, girls running wild and not going home, and occasionally it's ended in tragedy, but I'd have staked my job"—they liked the way she said job and not position—"Angela Toni wasn't like that."

"Chap seems to have let her off to go into the fryer's," Dace brooded, "but like they were saying, he could have been playing it cool."

"It doesn't bear thinking of," said Miss Benson with a sudden display of feeling. "Mind you, she probably knows a lot more about life than her mother would credit. She's an intelligent girl, too intelligent, I'd have said, to be taken in by such an old trick. And," she added with certainty, "if she were in any situation in which she could have communicated with her mother, she'd have done it, whatever had happened. I mean that—literally. Whatever had happened. And don't suppose she'd have tried to pull the wool over Mumma's eyes, because that's something even the Angel on the Gate wouldn't be able to do."

"They weren't like that in my school," confided Bill Davis to Trevor Dace as they returned to the car. "Let's try the Webb kid first—their house is nearer."

Mrs. Webb was in, though Hilda wasn't. Hilda had gone

to the pictures. *Werewolf in the Gloaming*, or some such title.

"Went with friends, did she?" asked Davis, wondering how a kid that age could be let in to see a picture that was surely marked X.

"She'd hardly be going alone," Mrs. Webb agreed. "Some sort of monster-from-outer-space thing, I understand. Why"— her expression changed in a trice—"what's all this about? You haven't come to tell me there's been an accident?" In her crazy mother's-mind eye she saw the cinema breaking into a flower of flame, heard smothered screams . . .

"Not to your Hilda," said the other policeman swiftly. "No one's reported it, anyway. We were asking about a girl called Angela Toni, a chum of your daughter, or so we were given to understand."

"What's happened to Angela?"

"That's what we're trying to find out. She was seen at the fish shop as usual on a Friday night, but she never got home."

"Knocked down by a car, I daresay," said Mrs. Webb, swiftly resorting to her original cool stance. "These new crossings, some genius may have thought them up, but you take my word for it, it was a man. May be all right for adults, but you've only got to see the young ones dodging over the road against the lights . . ."

"Hospital hasn't got any record," Davis told her. "Well, thanks, madam. When your Hilda gets in, if she does know of any plan Angela had for tonight or if she saw her going back from school with anyone—it's like the sergeant says, you have to catch at straws, and her mother's fit to be tied."

"I don't blame her," agreed Mrs. Webb soberly. "There must be something pretty wrong, or Angela would be home. She's a good girl, and it's not her fault if she hasn't got the usual number of parents to give her a settled background."

As if anyone wouldn't back Mrs. Toni against a dozen ordinary parents, the two young men reflected. You didn't need more than half an eye . . .

"Where does this other girl live?" asked Dace as they returned to the car. "Trelawny Street. Wonder who gives these streets their names? They do it better in the States. First Street, Second Street . . ."

"Okay, if you don't want 515th Street, and find you're at the start. Come to that— You'll lose your license, chum,

14

if you drive with your head over your shoulder," he turned to yell at a passing motorist. "We've got a First Street down Knightsbridge way. Don't ask me why. There's no Second Street so far as I know. Left at the traffic lights and it's the turning beyond the Methodist Chapel."

At Trelawny Street they got their first break. Here again they saw the mother. "Yes," Rose Hersey agreed, "my daughter brought Angela home to tea. Poor thing, no proper home, that mother of hers out till all hours . . ."

"Mrs. Toni works," said Dace shortly.

"If she had a husband—she should have thought of that, but of course these foreigners never do. Come over here and expect to enjoy all the privileges of the Welfare State, if you ask me, that's why they come . . ."

"Do you know when Angela left, Mrs. Hersey?" Dace asked ruthlessly cutting her short. They'd had trouble enough with race riots in Notting Hill, without importing them farther south.

"Let me see—it was after the rain started—'Didn't you bring an umbrella?' I said. But she hadn't. I daresay she doesn't even own such a thing."

"She couldn't know when she went to school this morning that the weather was going to break," Davis pointed out. "Even the Meteorological Office didn't know that. Clear and fine, they said, and warm for the time of year."

"It's nice to know the police have time to listen to the wireless," Mrs. Hersey snapped. "Well, she ran off—what happened after that?"

"We don't know. That's why we're here, to see if you could help us."

Mrs. Hersey scowled. "I said to Mary, I said and I said, there are plenty of nice girls in your school you can make friends with and bring home, girls who can ask you back, it'll only lead to trouble, picking up with a waif like that— Oh, I told her."

The door opened and Wilfrid Hersey came in, to stop abruptly at the sight of the police. "What's going on? I saw the car at the door, but I didn't believe . . . Rose?"

"The police are making inquiries about that girl Mary brought home, she seems to have vanished. They appear to be under the impression we might have got her hidden here."

"Why should you want to do that, madam?" snapped

Dace. His companion sighed. Trevor 'ud never get much beyond his present status, temper too quick. You had to learn to treat people the way bank clerks treat five-pound notes, nothing personal and fundamentally all alike.

"If she was able to proceed under her own steam, she'd have been home long before this," Davis insisted.

Mr. Hersey said, "You mean, Angela's gone missing? I say, that's bad. Have you tried the hospital?"

"That's the first place we tried."

"What made you suppose she might be here?" Mrs. Hersey demanded.

"The schoolmistress said she and your daughter were friends."

"Oh, Mary's always been like that. You remember, Wilf, when she was a tiny, she was always bringing in birds with broken wings and stray kittens covered with fleas . . ."

"We're talking about a child," her husband reminded her harshly. "And if Angela hadn't wanted to come she could always have said no. Have the police no idea . . ."

"She was seen getting out of a car at the fish shop, that would be about six-thirty."

"That's right," agreed Mrs. Hersey. "She spoke of getting some fried fish, and hoping the kind her mother likes wouldn't be gone. Her mother's a tartar all right . . ."

"She got the fish—she arrived at the shop in a car . . ."

"What?" Rose Hersey really seemed scandalized. "Well, that shows you."

"Shows you what?" Mr. Hersey inquired.

"The sort of girl she is."

"It did occur to us that perhaps, seeing what a wet night it turned out to be, someone might have given her a lift. I suppose no one here can help us with that?"

"What's that supposed to mean?" Rose demanded.

"The officer's only doing his job," Mr. Hersey pointed out mildly. You could tell this sort of scene was nothing very new to him. The kind of husband who drifts down to the pub of an evening to get a bit of peace, and who could blame him? "He's asking us if the girl could have been given a lift by anyone in this household, and of course the answer's no. I wasn't back till past seven myself."

"Seven?" snapped his wife. "You came in just a few minutes ago and don't blame me if the dinner's ruined."

"I won't," her husband promised. "But there's no sense

making the officers' job more difficult than it's bound to be, in any case. The process of elimination is a very important one. No"—he turned to the constables—"I didn't see the girl tonight, I've been at the Parrot and Pipkin since soon after opening time. Had to see a man there about a dog." His voice was solemn as the proverbial judge, but his eyes conveyed the wink he didn't dare pass on.

"I suppose that's meant to be funny," Rose Hersey jeered. "You know quite well there's no question of our having a dog, messing up all the new covers that I made by hand to save the expense of a seamstress— Oh, not in here," she added, seeing the young men's eyes move tentatively over the furniture. "In the lounge." Where you'll never find yourself, her voice implied.

"Where's Mary?" Wilfrid Hersey asked, diplomatically forsaking the argument about an imaginary dog. "Perhaps she could help."

"I don't want our daughter dragged into this affair. Policemen, indeed!"

"I've often thought it might be useful to have a policeman in the family," commented Mr. Hersey with another invisible wink. "If she's lucky enough to attract one in due course. I'll fetch Mary," he added, "though I wouldn't bank on her being able to tell you anything new. Now, Rose, just calm down and think how you'd be feeling if it was Mary who was missing."

"Are you comparing me with a woman like that Mrs. Toni?"

"If you would, sir," said Davis swiftly.

Mary was a cheerful extrovert, pink-cheeked, blue-eyed, thrilled to the bone to see policemen on the premises, and making no secret of the fact.

"Oo, Mummy, what on earth have you been doing?" she demanded. "Pinching from the supermarket? No, of course not, they don't let you come home then, do they? You go straight off in a Black Maria."

"Mary," said her father, before the outraged mother could speak, "we're in trouble and we think you may be able to help us. It's about Angela Toni."

The child's face changed at once. "What's happened to Angela?"

"That's what we don't know. She left here—when?"

"Oh, about a quarter past six, or it might have been half past. I know she said it was later than she thought, and she had to get the fish for their supper. They get it fried, with chips, from the shop in Makepeace Street, we never have ours from there . . ."

"Your fish, young lady, is properly cooked," scolded Mrs. Hersey.

"I expect theirs is just as good," muttered her mutinous daughter. "What's happened? Didn't she . . ."

"Oh, she bought the fish all right, miss, but she never got home."

"You mean, she's disappeared? How exciting!"

"Well, hardly for her mother," Mr. Hersey reminded her.

"Oh, poor Mrs. Toni. It must be awful. Doesn't anyone know?"

"I always told you she wasn't a suitable friend for you."

"I don't know why," flared Mary. "You don't seem to mind Ben going about with that awful Freda Gale, and everyone knows what she's like."

"I don't know what you're talking about, and I doubt whether you do. And you don't want to start any silly ideas in these officers' minds. Freda is a great deal older than you are . . ."

"Her sister, Alice, is in my class at school. She says," her voice dropped to a conspiratorial whisper, "she says Freda has the Pill."

Mrs. Hersey began to chatter with such rage that she became incoherent. Even Mr. Hersey seemed to be put out. "Don't talk about things you don't understand, Mary," he said. "In any case, what Freda Gale does or doesn't do is no concern of ours."

"Ben's all mushy about her. Goodness, brothers!"

"My son is not at home, Officer," Rose assured them. "He has not been home all the evening."

Mr. Hersey nodded. "I agree."

"And just to put matters on a perfectly clear footing, he doesn't have a car. He doesn't even have a driving license."

"He does, you know," piped up Mary. And just for a minute she had the floor. Even her mother was, like the famous greyhound, stopped in mid-career.

"What nonsense!" she said at last. "My son has not even taken his driving test," she assured her visitors.

"He passed it a month ago," retorted Mary calmly. "He's been taking lessons at the garage. He thought he might get promotion that way."

"He didn't tell us," Mrs. Hersey insisted.

"My son works at Singleton's Garage in Hope Street," Wilfrid Hersey elaborated. "Well, talk about your left hand not knowing what your right hand doeth. I assure you, it's news to me."

"Who told you, Mary?" her mother demanded.

"Why, Ben, of course."

"In any case, he has no car."

"He's employed at a garage, madam. You don't think he might be able to borrow one?"

"Not unless Singleton's more of a fool than I think he is. What are you trying to imply?"

"We're simply out to get information about a little girl who's gone missing."

"Angela would never take a lift from someone she didn't know," Mary assured them earnestly. "Her mother's always told her . . ."

"Her mother's no better than she should be," Mrs. Hersey snapped.

"I think she's wonderful," Mary protested. "She takes Angel to all sorts of places where you've never taken me, and— It *was* awfully wet."

"You can hardly hold us responsible for the weather. Now, I'm afraid, Officer, we can't assist you."

"You wouldn't even let me lend her my mac," Mary mourned.

"You will need your mackintosh tomorrow, if it rains. You know we're going to see Aunt Eleanor."

"Well," said Mary, with the outspokenness that characterized her generation, "she's a wet blanket in herself. What I mean"—she turned to the two officers—"is that if someone she knew offered Angel a lift, it's quite a long way back to Derwent Street, she might accept."

"How many people do you suppose a girl like that knows who owns a car?"

"Oh, she knows all kinds of people," Mary told her mother blithely. "She goes to the hospital sometimes on visiting days. She's invited because of her mother. Mrs. Toni delivers the morning papers there, so, of course, the people in the ward are interested when she tells them about Angela . . ."

"Well, madam and sir, thank you for your help," said Davis diplomatically.

19

"Afraid we haven't been able to do much for you," said Hersey. "I hope they find the little girl, though. It doesn't bear thinking about. That poor woman, it's a big responsibility."

"She should have thought of that earlier," snapped Rose.

"She couldn't know Mr. Toni was going to be swept up with the garbage," Mary protested. "Didn't you know? That's what happened. Angel told me."

"Talk about a wasp's nest," said Dace as the two young men regained the safety of their car. "Know what surprises me, Bill, not the murders that are committed but those that aren't. I bet she gives that little chap what-for for the next week. Where do we go from here?"

"Back to the station, what do you think? Mr. High-and-Mighty Inspector isn't going to be too pleased with us, he does like to see value for money."

"They should have him in the government, Bill, or would that be too much of a shock for them?" They drove off; from a window Mary wistfully watched them go.

 **3**

IT WAS STILL RAINING when Mumma came through on the telephone at about ten P.M. Normally she wouldn't have touched one of the nasty things, but it was some distance to the police station, and say Angel came back— The phone booth was on the corner and she could watch the house while she phoned.

"We know she was at the Hersey household immediately after school," the sergeant told her. "She went to tea . . ."

"A nice house for my Angel to go," exploded Mumma. "That Mrs. Hersey. That man of hers always at the Parrot and Pipkin and her son running after that loose girl."

We could do with someone like Mumma in the nick, the sergeant reflected. On one's own side she might be less intimidating. Certainly nothing escaped her.

"Mary Hersey," he began, and once again he was overborne.

"That girl! No shame they have, calling their daughter by the name of the Mother of God, an insult to the Blessed Virgin. A good Catholic will give her daughter such a name to put her under the Mother's protection"—the sergeant lacked the courage to suggest that in this case the Mother had fallen down on her job—"but what is Mary to them? Mary, Mary, quite contrary— Mary had a little lamb . . ." Her voice squeaked up the register, causing the sergeant to hold the receiver a few cautious inches from his ear. "One hour goes by, two hours, nearly three hours I wait, and for what? For nothing—nothing—nothing."

"We've got all our men on the alert, Mrs. Toni," he assured her, "and they won't be called off, right through the weekend, if need be."

"Men!" was Mumma's shattering comment.

"We've got the women police out as well, of course."

"Them! Why they not home looking after their own children, not walking the streets? What more do you do?"

"We haven't got such a lot to go on," the sergeant admitted candidly. "We've circulated a description, of course. It would help if we had a photograph."

"Where do you think is money for a photograph?"

"We've got a description of the car, too. We'll find her for you, Mumma, I promise you that."

"Like they found the children on the moors?" demanded Mumma crushingly. "I ask you—what do you do to find my Angel now?"

The sound of the receiver being slammed down nearly broke the sergeant's eardrum.

"She's got something there," he acknowledged, remembering another little girl who'd been missing for four days and was found in the basement of an empty house in no condition to be any consolation to her mother or anyone else. "As a rule I prefer this kind of search in a town, criminal's possibilities are more limited, but where there's a car involved"—he stopped, and both men thought of the wide, empty spaces, the rubbish tips, the ditches, under a blanket of black rain—"that's another matter."

Complaints of various crimes continued to pour in. (It hadn't, naturally, occurred to Mumma that the police had any other business of commensurate importance.) The victim of a hit-

and-run car was found in Hangman's Alley—"More like a lorry than a car if his face is anything to go on," reported the constable who found him (hoping he didn't look as green as he felt). There was a fracas at the Jolly Dustman, where a chap got his face cut by flying glass; the usual complaints about noisy wirelesses and anonymous phone calls of an obscene nature; and then, shortly after eleven o'clock, a man came striding wrathfully into the nick to complain of a stolen car.

"Taken from that free car park behind the public library," he said. "A Puma, bright green, not had her six months. I couldn't get a place anywhere near where I was visiting. Now they've installed meters in those residential streets beyond the cinema, you can't double-park any longer."

"Could be that's why they've installed meters," said authority grimly. "How long did you leave your car in the car park?"

"I was calling on a friend, we had some food at her place . . . Well, she didn't fancy going out in all that rain, we played some records, say it was half after eleven when I left her, I made for the car park and the car had gone."

"And you parked it?"

"Round about six."

"And you left it locked—of course."

"Well, of course." He hesitated. "Yes, of course," he repeated.

"Don't sound too sure."

"I always lock it. Well, I don't want to make a present of it to some long-haired git, do I?"

"So you think you locked it, but you can't be absolutely sure."

"What difference does that make?" Mr. Gordon started to get angry.

"Asking for trouble, I'd say, and here we have all the trouble we can cope with when owners do remember to lock their cars. Puma's a smallish car, isn't it?" the sergeant continued thoughtfully.

"I need a car for my job, not to take the choirboys for an outing."

He was very quick on the ball. The sergeant wondered if he'd had a stormy session with his young lady. It stood out a mile that the less publicity he had over this the better pleased he'd be.

"My point is it's not likely to have been taken in connection with a crime," said the sergeant. "Those boys go for something large and fast. Not to worry, sir, we'll probably soon get it back for you. It's not as though it's been stolen."

Mr. Gordon stared. "Not stolen? What do you call it, then?"

"A stolen car is one that's taken without any intention of its being returned. Those cars may be missing for weeks and turn up a couple of hundred miles away."

"You mean, it's just been taken for a joke? Very funny. Ha-ha!"

"I don't think it's a joke to anyone, least of all to the police. It's what we call being borrowed—some young chap wants to impress his girl, needs a car, no intention of hanging on to it— I don't say you'll find it back in the same car park, that'ud be asking too much, but it won't be far away. Now we know its make and number, our chaps 'ull soon pick it up."

"I hope to God you're right, and I hope you'll pick up the chap who did it, too."

"It's just possible it was used in a case we've started inquiries about—at all events the description tallies—in connection with a missing child. In which case you can be dead sure the chap who's got it won't want to hang on to it a minute longer than he needs."

"And you tell me I've no redress? Suppose the car's damaged?"

"I take it, sir, you're insured."

"And that's supposed to be a comfort to me?"

The sergeant sighed. These car owners, all their concern was for their own inconvenience, the wrong done to them. Look at this chap, not a thought for the child, not even a question. His own voice was hard as he promised, "You leave your address and telephone number and as soon as we hear anything we'll be in touch." Though if it really was the car that had abducted little Angela Toni, it wasn't likely the "borrower" would bring it back to the same neighborhood. Mind you, he had a pretty good notion why Mr. Gordon was in such a stew —whoever he'd spent the evening with, you could stake your davy it wasn't Mrs. G.

This fresh piece of information keyed everyone up. There is no crime more hated both by the police and by thoroughgoing evildoers alike than an offense against a child.

The car was located about three miles away, parked in a cul-de-sac, soon after 2:00 A.M. There were fingerprints on the steering wheel and the paintwork, but none of them tallied with any in the police records. And before the police could get weaving on identifications, a number of other things had happened.

The police were busy trying to identify the anonymous man in Hangman's Alley, who had nothing in his pockets to assist them; other officers were following up clues regarding a recent hold-up at a jeweler's; various cars were stopped by zealous policemen on the chance that they might be the missing vehicle—and the hunt for a missing child went on, without any success.

When she set down the receiver in the pay booth Mumma marched out, sweeping aside a group of youths waiting for their turn. One of them, more daring then the rest, jeered, "Stood you up, has he, Ma?" (they weren't local, goodness knew where they'd erupted from), and was rewarded by a resounding clout on the ear. He began to snivel about his mother.

"You tell your mother she come to me and I give her the same," Mumma promised. "I seen plenty dogs I sooner take home."

Back in her flat she swept over to where the Virgin simpered at the vase of fresh anemones that lighted even the darkness with their brilliant flame.

"So?" threatened Mumma. "You not interested? You listen. I give you till—till tomorrow, you work so many miracles, you work one for me."

But it seemed as though the aloof Virgin simply drew her blue painted robe more closely about her.

And not so far away Ben Hersey, eighteen years old, dark, attractive, but tonight definitely the worse for wear, and not only on account of the rain, returned to his parents' home about eleven-fifteen.

"Where have you been?" his mother wanted to know, sounding about as peaceable as Queen Boadicea, strapping the scythes onto the wheels of her chariot. "Ben, you've been drinking."

"I had a pint," he acknowledged. "Where's the harm in that?"

"And how many to follow?" demanded the hard thrifty woman who had borne him. "Why, you can only just about stand."

Mr. Hersey, self-appointed peacemaker and about as effective as peacemakers mostly are, said, "The boy's dead tired, probably glad to get off to bed."

"If it's that Freda Gale," Mrs. Hersey continued, ignoring her husband, as was her habit, "you're wasting your time. She's not going to take any permanent interest in a boy who couldn't even pass his G.C.E., and doesn't even go to night school."

"I've got better things to do than go to night school at the end of the day," her son growled.

"And you won't make much headway with any decent girl —not that I envy Mrs. Gale a daughter like that—if you come home in that state. Good thing you're not a car driver."

"You didn't tell us you'd passed your test, Ben," put in Mr. Hersey, trying to change the subject, with about as much hope as changing the color of his skin. "It's a first step."

"Everyone can drive," was his son's ungrateful retort. "There's nothing to it."

Mr. Hersey decided to try a little light humor—some people never learn. "You could have fooled me," he said. "Watching some of those cars in the High Street."

"Next thing I suppose you'll be wanting a car of your own," said Rose Hersey. "Or has Freda Gale got one already?"

"Not yet. She's only seventeen."

His mother snorted. "Someone slipped up when they made out her birth certificate. If you must go around with girls, why can't you pick one who'd be a credit to you? Well, go on, what did you do all the evening? You can't have spent the whole time drinking at the Ship."

"I haven't been near the Ship," Ben said sulkily.

"One of these classy night clubs, I suppose. Nice to know someone's in the money. Not that you need think you'll impress Freda Gale that way. If ever I saw a girl stamped gold-digger . . ."

"Oh, stuff Freda!" shouted her son. "Why can't you leave me alone?"

"That's a nice way to speak to your mother. Wilf!" She threw her husband an imperious glance.

"Your mother's right, Ben," said Mr. Hersey mildly. "That girl's no good to you. It doesn't pay off in the long run not to be able to say no. Oh, I daresay she's attractive, but there's more to married life than a pretty face."

He spoke with some feeling, the weak man who hadn't been able to say no when faced with his crisis. And look what it had brought him. A termagant wife and a son who despised him. It was a comforting thought that there was still Mary, who was, thank God, too young, too innocent, to feel contempt for her elders.

"Who said anything about getting married?" Ben flared.

"You want to watch out. I'm not having any affiliation order officer calling at my house," his mother said.

"Oh, for God's sake! You should be writing books, Mum. First you see me in court for drunken driving, and now I'm supposed to be putting some girl in the club."

"I won't have that kind of talk in my house. I'm telling you straight."

"You suggest a subject," her son proposed. "What high jinks have you all been up to while I've been out?"

"You may be interested to know we've had the police here."

"The police?" His face turned a greenish-white, though he did his best to disguise his dismay with a jaunty grin. "What have you and Dad been doing? Running secret bingo sessions with pot on the side? I'm surprised at you, Mum."

"It's not funny, Ben," Mr. Hersey said. "It's about Mrs. Toni's little girl, Angela."

"What about her?"

"She's disappeared. She was seen going into Billing's, the fried-fish shop, and no one's seen her since."

"But— I mean, why did they come here?"

"Because Mary invited her to tea," Mrs. Hersey informed him. "I don't know what children are coming to. When I was a girl I didn't ask anyone home without my mother's permission."

"Angela's all right," Ben said.

"Angela is Mrs. Toni's child and she's very far from being all right," Rose said. "I'm sure there are plenty of nice girls at the Fair Street school Mary could bring back, but no, she has to pick this—this gypsy's child, who hasn't even got a father. And then you go making a fool of yourself with Freda Gale, and coming back the worse for drink. If you ask me, it's a good thing you haven't got a car."

"Angela's all right," insisted Ben stubbornly, "and so's Mumma Toni."

"Where's the sense of bringing up your children right, slaving yourself to the bone to give them a nice home when all they do . . . If Angela's so nice what's she doing accepting lifts from strange men?"

He looked like someone stricken to stone. Then he said, "I don't know what you're talking about. Mumma would have her hide if she so much as spoke to a strange man."

"You seem to know a lot about her, Ben," Mr. Hersey said.

"She's my kid sister's friend. Mary's nine, I suppose Angel's about the same age."

"She's nearly ten and everyone knows these foreign children develop much more quickly," Rose said.

"Is that why the police came round? Because Angel was here this afternoon?"

"What other reason can you suppose?" his mother said. "You needn't look at me, I told them, my husband's down at the Parrot and Pipkin, as per usual, and my son doesn't have a car, and, anyway, he wouldn't be interested in little girls."

"What have you got in mind?" Ben asked. "You said she was seen in the fish shop?"

"That's right."

"She wouldn't have time to go joyriding," her son protested. "Mumma would be coming back from work. I mean, if she came to tea here she'd be a bit late going back, and . . ."

"I'm only telling you what the police told us," Mrs. Hersey said, "that she was seen getting out of a car."

"Perhaps someone did give her a lift home. It's been a wet night," Ben said. "But if some chap picked her up for the wrong reason, why on earth should he let her out at the fish shop where everyone would recognize her?"

"The boy's got a point there," interposed Mr. Hersey.

"The facts are good enough for me. She didn't go home, she hasn't been involved in an accident—she'd be in hospital if she had—and we've had the police round to the house. That'll give the neighbors something to talk about for a month of Sundays. I don't know about letting Mary go to school tomorrow."

"Tomorrow's Saturday, she wouldn't be going to school anyway," her husband reminded her.

"Well, this cinema club thing they go to on Saturday mornings."

"What on earth's it got to do with Mary?" asked Ben, mystified.

"Angela's known to have visited our house. The police even had the nerve to hint that your father might have driven her home, only naturally he was at his usual rendezvous at that time of the evening."

"Can't blame him really," said Ben coolly. "Chap needs a bit of peace at the end of the day. Besides, he gets orders at the Parrot, don't you, Dad?"

"How about some tea, Rose?" intervened her husband hastily. "I'm sure I could do with a cup."

"It's news to me that you recognize anything that isn't in a glass. Oh, please yourself."

"I daresay Ben could do with a cup."

"I should have thought a good dose of bicarb was more in his line."

"I'll put the kettle on," offered Ben, making for the kitchen.

His father followed him. "I don't want to come the heavy father with you, Ben," he began.

"Couldn't very well, could you? Not a lightweight like you. And if you want to warn me about getting involved with Freda Gale and that lot, you can save your breath. What I've seen of marriage isn't all that of an encouragement. All the same, Dad, there is something I wanted to tell you. Oh, don't look like that, I'm not going to confess to a murder or anything. Mother's got you so worked up you jump at a shadow."

Mr. Hersey took the kettle out of his son's hand and filled it at the tap. "What are you trying to tell me, Ben?"

"Now I've passed my test, old Singleton's going to put up my pay. When I've had a bit more practice he might put me on his list of drivers. He does quite a sideline in that direction, as well as repairs."

"Anyone can drive," his father reminded him. "Anyone can't be a good mechanic."

"No reason you shouldn't be both. I don't mean to be a garage hand all my days. I want my own business, and I'll need to know all sides of it. What I'm leading up to is when I've got a bit more money I want to get a place of my own, sharing, I mean. I know a chap . . ."

"You mean leave home?" Mr. Hersey looked flabbergasted. "Your mother isn't going to like that. She's taken so much trouble to have everything nice."

"She can't suppose I'd stay at home forever. Besides, I

28

want some place where I can see my own friends without having to produce a pedigree, where I can play a few records without her knocking on the wall, and take a girl out if I choose without Mum meeting us at the door with a chastity belt. It's all right for Mary, she's only a kid."

"Are you two having your tea in the kitchen?" called Rose in her hectoring voice.

"Kettle's just on the boil. Get the cups, Ben, will you, and don't forget spoons for the sugar."

Ben took a couple of aspirins with his tea and sloped off to bed.

"He's a nice, cheerful person to have around the house, I must say," his mother observed.

"You won't be having him much longer. He plans to get a place of his own. Well, most young chaps of his age feel the same."

His wife's laughter shrilled through the room. "That won't last long. I suppose that's what you were discussing in the kitchen."

"Not much discussing about it. He just told me what he was going to do."

"Who does he think is going to wash his shirts when he goes into lodgings?"

"I suppose he'll do the same as the rest of them, go along to the launderette. You should see the place of a Sunday morning. Rows of these young chaps reading the paper and waiting for the job to be finished."

"I suppose you encouraged him."

"There wasn't any question of encouragement. He just told me what he planned. Singleton's going to put up his wages . . ."

"There you go. Wages. Our son gets a salary."

"Working chaps don't draw a salary. They're paid wages. I'm only warning you so you won't come out with something that'll keep him away for months when he does tell you."

"So he does mean to tell me?" She laughed again, and he felt his face shrivel. "Well, I'm only his mother."

"Of course he'll tell you. I think I'll turn in now, Rose. It's been a heavy day. I wonder if they've found that little girl."

As he went up the stairs he saw his daughter's door open cautiously. "That you, Daddy?"

"What are you doing out of bed, poppet? If your mother

hears you . . ." In her present mood Rose would be quite capable of smacking the child. Mr. Hersey's blood boiled at the thought.

"I can't sleep. Daddy, do you think Angel's all right?"

"We must hope so, my duck."

"She's my best friend."

"I know."

"Mummy doesn't like her."

"Your mother doesn't approve of Mrs. Toni. No one could dislike Angela."

"She wouldn't let me lend her my mackintosh to go home, though it was raining quite hard."

"I expect she thought you might need it over the weekend," offered Mr. Hersey feebly.

"Angie would have brought it back, I know she would. Daddy!"

"Well, my duck?" He coaxed her back to bed and tucked her in.

"Angie's got a hair-slide her mother gave her. It's lovely, set with mother-of-pearl. She'd have given it me, I know she would, only her mother gave it to her . . ."

"You go to sleep now like a good girl and in the morning we'll see if we can get you one."

"Oh, Daddy! Promise?"

"Cross my heart and wish to die."

He kissed her, shut the door and came softly back onto the landing. To his dismay he could hear his wife rootling about in their son's room. No wonder the boy wanted to leave the house. Only wish I could do the same, he thought violently. And if it wasn't for Mary he would. No one had to worry about Rose, she could look after herself. She wasn't set about with little willful thorns, no, hers were huge daggers, like a giant cactus. For a few minutes he gave himself up to the luxury of imagining himself free once more. Then the door of Ben's room opened and Mrs. Hersey emerged.

"He won't last long in rooms of his own," she announced with grim satisfaction. "No landlady'll stand for him—clothes all over the floor, shoes chucked anywhere, doesn't even empty his pockets."

He cried, startled, "You haven't been— Rose, you should respect his privacy."

"Privacy!" she jeered. "Let me tell you one thing, Wilf Hersey. Whoever your son was out with tonight it wasn't Freda Gale. She'd never be seen dead in a trumpery thing like that."

And opening her hand, she showed him a mock tortoise-shell hair-slide set with mother-of-pearl.

 4

MUMMA'S WORK AT THE HOSPITAL stopped on Fridays. From seven-thirty on Friday night till early Monday morning her time belonged to Angela. On the Saturday after the child disappeared the papers were brought around by a substitute who simply distributed them willy-nilly and departed. The story of Angela's disappearance had spread like wildfire. Everyone in the hospital agreed it was too bad it should have happened at a weekend. Now they'd have to wait till Monday to get Mumma's reactions.

They looked eagerly in the press for news, but one little girl disappearing doesn't rate much publicity, not till she's been gone for more than a few hours. The boy who brought the papers knew nothing of her, and clearly wasn't interested. The nurses knew nothing.

"I expect she'll be all right," they said soothingly. "Gone off for a joke, I expect."

"Angela?" chorused the ward. They knew her, many of them—she sometimes came in of an evening, bringing things Mumma had undertaken to get for the patients.

"Anyway, it's not your worry," the nurses urged. "You leave it to Mrs. Toni."

"On the whole, it's probably just as well Mumma isn't doing her paper-round this morning," observed Miss Grainger candidly. "Mumma on the warpath would be more dangerous than the Luftwaffe. And I remember what London was like when

31

they started dropping their eggs. If anyone has cooked up something against Angela, I can't help feeling sorry for him. He won't have a chance if he comes face to face with Mumma."

In the Hersey household the day opened somberly. Rose Hersey was still seething; Mr. Hersey was nerving himself for the first showdown of his married life; Mary was impatient to go out and get the hair-slide before her father should forget and in time to reach the Essoldo Cinema, where there was a special performance of *Mary Poppins*, recalled by special request. There was at first no sign of Ben. Saturday was his late night at the garage, which remained open till 9:00 P.M., so he didn't have to go in till midday.

"If he's fit to go at all," said his mother repressively. "Don't fidget, Mary. What's all the mystery about?"

"Mary and I have a little private shopping to do. As a matter of fact, I wanted a word with Ben before we go."

Presently Ben came in, looking ghastly.

"He can't go to work like that," said Rose decidedly. "Sit down, Ben. I'll make you a fresh pot of tea."

"I expect it's that Freda," observed Mary sagely. "Alice says her mother's at her wits' end."

"It wouldn't take Mrs. Gale long to get there," snapped Rose, disappearing into the kitchen.

"You go and get ready, duck," Mr. Hersey adjured his daughter.

"Pooh! I know what that means. You're going to talk to Ben . . ."

"It means I want you to go and get ready, unless you want to call the excursion off."

"You promised. Cross your heart," Mary reminded him, skipping out of the door.

"What's all the mystery in aid of?" Ben demanded, taking a piece of cold toast and leaving it on his place.

"Mary and I are going out to buy her a hair-slide just like the one Angel was wearing yesterday—you remember? Set with mother-of-pearl. Very dashing."

"I don't know what you're talking about," said Ben. "Why should I know?"

"Because your mother took it—the slide, I mean—out of your pocket last night. And don't try to hedge," he added sternly as his son was about to speak, "because Mary can

32

identify it, though I don't want to drag her into this if it can be helped."

Rose pushed open the door with her foot and came in carrying a plate of freshly cooked bacon and eggs. "Get that inside you," she told her son. Then something in the atmosphere made her ask sharply, "What's going on here?"

"Ben's just going to explain how Angel Toni's hair-slide came to be in his pocket."

The words were simple enough, but their effect was explosive. "Nonsense!" Rose cried with so much conviction her husband began to wonder it he'd dreamed the whole incident. "You don't know what you're saying."

"You told me yourself you'd taken it out of his pocket, and that it couldn't conceivably belong to Freda Gale."

"That doesn't mean it belongs to the Toni girl. One old hair-slide's very like another."

"We can ask Mary, if you like. She noticed it particularly. She wants one exactly like it."

"Surely even you don't intend to drag a child into this."

"We're a family," her husband pointed out. "When there's trouble abroad you can't separate one member from another. Well, son?"

"He's got a name," Rose snapped.

"I thought he might like to be reminded he's also got a father."

"It's not my fault," Ben burst out. "If you want to blame anyone, blame Mother."

Rose was so much taken aback that for the moment she seemed to have lost her tongue.

Mr. Hersey said sharply, "You'd better explain what you mean by that."

"Letting a little kid go out without even an umbrella in the pouring rain, enough to give her pneumonia. Of course I offered her a lift, anyone would."

"You can hardly hold me responsible for Mrs. Toni's deficiencies where her daughter's concerned. It's up to her to provide the child with an umbrella—goodness knows, they're cheap enough."

"No one could have guessed it was going to rain like that when Angel went to school in the morning. She has school dinners, you know . . ."

"You seem to know a lot about her."

33

"Mary talks about her, says she wishes she could have school dinners, too."

"I wonder if all mothers have such ungrateful children. School dinners, indeed."

"And she came straight back with Mary—just called in at Derwent Street on the way— The rain didn't come on till about six, so how could she have an umbrella?"

"Do you suggest I should have rung for a taxi for her?"

"You might at least have let Mary lend her her mac. She wasn't going out again last night."

"She might quite well have needed it this morning."

"Angela would have returned it in time. Her mother would have seen to that. The kid was waiting at the lights by Trevanion Street, the rain was coming down cats and dogs—I had this car . . ."

"Whose car?"

"Well—I borrowed it."

"In order to take Angela Toni home?"

"Of course not, Rose, don't be so ridiculous. I suppose you were taking some girl out?" Wilf questioned his son.

Ben nodded miserably. "Freda said she was sick of standing in bus queues, all the other chaps had cars, only kids hadn't passed their test, so . . ."

"You mean to say Mr. Singleton lent you one of his cars on the strength of a three-weeks-old license?"

"Well, no. Actually, it wasn't one of his. I—I borrowed it."

"So you said. But who was mad enough to lend it to you? Ben, you didn't take it—even you can't be that daft."

"Of course he didn't take it," cried Mrs. Hersey. "In another minute you'll hold him responsible for Angela's disappearance."

"Whose car was it, son?" Wilf disregarded his wife's puzzled expression.

As for her, poor woman, she felt as though she were married to a stranger. Sixpennoth of ha'pence, that was how she was wont to describe him, and here he was, standing up to her, behaving as though he were the head of the household. The cheek of it, she thought wrathfully, after twenty years.

"I don't know," Ben confessed. "Some chap left it in that free park behind the public library." He grinned suddenly. "Must have been in a hell of a hurry to see his girl. He didn't even stop to lock it. Carrying flowers," he explained. "Well, chaps don't do that for their wives, do they?"

"Cheeky monkey!" said Rose. "You're not telling us you stole a car?"

"It's not called that, not if you don't mean to keep it," Wilf explained. "I take it you did return it?"

"Well, not exactly to the same place. I mean, I couldn't, I'd run out of juice."

"Never heard of garages?"

"I couldn't go to one of those. There might have been a call out for the car. I left it in a cul-de-sac—someone's bound to notice it as soon as it's reported."

"I see you kept a portion of your wits about you. How about Freda? Didn't she mind walking back in the rain?"

"Freda wasn't there," acknowledged the boy, bitterly. "I rang her from the call box outside the hairdresser, when I'd got the car, but it was Mrs. Gale who answered. 'I'm afraid there's been some mistake,' she said." His voice mimicked the absent woman. " 'My daughter is out with her fiancé. Who is that calling?' Her fiancé, Dad! And all this time she'd let me think . . ."

"That girl's a trollop," pronounced Mrs. Hersey, "and I daresay that mother of hers is no better."

"I do wish you'd guard your tongue, Rose," her husband protested. "One of these days you'll land me in a slander action. Well, son, I can't pretend to be sorry about this girl. She's not the kind you want to get lumbered with. Well, go on. No, Rose, don't ask any more questions, let him tell it his own way."

Ben looked from one parent to another. It was a despairing sort of look, the look of one who knows you can't expect the old to understand anything.

"As I'd got the car," he went on, "there didn't seem any point in taking it straight back, so I tooled on, with no special plans in mind, and after a few minutes I stopped at the lights by Trevanion Street. I saw Angela waiting, and I thought, If I can't take one girl I may as well give another a lift, so I leaned out and said, 'Like me to drive you home?' She said she had to go to the fish shop, she'd been having tea with Mary and they got talking and she hadn't noticed the time. She had a bit of paper in her hand which she said her mother had left for her. I took her to Billing's and there was a sizable queue. I knew I couldn't wait because there was a double yellow line, but she said not to worry, she'd probably see someone she knew, and anyway it was so close. I couldn't stop to argue, so I drove round the corner and—oh, Dad! It sounds phony, I suppose, but I hadn't been at the wheel more than a few minutes when even Freda started to seem less important. She went like a bird, the Puma, I mean—it was marvelous to feel her response, all that power in my hands. You don't know."

"I wasn't always a henpecked husband," his father contributed mildly. "And though I seem half as old as Methusaleh to you, I can still remember my first car—well, that's what I called it. It cost fifteen pounds and you had to wind it by hand, and sometimes it went and sometimes it didn't. But there's never been another like it."

Ben nodded. Then he said, "Dad, what do I do now?"

"What do you think? You'll have to tell the police, naturally."

"No," cried Ben's mother. "He's not going to be involved in a case like this. It would ruin him. It's not as though he can help them. They know Angela went to the fish shop. Ben's told us there were half a dozen people there, probably they all saw her since he did. Do you want him to lose his job? It may not be a very good one, but . . ."

The door was pushed open and Mary's face appeared in the crack.

"What do you want?" her mother said.

"Daddy said we were going out. And I promised to meet Clara . . ."

"Look, duck." Wilf turned to her persuasively. "Something's turned up. It's Ben, he's—he's not well."

"You mean, he's got to go to the doctor?"

"Perhaps. Look, why don't you pick Clara up a bit early, and you can go off together and buy a hair-slide, whatever you fancy. You may see one you like even better than Angela's." Putting his hand in his pocket, he produced two half-crowns.

His daughter's eyes widened. "All that?"

"If there's any change you can buy yourself on ice-lolly to suck in the cinema."

"I don't know that I care for the idea of Mary going out by herself in the circumstances," Mrs. Hersey fussed.

Mary's eyes opened wider still. "What circumstances, Mummy?"

"Just because Angela's gone missing, there's no reason why Mary should follow her example," added Wilf Hersey.

The child broke into a peal of derisive laughter. "Why Mummy, I go to school by myself every day. What's happened?" she added curiously.

"We don't know, darling, and whatever it is was happening before you and Ben were born or thought of. Nip off now, or you'll miss your film."

Mary nodded. The door closed with a bang, and they heard the sound of young feet running through the hall.

"Go on," invited Rose Hersey discouragingly. "You were telling us about stealing a car."

"I told you, Rose. The word is borrowed."

"I hope the police are as broad-minded as you are. I don't know what I've done that my children should have no moral sense."

"Infatuation is responsible for a lot more wrongdoing than most people realize," her husband assured her.

Both wife and son stared. This meek little man, suddenly rising like a phoenix from a bed of cold ashes to dominate a situation that might well have flummoxed a far more masterful personality, was new to both.

Pity he wasn't like this a bit earlier, Ben thought.

Must have taken leave of his senses, was Rose's summing-up.

"Well, when I realized that Freda had stood me up, I started to drive around—I told you—and suddenly I heard a clock strike and I realized if I didn't want any more trouble I'd better get the car back before the owner came looking for it. I didn't think on a wet night like this his girl . . ."

"You don't know there was a girl."

"I didn't suppose he was taking flowers to the cemetery at that hour," retorted Ben pertly. "Then I realized I was out of petrol and I couldn't run her into a garage in case the alarm was out, so I left her in a cul-de-sac and came back on the bus. On the way home I dropped into a bar for a drink."

"When did you find the slide?" Wilf asked.

"I was going over the car to make sure I hadn't left anything of mine in it, and— It must have slipped off her hair, which was dripping, almost behind the seat. I put it in my pocket, meaning to leave it somewhere in the house where it might seem as if Angie had dropped it. It didn't occur to me," he added drily to his mother, "that you'd go through my pockets."

"If you took proper care of your clothes it wouldn't be necessary."

"Yes, well, the first thing for us to do is go to the station. I'll come with you, Ben."

"Are you out of your mind?" Rose fired up. "He's not going near any police station."

"You can be dead sure the car will have been reported. It's much better for Ben to own up now, than for them to find out."

"Why should they ever find out?"

"You can't bank on that. And if he keeps his mouth shut, then they may start to think he's really got something to hide."

"You sound as if you really want to see your own son in jail."

"They don't put you in jail for borrowing a car for joyriding. Have to build a couple more prisons in the London area alone if they did that. Come on, Ben."

"I suppose you know he'll lose his job."

"That'll depend on Singleton. Anyway, you've never liked him working there."

"Who else do you think will give him one after this?"

"It's not a crime that he's committed."

"And if they don't believe his story, that he left Angela in the fish queue?"

"Why shouldn't they? If he was the sort that went after little girls he wouldn't choose his sister's best friend. You're not being very complimentary to your son, Rose."

"So I'm supposed to be paying him compliments now."

"He could do with a little support from his own family. Anyhow, he hasn't lost this job yet. Come, Ben, no sense wasting any more time."

Without another word Ben followed his father out of the room.

Wilfrid Hersey might not be a very impressive figure but he was treated at the police station with a respect that impressed his son. As soon as the duty sergeant realized why they were there they were passed on to the appropriate authority.

The inspector in charge was taking a jaundiced view of the

public that morning. "Two more publicity hunters?" he suggested, but the sergeant said, "I don't think so. The boy's as white as a sheet, and the father's like a cat on hot bricks, though their story seems to hang together well enough."

"Abominable cruelty, cats on hot bricks," said the inspector, nowise mollified. "You've got their names, I suppose. They'd better come in." A minute later he was facing father and son.

"Let's get the position quite clear," he told them. "You're Ben Hersey and you're making a statement of your own free will. It's my duty to caution in case you tell me something detrimental to your own interests." He repeated the official caution. "Now, if you're still ready, go ahead."

Ben was surprised to discover how much reassurance it gave him to have his father present. "My mother's right, I'm afraid. What I have to tell you won't get you very far where Angela Toni's concerned . . ."

"We'll be the judge of that."

"I'd like to stay while you talk to my son," Mr. Hersey put in. "He's a minor and I fancy this is his first visit to a police station."

"We're not going to eat him, you know. Fire ahead, lad. Anything you can tell us about the little girl—her mother's fit to be tied and we don't want mass murder at the station."

He listened to what Ben had to tell him. "That's the last I saw of her," declared the boy desperately. "There was quite a queue, nine or ten people I should say, they go to one counter for chips and another for fish, it all adds up, and it's a No Parking area, and Angel said she was quite near home, and anyhow I wouldn't have dared drive up, goodness knows what Mrs. Toni would have thought."

"So you just drove off?"

"Yes."

"In the rain?"

"I couldn't help the rain."

"Knowing your young lady had stood you up?"

"If she hadn't I wouldn't have picked up Angela."

"It didn't occur to you the sensible thing would be to return the car right away? You didn't need it . . ."

"Ah, but I did."

"You did?"

"It's not far, not in a car, from our house to the fish shop, but it was long enough for me to get the feel of the car—I couldn't have given it back right away. Anyway, I'd nothing else to do. I couldn't go home, I didn't want to go to the pictures on my own—anyway, she might have been there. I didn't do the car any harm, not so much as a scratch. I left it . . ."

"We know where you left it. It's been found—around two A.M."

"I suppose I owe the owner something for petrol," said Ben awkwardly.

"That's the least of your troubles."

"He's not saying I did any damage?"

"You'll soon hear from him if you did. But no, he's made no complaint."

"I wouldn't have hurt her for the world," explained Ben reverently.

"You're sure you didn't pick up anyone else?"

"Of course I didn't."

"Or meet anyone you knew?"

"Not even in the Fighting Cock."

"Known there?"

"I'd only been there once before."

"You didn't think of picking up a pal. It 'ud have been safe enough before the owner gave the alarm. I mean, I'd have expected you to—well—peacock it a bit. Your first car—in a manner of speaking—"

Ben replied simply, "Any chap I'd picked up would have wanted his turn at driving at least, and do you think I could have been a passenger with some other fellow at the wheel? But I don't suppose you'd understand."

"What I don't understand is why the public always assumes policemen were born the way they are now," commented the inspector drily. "Now, about the slide."

"I've explained about that. I found it when I was going over the car."

"Didn't mention it to anyone when you got back?"

"Well, how could I?" Ben sounded amazed. "Not unless I was going to tell them about the car."

"If there'd been any monkey business about the slide, the boy wouldn't have brought it home at all," Wilf Hersey pointed out.

Ben looked sick. "The minds you people have! First Mother, then you. This wasn't a girl like Freda Gale, this was a little kid who was my sister's best friend. What do you mean by monkey business?"

"Simply a routine inquiry," the inspector told him.

"You could have fooled me," said Mr. Hersey bitterly. "What is this? The Star Chamber?"

But you couldn't shake the inspector. On it went, question after question, but he found he couldn't shake Ben either. "I can't tell you anything different," he protested, "this is the way it was."

Mumma identified the slide on sight. "So you have that?" she demanded. "Where is my daughter?"

"We don't know yet. This was dropped in the car that gave her a lift to the fish shop."

"You know whose is the car?"

"It wasn't being driven by the owner at the time. It had been 'borrowed.' "

"That is what he says. And you believe him?"

"He has an alibi, Mrs. Toni."

"Alibis? That is nice for you, is it not?"

"He was visiting a friend, and left his car parked behind the public library. It was taken and later found abandoned about four miles away."

"And this—this thing that took it?"

"We'll identify him, never fear."

"And perhaps he will tell you where my Angel is?"

"If he just dropped her off at the fish shop and didn't wait . . ."

"So you defend that—murderer?"

"We've no evidence to date that any harm has come to your daughter, Mrs. Toni. Believe me, we are leaving no stone unturned."

"If no harm has come, why is she not with her Mumma?"

There are no two ways about it, there are occasions when a policeman's lot is far from being a happy one. They hadn't yet traced the perpetrators of the jeweler's raid, they didn't know the identity of the dead man found in Hangman's Alley and they'd no clues they could follow up about Angela Toni's whereabouts. O Death, where is thy sting?

When the officer had departed, Mumma stomped over to the niche where the little Virgin stood, unmoved, gazing on the rich red and purple anemones. Today was a crisis, today she got no Hail Marys or intercessions.

41

Mumma took the flowers from their vase and threw them into the trash bucket. Then deliberately she picked up the little statue and scornfully she stood it on its head.

The late editions carried a paragraph to the effect that a man had been at the local police station for a good part of the day assisting the police in their inquiries as to the whereabouts of the missing girl, Angela Toni.

 **5**

To ARTHUR CROOK, Sunday was simply another day of the week—the first or the seventh, according to your beliefs. On this particular Sunday he was up earlier even than Mumma Toni, following up some information that might clear a particularly unpromising client, and shortly after midday he stopped his car opposite a rather gloomy-looking public house called the Drover and went in for a pint. A glance around the bar assured him there was no one here whom he knew. This was slightly outside his normal perimeter, but he thought if ever a man had earned his pint, he was that man. A couple of sips of the muddy liquid they miscalled beer were enough to convince him he'd never cross this threshold again unless business compelled him, and was even grateful to the Breathalyser Racket, as he called it, that had stopped his normal practice of engulfing his first pint at a gulp. No one here appeared to recognize him—not that that disturbed him, a little anonymity never hurt any man, but he didn't care for the barman's indifferent manner any more than he liked the atmosphere. He was halfway through his nauseous draught when his attention was caught by a man's unpleasant voice shouting scornfully, "You're surely never on that old game. You want to grow up, Dad." Crook turned sharply. A pretty ordinary sort of man, fortyish, slightly undersized (like the pub's glasses, he shrewdly suspected), with a face too pale for health and a manner too subdued for his own good, was standing at the counter, going feverishly through his pockets, while the barman and some other chaps who clearly didn't deserve anything better than the swipes that were sold here looked on and grinned.

The little chap looked harassed, as well he might. "I had it," he was saying. "In a purse."

"So you keep your money in a purse, do you? That's a bit girlish, isn't it? What the hell do you think this place is?"

"He wouldn't like to tell you, not on the Sabbath," interposed Mr. Crook, and the smiles were wiped off all the faces like someone demonstrating the efficacy of a new kind of furniture polish.

"I don't know who you are," observed the barman insolently, and Crook put his hand in his pocket and slapped an equally insolent card down on the counter. "Say you can read," he observed in a genial voice, "take a look at that."

The barman looked. ARTHUR G. CROOK—two addresses: one in Bloomsbury Street and the other comparatively local—*Your worry our opportunity. Trouble is our business. Round the clock service.*

"What do you suppose you're advertising?" demanded the barman angrily. "Don't you know you're not allowed to advertise in a bar?"

"Just supplyin' your deficiencies," said Mr. Crook, unmoved. And turning to the harassed man he said politely, "Be my guest," adding blatantly, "Though if you knew what you'll get you might doubt my motives."

"Your old lady won't like it," the barman said. "Probably took your purse away to stop you having a wet."

"There speaks Benedict, the married man," quoted Crook.

"You take care who you're calling names," the barman warned him angrily. He picked up the card, read it again, and his expression changed. "What do you want here?"

"I thought I wanted a drink, but they say, don't they, you live and learn. Ask my friend what he's having— Take my tip and avoid the beer," he added. "As you'll see from my card, advice is free."

"I could certainly do with some of that, Mr. Crook."

"Better make that two of Scotch," Crook told the barman, and waited to see the spirit drawn.

"That's best old Scotch," said the man, setting down the glasses.

"It's very small for its age," Crook quoted. He picked up his glass and his companion followed his example. There were two or three uncared-for small tables against the wall and they sat down together at one of these. "I was wondering why Providence directed my steps into this dump," the lawyer continued in cheerful tones. "Maybe now I know why."

"It's very good of you, Mr. Crook. I'm afraid I don't know . . ."

"Shows you've never been in trouble," Crook assured him. "More than can be said for Soapy Sam there."

"I noticed. I did wonder why."

"Could be a spiv pub, might even pass pot, no telling—wolves get into some funny clothing these days. Didn't happen to mention your name, did you?"

"Hersey—Wilf Hersey. It's not me—that's in trouble, I mean—it's my lad."

"He's the right age for it," Crook offered.

"Not this sort of trouble, Mr. Crook. Oh, I don't mean taking the car, lots of young fellows would have done the same and think no worse of themselves. I don't feel that way about it myself, but you have to try to keep abreast of the times. But this thing they—the police, that is—seem to think he's done—I mean, it doesn't make sense. Ben's no angel . . ."

"Wouldn't still be with us if he were," Crook murmured.

"But when it comes to harming a little girl—his own sister's friend—why, she's not ten yet."

"Wait a minute," said Crook, who always found time to read the juicier Sunday papers in the way of business, "you're not on about the kid in the fish shop?"

"That's the one. Apart from anything else, no one who wasn't off his rocker would lift a hand against Mumma Toni's kid. Why, she'd cut off your head with a breadknife as soon as look at you."

"I like 'em to have a bit of spirit," said Mr. Crook enthusiastically. "A man has been at the station—that your lad?"

"That's the one. To tell you the truth, Mr. Crook, he hardly knows if he's on his head or his heels. I'll get you a lawyer, son, I told him. Well, chaps like us can't expect to measure up to the police—and I've been trying to do that thing all day. Started yesterday afternoon when I saw the way things were going to break."

"No legal beagle of your own?"

"We've never needed one. I mean . . ."

"I know what you mean," said Crook. "You've done your share of trudging through the Valley of the Shadow, but never come up against anything where the law can help you."

"One of my mates recommended a man—but he didn't want to know. I tried a couple of others, but it's the same with them. Young chap who goes after little girls deserves all that's coming to him—that's their attitude."

"Where's the boy now?"

"Being detained in custody, just for the weekend. Mind you, I don't think he's any worse off there than he'd be at home, all things considered . . ."

"If your Mumma Toni's anything like you say she is, he could easily owe his life to the police. It's a funny thing, even chaps with records as long as your arm don't have a word to say in a case like this."

"He's only eighteen and crazy about some girl of his own age. He'd hardly know the girl if he saw her again—Angel, I mean. Only—what's he to do? He's all at sea."

"Not much time to spare," said Crook consideringly. "And Sunday ain't the best day for finding people at home. Still, you say the word and I'll get cracking."

Wilf Hersey clearly wasn't accustomed to moving at this rate. "You mean, Mr. Crook, you'd take it on?"

"Up to you," Crook told him.

"The police will have seen everyone," Hersey said.

"Sure. But the police and me don't always see eye to eye. And you know why? Because we don't always see the same things. Like two chaps in a room looking out of two different windows—you wouldn't expect them to have the same view, would you? Now, about this little girl. Know anything about her, beyond the fact that Mum's a female dragon?"

"She's my Mary's special friend, and that means a lot. And whatever people may say about Mumma's morals—and no one's ever set eyes on Angela's father—she's brought the little girl up well enough."

"Mumma have a job?"

"About three. Well, she's the family's prop and stay. Out at crack of dawn—that is, as soon as she's given the girl her breakfast—back about five-thirty. Child has her dinners at school. Angel's a latchkey kid."

"And she'd come out of school—when?"

"Three-thirty or four—something like that."

"What does she do till Mumma gets back? She doesn't always come to your place?"

"I don't know what she does. Mumma doesn't get home till about seven-thirty on Fridays. Stops to do a bit of overtime. That's why Angel buys the fish. Mumma leaves a note what she wants—and the money. I got all this from Mary."

"So two hours a day she's on her owney-oh and nearly twice that on Fridays. She may be only nine, but you'd be surprised some of the capers these kids can get up to, and all the time looking as though they'd just come back from choir practice. Mind you, I don't say this one doesn't live up to her name, but that's a gap I'd like to see filled."

Don Billing of the Pemberton fried-fish shop worked hard all week, so took it easy on the Sabbath. At around one, when Crook came knocking at his door, he was still in his shirt sleeves and had just finished shaving. When he saw a large bright-brown figure on his doorstep—brown suit, brown overcoat, abominable brown bowler hat—he said promptly, "Sorry, mate, we're not open Sundays, not before six. And that's my private bell you rang."

"That's what I thought," agreed Crook. "Had the police round already, I daresay."

"Strewth, don't tell me you're the C.I.D." Don sounded really disturbed. "I told your other chap all I know, which wasn't much."

"I'm like George Washington, I cannot tell a lie. Representing this chap they seem to be hanging on to in the nick—the one who dropped Angela Toni at your place."

"Don't mind sticking your neck out, do you?" suggested Don. It was a good thick neck, as sturdy as a bull's.

"If he's innocent he needs someone help him prove it. So far he's got his dad—now he's got me. Of course, if he ain't —innocent, I mean—he needs help even more. Not afraid of catching a chill standing on the doorsteps in the cold, I take it?"

"I suppose you'd better come in," Don agreed. "Maggie"— he called up the stairs—"someone about Angel."

Maggie Billing, a dark, fresh-faced young woman—no hair curlers, no bedroom slippers and a mouth as inviting as a cupid's bow, Crook noted with approval—came hurrying into

46

the hall. "Oh, Don, any news?" She looked at Crook with frank curiosity.

"Only that he's acting for the son of a b—, that chap they're holding in the nick."

"What sort of justice is that?" demanded Crook, offering a hand no larger than a leg of mutton. "Chap says he never saw her after he deposited her at the shop front."

"Who else is it likely to be?"

"Well, we don't know, do we? Me, I'm not like the police, grasp at any straw. You saw her that evening, Mrs. Billing?"

"I wasn't working in the shop on Friday," Maggie said. "I had a bit of a cold and Don thought— But he remembers her."

"Anything special about her that night? Didn't notice, f'r instance, she was wearing her hair loose by way of a change?"

Don considered. "No—no, I don't recall. The police did ask. But there are such a lot of a Friday."

Maggie spoke unexpectedly. "Wait a minute, Don. I do remember one thing. When you came in that evening you happened to say it was a shame really that a kid like Angel Toni had to stand around in the rain—something about how young she looked. You'd never said anything like that before."

"What's that supposed to mean?" inquired Don.

"It impressed you that she looked so young—so perhaps her hair was loose, it would make a difference to her appearance, you know."

"Could have been that," Don agreed thoughtfully. "I wouldn't like to swear. Is it important, Mr.—?"

"Crook. Arthur Crook. Didn't I say? Yes, it could be important. You see, if her hair was loose, then she lost the slide in the car before she came into the shop. But if it was fastened back, then she must have gone back to the car, since that's where the slide was found."

"And he says he didn't see her after depositing her here? Well, I'm sorry, I couldn't really say one way or the other. And they'd crucify me at the station if I tried to tell them I *was* sure. They'd want to know why—now, I mean—when I wasn't sure before. And come to that, I'm not sure."

Crook nodded. "Anything else you remember? She just asked for the fish . . ."

"Not asked. She passed me Mumma's slip. Mumma always

47

wrote down what she wanted—two rock salmon, three of chips. We were out of vinegar."

"Vinegar?" Crook's thick red brows rose. "Nobody mentioned vinegar."

"Well, I daresay it's not important."

"Did you mention it to the police?"

Don looked surprised. "I don't remember. Most likely not. They didn't ask me."

"Why's it so important, Mr. Crook?" Maggie asked.

"You tell me something. If Mumma wrote vinegar on her list and you hadn't got any— Do you usually sell vinegar, by the way?"

"We have a clientele that eats on the premises—Maggie deals with them—and of course they want vinegar. Where's the sense of fish without it?"

"And you sell it—quite apart from serving it at the table?"

"If we're asked. Sometimes chaps draw up with their cars—we're open midday five days a week as well as in the evening—and they take the fish with them, and naturally they want vinegar as well, so we keep small bottles . . ."

"If Mumma left a note for Angel to bring back some vinegar and you hadn't got it, would she go back and tell Mumma or shop around for it somewhere else?"

"If Mumma says bring back vinegar, you bring back vinegar —if you have to knock at a private house and bring it back in a teacup," said Don simply.

"So Angel would go somewhere else. Where would she go?"

"She might go to Hanna's in Main Street, they're what's called continental delicatessen—ham from Silesia, you know."

"Can't say I fancy my bacon from behind the Iron Curtain," said insular Mr. Crook. "They stop open late?"

"All hours. It's a family concern, see?"

"The only other place 'ud be the supermarket," Maggie put in. "That's nearer, only about a minute, but that closes at seven."

"And she left here?"

"Oh—say, twenty to. I couldn't be dead sure," said Don.

Maggie suddenly produced a steaming cup that she set in front of Crook. "Don doesn't drink," she explained, "but that's ever so good. None of your instant kind. I grind it fresh every day and we get it once a week from a chap who roasts his own."

"At Hanna's." Don grinned. "Mind you, I'm like you, Mr. Crook. I don't buy foodstuffs there, couldn't be sure what those Soviet pigs were fed on . . ."

Mr. Crook stirred his coffee, which was remarkably good. "Might even take to the stuff myself if it always tasted like this."

His experience was mostly limited to Parkinson's Caff, where he breakfasted, and where the coffee was as black as your boot and as strong as Cassius Clay. Maggie's brew was a ladylike concoction by comparison, but there's times when you don't object to being treated like a gentleman.

"If Angel wasn't abducted by one of these sex maniacs," Maggie went on (Crook liked her Saxon proclivity for calling a spade a spade), "what is the motive? It's not as though Mumma's got any money, so they couldn't expect a ransom. She's lucky if she has something left on a Sunday morning to put in the dish at Mass."

"There's something no one seems to have considered to date," said Crook thoughtfully. "And that is that the little girl might be being used as a pawn. Blackmail ain't always a matter of hard cash."

"You think *Mumma* . . .?" Words seemed to fail Maggie.

"I'll tell you what strikes me," said Crook, "and that is that everyone talks of Mrs. Toni in the present tense—she does this, is that—but does anyone know a thing about her the day before yesterday, so to speak? I mean, she wasn't born hereabouts, she just appeared one day—right?"

"I hadn't thought. She must have been here ten years and more for Angela to look the way she does. I mean, no one can tell you anything about her father, but you can be pretty sure he wasn't Signor Toni."

"I had worked that out for myself," Crook acknowledged. "Now, for all we know, in her younger days Mumma may have been what in my boyhood was called a hot number. She might have information—don't ask me about what—that could be dangerous, she might have met up with an old flame—anything. And I wouldn't say she was one to pull her punches."

"I wouldn't have said she had the blackmailer's temperament, either." Maggie's voice matched the east wind for bleakness.

"I don't doubt you're right," Crook hastened to assure her. He didn't care for east winds himself, a nice healthy fug was his choice. "But would X know that? Conscience doth make cowards of us all, and if Mumma should happen to have something on him, the odds are he'd take pretty drastic steps to keep her mouth shut."

"So, in a sense, Angel is ransom money. But, Mr. Crook, in that case, would Mumma have gone to the police?"

"I don't say it is that way. It's just a suggestion. And she might have gone to the police before she knew the score. And now she's committed."

"Wouldn't she tell them, because if you're right she must know X's name?"

"If I'm right, she wouldn't dare. But this is all speculation. It could be something the child knew or saw, which made it safer to remove her from circulation. What we need now are a few facts. No chance of seeing anyone from the supermarket before tomorrow, I suppose. How about the chap at the classy delicatessen?"

"Hanna's is open till five on Sundays," Don told him.

"Nice to know some chaps don't mind a job of work. Well, thanks for everything. Be seeing you. Oh, and if you want to do your customers a good turn, keep 'em off the Drover. Chaps have worn rope neckties for dispensing draughts less poisonous than the swill they call beer."

At Hanna's he found a smiling young Pakistani, prepared to sell him everything but evidence, and after a few minutes' conversation, Crook believed he'd have sold him that, if he'd had any under the counter. But he'd no sooner made his position clear than the smile vanished, flattened out like a penny run over by a tricycle.

"If there is any little girl missing, we do not know," the young man announced.

"Well, I didn't really suppose you did," Crook acknowledged, "but in my job you can't afford to leave any stone unturned, even if it only results in a dishonored graveyard. The one I have in mind could have come here on Friday evening, round about seven P.M. Came for a bottle of vinegar," he added encouragingly.

The young man's face cleared, though he still remained aloof. "Friday is the day we close at half-six, sir, because of my uncle who has died. The family attended a dirge . . ."

This was a new one to Crook and it delighted him. "Meaning that anyone who came after six-thirty would find the shutters up?"

"That is so, sir. On the clock, half-six. You cannot keep a mourning family waiting."

"Very nice feeling," Crook approved. "I wish everyone was as delicate. This little girl," he added. "You'd know her if you saw her on the street? Name of Angela Toni."

The young man was galvanized into sympathetic interest. "That one?"

"Well, don't tell me there's more than one missing. Don Billing—you know him?—yes, well, he thought she might come along here for vinegar, seeing he'd run short, and Mumma prefers your kind to the supermarket. Still, if she didn't get it from you and she wouldn't go home without it . . ."

"No, sir," said the Pakistani gravely, "she would not return without it."

"Mumma's got quite a reputation round here," murmured Crook. He meant it as a compliment and as such it was understood.

His companion opened a drawer and took out a hand-printed notice. This said that the shop would close at six-thirty sharp on the previous Friday, owing to a family bereavement.

"All according to Cocker," Crook approved. "The police should love you. They're dead nuts on corroborative evidence, if they can get it—the other chap's word ain't enough for them, as it might be you or me" (though, in fact, not often for him, human nature being what it is), "and that sort of thing ain't usually handed to them on a plate. You hadn't heard?" he added curiously. If they hadn't they must be the only two chaps in the neighborhood (the caption over the shop said Brothers, so presumably there were two at least) who didn't know about it.

"We hear talk of a child, but not Mumma Toni's child."

"Been here long?" asked Crook.

"Two years, sir." His expression changed. "We have our permits."

"Nothing to me if you hadn't," Crook assured him.

"You then are not the police."

"You should ask them. Mind you, I was once taken for a superintendent, in the country that was. And if ever you do think you're being fried by 'em you take my tip and ask to see their warrants. It's your right, and the public should exercise its rights from time to time, otherwise officials are inclined to forget they exist."

He didn't for one instant suppose he could learn any more here, though as a matter of form he'd check up with the records. Probably there'd be a note in the local paper, which specialized in obituaries—particularly, he thought with a faint grin, when accompanied by a dirge. On his way to visit Mumma, who presumably would be home on the Sabbath, he rang Michaels, the editor of the local rag. He and Michaels had got together on a number of occasions before now and the man had an elephantine memory. And sure enough Michaels could corroborate the Pakistani's story.

"Might have guessed you'd inveigle your way into this," he observed. "Who do you represent?"

"Well, who do you think?" Crook said. "And, Joe, do try not to sound like a professional scavenger. I don't like this case, not one little bit, and that's a fact."

"Seen Mumma yet?"

"I'm on my way."

"Remember the advice to the Christian soldiers, gird your armor on. Mumma's the kind that uses the knife and asks questions later."

"Thanks for the tip," said Crook. It seemed to him the safest person to be at the present moment was young Ben Hersey. "Be in touch." And he rang off.

Mumma, looking like a female howitzer, opened the door suspiciously. "What you want?"

"Mrs. Toni?" Crook tipped the horrible brown bowler. Mumma looked as if she thought he expected her to put sixpence into it.

"Ho no," cried Mumma, "how should it be Mrs. Toni when this is her house? I am, of course, the mother-in-law of the Wizard of Oz. You come from the press?"

Crook, thanking his stars that he could honestly say no, produced one from his illimitable collection of cards.

"You sell something?" demanded Mumma, paying no attention to it whatsoever.

"I thought I might be able to help you about your little girl."

"You read the cards, perhaps? Or you look at the stars?

Or we put out the light and you talk to some dirty devil who says if I give you money, much money . . ."

"Be your age, Mumma," exclaimed Crook. "It doesn't pay any of us to take chances like that nowadays, not with income tax what it is. If you'd look at that card you'd see I'm a lawyer, even if some chaps do tell you different."

"Do I ask you for a lawyer?"

"Not for you. I'm acting for this young chap who's being held on suspicion . . ."

Mumma prepared to release her charge. "You come for *him*?"

"Well, you didn't ask me to act for you. Anyway, as you say, you don't need a lawyer. You're in the clear."

"I would like to hang him with my own hands."

"You do that and you'll find yourself behind bars for life, and then when Angela gets back . . ."

Mumma leaned forward and caught his great rough coat in both hands and shook him to and fro. It was like shaking a sack of potatoes.

"You know where my Angel is, you come here, you talk, you think this is a joke, perhaps . . ."

"You must think I have a rum sense of humor. Do you always carry on like this?" demanded Crook, freeing himself with some difficulty. "I mean, I do understand if you want to see your picture in the paper . . ." He saw two men passing at the end of the road, and indicated them with an eloquent glance and the implication of a jerked thumb.

"Who are they?" Mumma demanded. She'd have made a good mate to the snake that crushed Laocoon and his two sons single-handed, if you could speak of a snake being single-handed. She could probably have taken on Laocoon's wife as well, for good measure.

"Never saw them in me natural," Crook assured her. "But you're rather handing it to them on a plate, ain't you? And I haven't come to rob you of your earnings, I have the sense to know I wouldn't stand a chance . . ."

Mumma retreated two or three steps, her tongue going like a pendulum. Tick-tock, tick-tock, it 'ud run you off your feet in a matter of minutes. "You come here, you send no warning, you talk of my Angel, you threaten me, isn't it? So what do you know?"

The chief thing Crook knew was that he wished himself somewhere else, but that's not the kind of thing you can say to a lady. "Nothing much to date," he acknowledged, "beyond what I've been able to persuade chaps to tell me. I was hoping you'd be able to help."

"You think *I* help to save that—that—" She turned her back and marched into her premises.

Crook meekly followed, wondering if he'd come out as comparatively whole as he went in. Mumma led the way into the big living room. Crook looked around him with approval. It wouldn't have won even a Highly Commended at the Design Center, but it was his cup of tea all right—cozy, homely, the sort of place that invited you to sink down and relax, possibly with a glass of something that didn't emanate from the Drover. One thing, though, was out of character. He walked across the room to where the little plaster Virgin still stood ignominiously on her head. Not for an instant did it cross his mind that this could be accidental. He didn't know a lot about any church's dogmas, but he respected them as he respected the sincere witch doctor. Carefully pulling off his glove, he upended the little Virgin and set her on her feet. "You have to show respect," he told the dumfounded Mumma.

Her face expressed only an enormous contempt. "Me—respect her? What she done for me? She think she the only one worried about her Child?"

"If I can respect the police," Crook argued, "and no one can say they're backward at coming forward, you can show some respect for a lady."

"The police . . ." began Mumma, prepared to dismiss the lady in question. But Crook bore on relentlessly. "I've heard a copper called a lot of things, but I've yet to hear him called a lady. And this one's a very courageous member of her sex," he added, his eyes on the changeless smiling figure. "I wouldn't fancy treading on a serpent myself, bare feet and all."

Mumma tossed her dark impious head. "I bet you, that phony snake, he come out of a tame circus," she scoffed. "Or maybe you think *she* sent you?"

"Haven't the honor," murmured Crook deferentially. "Now, about Angel."

"You have news? No." She answered her own question. "All you care for is the one who took her away."

"Gave her a lift as far as the fish shop and didn't see her

thereafter," Crook corrected her. "No, don't ask me for proof, because if I had that I wouldn't be badgering you now. And show a bit of common, Mumma. If he had meant to abduct her, would he have let her out at the fish shop? And we know she went there, because Don remembers her. So just for the minute lay down your bow and arrow—me, I aim to leave this house with two eyes, same like when I came in—and just consider—maybe the young chap is telling the truth. Believing he's the guilty party hasn't got us anywhere to date. Which means there's someone who does know where she is. Now, Mumma, if you've got any cards up your sleeve you didn't want the police to see, now's the time to lay 'em on the table."

"You make a joke?" Mumma inquired dangerously.

"Do I look like a funny man? No, is there anyone anywhere who might harbor a grudge against you and take this way of getting even? Think before you speak."

But Mumma clearly had no time to waste on thought. "You mean an enemy?" She looked at him scornfully. "Poor people, they don't have enemies, they don't afford them."

"Which brings us back to Square One. Which is Angel at the fish shop, asking for vinegar, and Don Billing saying he hadn't got any."

"He call himself a shopman . . ."

"So Angel would go somewhere else—yes?"

"If I say bring back vinegar . . ."

"She bring back vinegar? Well, Don suggested Hanna's . . ."

"Hanna's shut Friday six-thirty. The uncle die. And they keep watch."

"Same as you'd do if it was your uncle?"

"My uncle marry a heathen girl and go to America," Mumma informed him. "The Hannas heathen, too, maybe, but they do right by their uncle."

Crook presumed that by her standards he was a heathen too, but that was beside the point.

"So that only leaves the supermarket," he offered.

Mumma scowled. "That supermarket. Always trouble, police called, some poor woman take a pat of butter, an apple maybe —what a country, no charity."

"Well, it is their living," Crook pointed out mildly.

"Maybe the butter or the apple someone else's living. No, I tell my Angel, stay away from the supermarket."

"So you think it's more likely she'd come home without the vinegar."

Mumma threw up her defiant dark head. "If I tell my Angel bring vinegar—then she bring vinegar."

I'm not surprised your husband melted into thin air, reflected Crook, retaining sufficient wisdom to keep his opinion to himself. Aloud he said, "Supermarket stays open till—when?—on a Friday?"

"Till seven— I do not know, we never go there—seven-thirty maybe."

"Someone could have remembered her at the supermarket."

"In that—rabble?" Mumma considered. "Yes, it could be. You not see a girl like my Angel every day."

"No harm asking," Crook said.

"You think they tell you yes, we see her, we kidnap her, we take her away?"

"Well, what do you think? No, but they might remember her, and if she was by herself . . ."

"Why would she not be by herself?"

"Come, lady, you're not suggesting she ran away from home, I take it. Well, of course not. And she wasn't knocked down by a car, and nobody seems to have seen her, though plenty of people would recognize Mumma Toni's daughter, so the odds are she wasn't alone when she went missing."

"Of course she was not alone." Mumma looked at him if possible with a greater scorn than she had bestowed on the plaster Virgin. "Some evil creature . . ."

"Whom we're trying to trace. I can't say you're helping much. Now, hold everything. Who were her special friends? She must have had some. I mean, what did she do of an afternoon when she got back from school before your job was through? Did she visit anywhere in particular? She wouldn't go to the pictures on her own, I take it?"

"Where is money for the pictures?" demanded Mumma indignantly. "She iron, perhaps, she is a good girl. She listen to the radio, perhaps she visit a little with a friend, or she read. She is a great one for books, my Angel."

"That's a thought," said Crook. "Wonder it didn't occur to us. Say she went to the children's library."

"The children's library close at six."

"Adult library?" hazarded Crook without much hope.

"She don't have no adult's ticket."

"So the library's out. We know she went home with the Hersey girl . . ."

Mumma Toni sniffed loudly. "You ask that Mrs. Hersey how often she wash her curtains?"

"Mary sounds a nice kid," offered Crook placatingly.

"How can any girl grow up nice if her Mumma don't wash her curtains right?"

Crook had begun to feel he was interviewing an inmate from a foreign zoo, a striking inmate, in every sense of the word, but there seemed to be a language difficulty.

"We know she left there, got a lift from this young chap, didn't get the vinegar from Don, didn't get it from the Hannas because the place was shut, so—she'd go to the supermarket. It's not likely this young chap 'ud hang around waiting, he'd be picked up for parking before he had time to blow his nose. So—if he's out, who's in?"

There was a quotation he'd heard once—the wheel has come full circle—and it occurred to him now.

Mumma changed her tactics. "Why should anyone wish to harm my Angel?"

"Maybe they wanted to hurt you. Now, Mumma, put your thinking cap on—have you got any enemies, someone who might want to do you a bad turn?"

Mumma said scornfully, "Enemies are a luxury, we don't have no luxuries in this house."

"No anonymous letters, anything like that?"

"And we don't have no time to write letters. I don't write so good myself," she added candidly.

"No one in the neighborhood happened to clap eyes on her —no, don't bother to answer that. Ask a silly question and you get a silly answer. Now, there isn't anything you know that might, if publicized, make trouble for someone else?"

Mumma looked stubborn. "I know what everyone know, and that is—nothing. Just nothing."

"Knocking around the way you do, you're bound to hear quite a lot, perhaps something you don't even realize you know."

"So now I am crazy. I don't know what I know."

"It could even be Angel. And not crazy, Mumma." (Though privately he thought if they went on like this much longer, he'd be ripe for the bin himself.) "Just a bit of a puzzle—like picking up the essential clue in a jigsaw." But he saw he'd lost Mumma altogether.

"So now we are doing jigsaw puzzles—that is nice, yes? That helps my Angel?"

"Kids can be just as bright as their elders, if that's saying much."

Mumma began to catch on. "You think she know something?" Mumma shook her head. "If she know anything she tell her Mumma. My Angel don't have no secrets."

Crook had heard that statement a thousand times, at a conservative estimate, but for almost the first time he was inclined to believe it. He was surprised to discover how real to him was this child he'd never seen, partly, he supposed, because the various people who knew her all told the same story. All the same, he reminded himself, it's the ones I haven't contacted to date who might be the biggest help. He knew, none better, how two characters can inhabit one skin, and each have a circle of acquaintances unknown to the other— witness the famous case of Dr. Jekyll and Mr. Hyde. You might roar at the idea of a kid not yet ten years old being so devious, but though Crook had never found time for trick cyclists, he knew enough about them to realize they would at all events entertain the notion.

"Know who I wouldn't like to have against me if I was in the dock?" he asked. "That's a child, and particularly a nice, straightforward kid like your Angel sounds to be. That sort of witness doesn't know there's anything to hide, she ain't learned in the ways of corruption, she wouldn't even be tempted to lie. You've always taught her to tell the truth—yes?"

Mumma sent a baleful glance at the restored Virgin. "My Angel is a good Catholic. Why she not tell the truth?"

"It's a good idea," Crook acknowledged, "only sometimes it's like pearls before swine—I mean, it ain't always appreciated. What I mean is, the kid who can't be bribed to keep her mouth shut is about as dangerous an enemy as you can find."

"You think"—for the first time Mumma found the courage to put the dread question—"you think they do something— dreadful—to her?"

"I think anyone who'd kidnap a little girl is capable of anything," said Crook candidly. "You don't get anywhere, not in this world and I daresay not in the next either, by shutting your eyes. That's a sure way to fall down flat on your kisser."

He spoke with more than his normal passion. He'd never, not after eight pints, describe himself as a child-lover, but even his blood boiled at the thought of a little girl being the object of revenge. If adults chose to go to war, well, that was their affair and no skin off his nose. But kids and old people, the defenseless and, to a large extent, the unrepresented, they needed a bodyguard, and this side of the Kingdom of Heaven, it couldn't be too strong. Hell, I'll be equipping myself with wings in a minute, he thought, genuinely alarmed.

"You think she carried away like a bird carry a field mouse?" The emergency was equipping Mumma with flights of fancy of which she hadn't believed herself capable. "In a crowded street, in the rain, on a Friday, with all the people coming from the market—Mr. Crook, someone would see."

"We don't know that they didn't, but there's quite a crowd will say, 'I can't help, I don't want the limelight, I don't want this chap turning his attention on me'—self-preservation, see —or chaps who can't afford to invoke the law, chaps who'll tell themselves, 'Well, I don't know it was that kid, do I?' You have to remember Angel's someone very special to you, but to a stranger she's just another little girl. Now, if it had been you or me—well, we ain't so easy to forget—but to the man in the street kids come a dime a dozen."

"You think that—and you work for this—this—" She stigmatized Ben with an expression that doesn't bear any printable translation. If Crook didn't know the meaning of the word, he got the message.

"Listen, Mumma," he said, "and remember you can't afford to chuck away any chances. There was a mouse once released a lion, pretty tall story you'd have thought, but it's a matter of history. Now, I ain't no mouse, but I'm working to establish the truth—and tell that to the police and it'll give 'em a good belly laugh and I daresay they could do with one. Crimes against children get under everybody's skin. That means I'm workin' as much for you and Angel as I am for this young fellow. If I've backed the wrong horse and he's responsible, well, you can't win them all, can you? But I don't believe he did do it. The facts don't add up. And if the lad's father hadn't asked me to hold a watching brief, which is all it is, since he hasn't actually been charged yet, I couldn't be in on it at all. I mean, you couldn't ask me to make inquiries, you've got the police on your side. And I may only be slinkin' in by the side door, but even side doors give you an entry into the house. Come to think of it, you've got me and the rozzers on the same side for once, and that must be something of a record."

6

THE MANAGER OF THE SUPERMARKET, a brisk, suet-faced fellow wearing black horn-rimmed glasses and no hair on his face (and not as much as he himself would probably have liked on his scalp), looked at Mr. Crook in amazement. "But, Mr. Crook" (it was obvious the name didn't register with him), "just think what you're asking. Friday night's one of our busiest nights. Honestly, the turnstiles never stop, our girls are literally run off their feet."

"My mistake," murmured Crook. "I thought they clocked everything up by computer."

"You know perfectly well what I mean." He looked suspicious. "The police haven't approached me."

"Are you blaming me for that? No reason why you shouldn't want to answer my questions, I suppose? This is a local kid . . ."

"I thought I heard they'd got someone . . ."

"Ever been for a country walk?" Crook inquired, though it didn't seem probable in view of the man's figure and complexion.

"I don't follow."

"Come to a bend in the road, one way forks left, one right. You plump for the left, and it leads into no man's land. You should have gone to the right. Police are only human, though that's sometimes a matter of debate . . ."

"You mean, you think they've got the wrong fellow?" discovered the manager intelligently.

"That's what his family hopes I'm going to prove. And if you haven't had the police round yet, that's your good luck. Now, I have a hunch this little girl came in about closing time on Friday night— No, don't give me that spiel about the turnstiles, I got the message the first time, but there wouldn't be so many little kids buying just the one item . . ."

"We don't know that she did buy just the one item," contended the manager, Mr. Butts, stubbornly. "Most of these kids have plenty of spending money. She could have bought a packet of chips, a chocolate bar . . ."

"This kid wouldn't have much spending money, and whatever she bought, it wouldn't change her appearance. So how about letting me have a word with any of the cashiers on duty that night?"

Mr. Butts hedged. "I don't know that they'll all be in today. Our employees only work a five-day week."

"Then we can get the others on the blower. Wake up, man, there are two lives at stake, three if you count Mumma, and I warn you, if anything happens to that child she'll do her nut, and she might very well do it on the floor of the supermarket. So if you don't feel like cooperating, I'm going along to the store to buy a packet of chips myself, and join the queue and do my own questioning. And if I get nothing from the first young lady, I'll buy a bar of shaving cream and start all over again. And one of them will give me the names of the spare staff. Well, of course they will. Even criminals cooperate where a child's a possible victim. Now, how many turnstiles do you operate?"

Mr. Butts knew when he was defeated. This lunatic would do precisely what he threatened, and there was nothing he, Butts, could do to stop him. Bottlenecks in a supermarket are one of the manager's big headaches, and Monday's always a busy day. Moreover, this chap wouldn't put his question in a discreet, retiring way, he'd yell it at the top of his great bull's voice, so that even customers in the remoter areas, refrigerated goods and fish, would hear him.

"If you'll wait here, Mr. Crook," he said with as much icy dignity as he could summon, "I'll see what can be done."

"You do that thing," Crook agreed, not feeling particularly optimistic.

If only he'd realized it, his first big break was on the way.

Not that it seemed like it at first. The four duty cashiers said they didn't know anything about a little girl buying a bottle of vinegar.

"Any of you not on duty Friday?" Crook said, and one of them, a girl called Marion, agreed it had been her turn for a long weekend, and anyway the store employed substitute staff Friday nights and Saturdays.

"Any idea who was on last Friday?" Crook wanted to know, and Marian said, "I think it 'ud be Miss Christie. She hasn't been with us long, but it's not so easy for the management to get substitutes at the weekend, they have to take more or less what offers. Old Christie isn't bad, except she makes herself look such a figure of fun, and she does get so flustered. Mind you," she added shrewdly, "I think a lot of it's put on. You know how it is, probably wanted to go on the stage as a kid but had an invalid Mum or something or Daddy thought the stage was the scarlet woman, so she puts on an act whenever she gets the chance. Mind you," she conceded generously, "I could be wrong, but I've noticed she can be sharp enough when she likes, and sometimes—well, honest, Mr. Crook, no one could be as stupid as she makes herself out to be and not land herself in the bin."

"How about ringing up the right figures on that computer thing?" Mr. Crook wanted to know.

"We-ell." Marian considered. "She comes a purler now and again and goes round wringing her hands, but that's one way of attracting attention—you know what they say, you'd be looking at a chicken a long time before you thought of her —and it's never much, six-and-four when it should be four-and-six."

"Gets worried about having to make up the difference?"

"Not her. That's the computer's worry, not mine, she'll say. I tell you, she can be bright enough when she likes."

"You're wasted in your present job," Crook told her frankly. "I could do with someone like you in my setup. You think she might remember a little kid buying just the one item?"

"I wouldn't like to say," Marian answered. "Only—she's more likely than anyone else. You should hear her take off some of our customers, as good as a play she is. But by the end of the evening you hardly see the customers as people at all—just so many baskets or trolleys, ring up the goods and go on to the next."

"Say she did remember one—is she the kind that 'ud go to the police if there was trouble?"

"What sort of trouble?" Marian's voice sharpened. "You mean, there was more than just the one item? The management doesn't usually get the police in when it's kids. It's different for adults, of course, you can't afford to shut your eyes, even if it's some old bunny trying not to starve on the pension."

"It's not quite like that," said Crook slowly.

"You mean, it's this kid who's gone missing? Well, why didn't you say so? As for going to the police, well, no one does that if they can help it, do they? The questions they ask —and they might think it funny she remembered one particular child. Why don't you ask Miss Christie herself?"

"I could do that," Crook agreed. "Any notion where I could contact her?"

"She rooms at 49 Rembrandt Street. My flat she calls it, but they're mostly rooming houses there. She chose forty-nine because seven's her lucky number and forty-nine is seven squared, if that makes sense to you. It sounds crazy to me."

"All articles of faith sound crazy to people of other religions," Crook assured her. "And belief in luck's as much a religion as anything else. Don't forget what I said if you think of changing your job." Out came another of his monstrous cards. "And thanks a million." And like the genie in the bottle he was gone.

When he reached 49 Rembrandt Street, a small, spry woman opened the door and said sharply that Miss Christie wasn't at home.

"When's the best time to catch her?" asked Crook.

"You didn't state your business." The suspicion deepened.

"Legal," said Crook briefly. "And urgent."

"What does that mean? Does she owe you money?"

"If she does, I haven't got round to it yet. Come to that, I haven't got round to meeting her yet. And anyway, if she did, that 'ud be strictly between her and me, wouldn't it?"

"I don't know about that," said the little woman in a voice as dark as the trim little mustache she wore on her upper lip.

"You don't know how alert you have to be with these roomers. The tales they tell you, as if they were the only ones that ever had bad luck."

"But Miss Christie doesn't have bad luck," Crook protested. "Isn't she the seventh child of a seventh child or something?"

The landlady delighted him by saying, "Might have been more sensible of her mother if she'd stopped at the sixth. Well, she's gone to Brighton today—Miss Christie, I mean—to see an aunt living in a nursing home there. Hurstleigh, rather."

"Kind heart," volunteered Mr. Crook.

"If you ask me, she likes any excuse for the trip. This aunt's been paralyzed for about three years—had a stroke, can't recognize anyone, can't speak, can't even feed herself. But you try and tell Miss Christie she's wasting her energies. 'We don't know,' she says, 'how acute the life of the mind is, even when the body's helpless.' According to her, she was a schoolteacher once. All I can say is there must be a lot of screwballs going round if they listened to her."

"Oh, Life, how grand, how rich, how rare," caroled Mr. Crook to himself, clumping down the steps into the street. Mumma, the girl at the supermarket, and now this Christie woman. He proposed to call around again this evening, though he hadn't told the spry woman that. He had an idea that if Crazy Christie knew of his intention she'd jam on her bonnet and go to the flicks.

But it so happened he didn't get around to talk to her that night, after all, because before her train brought her back to London, something else happened that seemed to give a new twist to the affair.

Crook was working in his flat in Blandford Street when his bell rang, a rather timid sound that made him wonder if Miss Christie's auntie had considerately died and allowed her to return by an earlier train. Then he remembered she wouldn't know where to find him, so he came out onto the landing, after pressing the automatic porter, and saw a female figure entering the hall. The woman started to ascend the stairs, rather in the manner of someone who expects to find a lift in any building she visits.

"Up as far as you make it," he called cheerfully into the well. "A long climb, but nearer heaven if the skies should fall."

He didn't know who the lady was, or even whether she

packed a rod in her muff, but these are chances you have to take, and no bullet can get you unless your name's on it—that's what he believed, anyway—so he waited, cheerful with anticipation.

Whoever his visitor was she was a stranger to him, a plump forty to forty-five, a snappy dresser with a slightly exotic taste in chains and earrings. The stairs had clearly winded her, and Mr. Crook considerately put her into an aged armchair she wouldn't have had in her house for the dog, before he started to ply her with questions. He saw that she was surreptitiously eying her surroundings with a sort of wonder that anything human could live in such confusion and lack of grace. Crook was used to that expression, had even heard his home described as a midden, but as we all know, lilies grow on middens, so what? Then when her glance met his squarely, she seemed reconciled, as though he and his extraordinarily uncomfortable, overcrowded place were all of a piece. A bull would look more at home in a china shop than this creature in her smart bijou Chelsea home.

"I suppose I should have rung you up," she said rather abruptly, and he wondered why she was so nervous. He excited a lot of feelings in the female of the species but nervousness wasn't usually one of them. "You are Mr. Crook? Mr. Arthur Crook?"

"There ain't two of us, I hope," Crook ejaculated fervently.

"I think I ought to explain that my husband doesn't know I've come to see you," his mysterious visitor hurried on, and she paused, looking at him expectantly.

"I wish I had a sovereign for every time I've heard those words," Crook reassured her.

"And I may be wasting your time, anyhow. Charlie—Mr. Tuke—says women can never resist putting their fingers into other people's pies, but I can't help thinking about this little girl . . ."

"Meaning?" If Crook had been a horse his ears would instantly have pricked.

"This Toni child. I've read about her in the papers and—oh, Mr. Crook, I believe I saw her on Friday night."

"Now we're going places," said Crook approvingly. "Now, loosen your wraps, get yourself cozy." He wondered if he should offer her a cup of tea. Beer seemed not merely out of place, but actually a waste of the real stuff.

65

"It was at the supermarket," Mrs. Tuke continued. "I was rather late, I'd been to see a film in the afternoon, and it ran longer than I expected, so like everyone else there, I was in rather a hurry, and on top of everything else, there was that unexpected rainstorm. It was almost seven when I wheeled my trolley up to a desk where a quite crazy woman was arguing with a customer, the kind who has to be persuaded at every turn that she isn't being cheated. 'I'm sure that's a special offer,' she said, and the clerk told her that was last week. So she said, 'Well, I couldn't come last week, I was in bed with the flu.' And the assistant, she's a temporary, terrible dyed hair and her lipstick on all crooked, said, 'Well, I can't help that,' and then she couldn't remember if she'd rung up the item or not. I can't think why a modern store like that employs such a woman."

"Hobson's choice, perhaps," offered Mr. Crook, but he saw the allusion was wasted on her.

"I was thinking I'd never get home, my husband wouldn't know what had happened to me, when this little girl spoke from behind me. I hadn't noticed her coming up, I quite thought I was the last, and she said, 'Oh, please, I've only got this one thing'—it was a bottle of sauce or something—'and I've got the right money. Please, my uncle's waiting for me, he's going to ride me home in his car because it's so wet, and he won't like waiting.' Well, this woman who was holding us all up, she turned and said, 'Don't you listen to her, always putting themselves forward these days, kids are. Now, when I was a girl—of course, that was a long time ago.' "

"When dragons walked the earth," agreed Crook amiably. "So?"

"I daresay I'd have let her through anyway, after her saying what she did about her uncle . . ."

"Hold everything," interrupted Crook. "You're dead sure she said uncle, not friend?"

Mrs. Tuke looked astonished. "Well, uncle and friend don't sound very much alike, do they? Besides, if she'd said friend, I daresay I'd have paid a bit more attention. I mean, when a girl says friend she usually means a boy, and this one looked pretty young—I know they all have their hair hanging down their back these days, but this one really was a child."

"You really think she may be the one the police want?"

"Since you ask me—yes. But Charlie's different. He says there's no sense me going to the police, I couldn't swear to the kid—and that's true, I couldn't. Only it does seem rather a coincidence—I mean, a child missing—and she was carrying these parcels of fish."

"Ah! So you noticed them?"

"I asked her what she was carrying, and she said it was fish for their dinner. I supposed this sauce, or whatever it was, was to go with the fish."

"Anyway, you let her through?"

"It only took a second, she just put down the money, didn't even stop for a bag, not that they're keen to give you one just for the one item . . ."

"And off she went?"

"Yes."

"I suppose it's too much to ask if you remember which way she went when she left the supermarket?"

"Well." Mrs. Tuke looked astounded, almost outraged. "I had all this stuff, and the counter clerk, whatever they call them, seemed to have gone into a daydream, and I knew Charlie would be wondering where on earth I was— No, I'm afraid I didn't give her another thought till I read this bit in the paper."

"I suppose you didn't see a car? Well, I had to ask, didn't I?"

"It couldn't have parked outside. I suppose it could have been on that bombed lot round the corner. Or I suppose it might have parked in Hangman's Alley—that's over the road —only it's less likely than the other."

"You didn't see one?"

"I daresay I wouldn't have seen one if it had been there. I had a lot on my mind . . ."

"And a lot more in your trolley. Why would the child, if it was Angela Toni, go into the alley?"

"It's a short cut to Parker Street, and Derwent Street's off that. If she was walking—but there was that bit about the uncle waiting."

"Told this to the police?" But of course he knew she hadn't. All the same he was a bit surprised at the shock she displayed.

"No. I promised Charlie. 'You don't want to go getting mixed up in a thing like this,' he told me. 'It's not as though

67

you could swear to the kid or know what she did when she walked out of the supermarket. Come to that, we don't even know she was in a supermarket.' "

"We don't even know she had an uncle, not if this is the one we're looking for. And if it was seven o'clock when you saw her, and Mumma was expecting her back at seven-thirty, she was running it pretty fine if she was going for a drive with Nunkie."

"I took for granted he was driving her home, as she said. Well, I didn't really think much about it. I did wonder how she got so wet if she was going back in a car, because she was wet— Charlie's right, I suppose, I can't really swear to its being the same girl."

"There's such a thing as the law of probability," Crook pointed out. "I mean, it ain't very likely there'd be two with hair flowing down their backs, carrying packets of fried fish and buying a bottle of sauce or what-have-you on Friday night, just before closing time."

"I did tell Charlie that, but he says that probability isn't enough for the police—they've got to be sure, and coincidence has a long history."

"Your Charlie knows how many beans make five, I'll say that for him."

"He's usually right, I have to hand it to him. Only—I can't get that little girl out of my mind. Of course . . ." she hesitated. "You have met Mrs. Toni?"

"I'll say I have."

"I mean—before this case."

Crook shook his big red head. "God is good to the fat, and sees to it that they stay in good health— Anyway, speaking for myself, you don't find me in a hospital, not while I have my wits about me. I aim to go to my grave without any discounts, if you get me. Why did you ask, Mrs. Tuke?"

"It sounds a dreadful thing to say, but even children who look angelic aren't always. And what does anyone know about her? I know she was very young, but—well, she definitely did say what I told you about an uncle. But of course that could have been just to get in ahead of me. I do hope she didn't go down Hangman's Alley, though I suppose, if she did, you could argue she'd been that way before. Only—isn't that where they found the hit-and-run man? Mr. Crook, what's the matter? What have I said?"

"I'm not sure," said Crook. "But, you know, it could be the case of the golden thread that takes you straight into heaven's gate, set in Jerusalem wall. Funny how you keep remembering these tags you learnt at school. That verse—chap called Blake, ain't it?—used to hang over my bed when I was a kid. My Mum won it at a bun competition at a Mothers' Union. What I'm trying to say is I'm not half sure you haven't put the end of the thread into my fingers."

"Well, I don't know, I'm sure." Mrs. Tuke sounded flustered. "Charlie isn't going to be pleased about this."

"Why, don't he want you to be a good citizen?"

"He says it's just me wanting a bit of the publicity I missed."

"Missed?"

"I was on the stage when I met Charlie. Mind you, I was never a big star or anything . . ."

"If all the stars were life-size, a whole lot of the others 'ud be crowded out of the heavens," offered Mr. Crook generously.

"I wish I'd thought of saying that to Charlie. Well, naturally, I did miss the life at first, especially when I realized we weren't going to have a family—well, we did have a baby but it died. And Charlie's got so many irons in the fire— Every now and again I meet someone I used to know— Mind you, we're all getting on, but these rep companies always have some nice fat parts for the older woman—have you noticed in a thriller how often the body's found by a landlady or a grandmother or some old trot taking the dog for a walk? I don't say they're the chief parts, but you do stay in the swim. 'I'm sure I don't want to see my picture in the papers,' I said to Charlie. 'Not in this connection,' and he said, 'You stay out of this, May. The police are like a cold, once you've got it you don't know how long it may hang on.' And he says his boss wouldn't like the notion of him being mixed up in a criminal inquiry."

"Seems like he has a very tender conscience," was Crook's comment. "What's his job—Charlie's, I mean."

May Tuke looked embarrassed. "You'll think it sounds absurd, me being his wife, but I'm never quite sure. He calls himself a liaison officer, but who or what he liaisons— It's a good thing I trust him, I tell him, or I might start getting some funny ideas. Liaison officer, indeed! Between ourselves,

Mr. Crook, I do wonder if there's something in his past I don't know about. I mean, something before we were married —not criminal, I don't mean that, but something like being a bankrupt—he's a great gambler and they never learn, do they? And isn't there something about bankrupts not being able to sign agreements or something? It's only just an idea, because he made me promise not to go to the police."

"And you keep your promises?"

"I'd keep any promise I made Charlie. It 'ud be as much as my life was worth not to. I don't ask a lot of questions, either. Men don't like it."

It seemed to Crook by no means out of the question that Charlie Tuke was a bigamist, which would explain his wanting to stay away from the police, but he didn't voice the thought aloud. He didn't want a hysterical female on his hands or to be made to feel responsible for another murder—and the police, poor sods, had enough on their plate as it was. Mrs. Tuke was speaking again.

"He didn't say anything about not telling anyone else, and I got to thinking about that young man. I mean, it must be so terrible to be innocent—if he is innocent—and know you can't prove it. Because if he could prove it he'd be free, wouldn't he? So I thought and I thought and then—it's what's called a compromise—I knew you were acting for him . . ." She offered a pleading uncertain smile.

"I wouldn't like to guess what Charlie would call it," Crook told her. "Going to mention our conversation?"

"If he asks me I shall say I haven't been near the police. I don't suppose he'll think of me coming to you. I suppose you think I'm awful."

"I'll tell you what I think," said Mr. Candid Crook. "I think that serpent that tempted Eve was a female, and the two of them got together to bring old Adam low. Mind you, if anything should come of what you've told me, the police 'ull have to know. I'll keep your name out of it if I can, say it does come to that, but no sense making promises. I never did much care for piecrust."

When May Tuke got back she found her husband talking to a man called Penrose, whom she had met before. She understood he was some kind of a lawyer, though the disparity between him and Crook was as stunning as the difference between chalk and cheese. Charlie was looking a bit tense, which probably meant breakers ahead. He was a square pale man, who clearly didn't buy his clothes off the hook, and normally he carried himself with a remarkable degree of confidence.

"Well," he observed as his wife came hurrying in, "this is a nice time of night to come home." Disregarding her murmur that it wasn't really so late, he went on, "You want to be careful, May, or you'll start giving me ideas. Late on Friday—I nearly got a parking ticket—late on Monday. What are you planning to do tomorrow night?"

Penrose, a perennial bachelor, thought it a pity that a fellow who had forged ahead as Charlie Tuke had done should retain such an infantile sense of humor. Mrs. Tuke actually looked alarmed, as if she were afraid of getting a black eye or something.

"If that's the kind of welcome your wife can anticipate, I wonder she comes back at all," Penrose observed drily, shaking hands. He noticed hers were trembling a little.

"Oh, she knows which side her bread's buttered, don't you, old girl? You wouldn't want to go back to the chorus." There was no need for him to add. "Even if they'd have you."

May looked at Penrose with a smile as artificial as a beauty patch. "Charlie likes to rib me about my career," she said, "but actually I did have a number of speaking parts."

Penrose was convinced that Charlie was going to say something flip about a wife's position giving her an opportunity for speaking all around the clock, so he intervened again. "I'm afraid you've had a heavy day, Mrs. Tuke. You look quite tuckered out."

"I do feel like something they've put in the bargain basement," May agreed.

Her husband's face darkened. "What have you been at? May, you never, not after your promise!"

"Of course not, dear, of course not. I'll say it on the Bible, if you like," she added quickly.

Charlie smiled and looked like a different person. "I was only having you on. My wife"—he turned to Penrose—"has some idea that she saw this missing child—you've probably seen about it in the press—at the supermarket on Friday night. So far as she knows, she'd never set eyes on the kid before, and there must be about ten thousand of them milling

71

around the London streets, playing last across the road and turning the motorists' hair gray, and even if she did see her, I can't see how it would help the police."

"It's not the police so much I'm thinking of as that boy they're holding in connection with her disappearance. You see, Mr. Penrose, it did occur to me that if she was at the supermarket at seven o'clock—well, he dropped her at the fish shop soon after six-thirty, everyone's agreed about that, so if he'd had *designs,* as they say, he wouldn't have hung around while she went shopping from one place to the next."

"You have a point there, Mrs. Tuke."

"But we've no evidence it was the same child," Charlie fairly howled.

"She had this fried fish," May whispered placatingly.

He stared at her. "That's the first time I've heard you mention fish."

'I suppose I forgot. But I did tell . . ." She stopped abruptly. The eyes of both men were fixed on her. "I must go and hang my things up," she hurried on. "And change my shoes. If we lived in the country, Charlie, I could wear these bumble-puppies or whatever they're called . . ."

Charlie's voice had changed. It was quiet as a dove and stealthy as a snake. "Finish what you were going to say, May," he invited her. "You told—who? Have you been gossiping to one of your big-mouthed friends?"

May shook her head.

"Who, then? You weren't lying when you said you hadn't been to the police?"

"Of course I haven't been to them."

Mr. Penrose intervened. "I'm not sure you shouldn't, Mrs. Tuke."

That caught them both off balance. "Look," Charlie urged, "you don't know my wife the way I do. She's only got to talk to them for ten minutes and she'll remember the kid actually told her her name. I mean, why didn't she mention the fish before? I'll tell you why, because this particular kid wasn't carrying any."

"You didn't see which way she went when she left the supermarket, Mrs. Tuke?"

Charlie answered for her. "No, she didn't. Though, mind you, she won't have been talking to a sergeant for five minutes

72

before she'll remember clearly. Look, love, you don't know the way those chaps can tie you up in knots."

"But I haven't got anything to hide," protested May.

"Think of it like this. If they put that kid and a dozen others in a line, could you swear on the Book you'd know which was the one you saw?"

May hesitated. "I suppose it would depend how much alike they were."

"And if you picked one and it turned out she'd been at home all evening on Friday . . ."

"Then I'd have got it wrong, wouldn't I?" said May.

"God give me patience," muttered her husband, who didn't believe in Him anyway. "Well, go on, who did you tell?"

She threw up her head, giving an impression of a fresh access of courage. "I went to see Mr. Crook."

"Crook? What sort of a name's that?"

Mr. Penrose intervened. "I understand the Herseys have called him in on their son's behalf. In the circumstances, Mrs. Tuke, I wouldn't worry too much. He can, as they say, run rings round any opponent. That young man's very fortunate to have him, particularly as he has his own legal code, which is, shall we say, somewhat more elastic than that of most lawyers."

"Crook by name and Crook by nature, eh?" Charlie seemed to be recovering his good temper.

"You want to watch yourself, Tuke," Penrose warned him. "That could be ground for slander. No one's ever been able to prove any malfeasance against him, and to give him his due, I doubt if he's ever actually infringed the law, just sidestepped it from time to time. And the man certainly earns his fee. Crook not only leaves no stone unturned, he wouldn't leave any coffin unopened if he thought he could find the ghost of a clue inside."

May looked happier. "I've been feeling so responsible," she explained. "That's why I thought perhaps I should see the police . . ."

"I still consider it would be to your advantage," Mr. Penrose told her. "One can't at this stage see why your evidence, such as it is, should affect a verdict, but the police can put two and two together as well as anyone, and with all the publicity this case has had—there was a picture of the child,

73

a snapshot provided by a school friend, I understand, on the screen at midday—it might seem strange that you had withheld any information that could conceivably be of assistance."

"I told you, Charlie . . ."

Charlie Tuke looked stubborn. "Well, it hasn't come to that yet," he said. "You'll have something to drink, Penrose?"

Mr. Penrose said sedately he'd take a Scotch. When May brought it back, he told her kindly, "If you wish it, Mrs. Tuke, I'd be prepared to come with you to the station—not that I believe you've anything to hide, but it's quite an ordeal for someone who's had nothing to do with the authorities hitherto, which I take to be your situation."

Charlie gave a great belly laugh. "If she has, she's kept it dark from me, and May's not very good at keeping secrets, as you must have realized for yourself by now."

May went to fetch some ice. "She doesn't drink much herself," Charlie explained, "so she never remembers the ice."

If Mr. Penrose thought Charlie might have done the hospitality, he prudently kept it to himself. But when he was going home, he reflected, I wonder what tricks Charlie Tuke is up to that he's so anxious to avoid the police. Tuke called himself a middleman, a phrase that like "love" or "cousin" can be made to cover practically anything. A smart operator can drive a horse and carriage through some of our rules and regulations even now, and Charlie Tuke appeared to the lawyer to be pretty smart.

 7

BEFORE RETURNING FOR A SECOND VISIT TO Rembrandt Street, Crook went to see Hangman's Alley for himself. It was a narrow road opening off the main traffic street, almost exactly opposite the supermarket. There was a public house on the corner called the Horse and Cart, a singularly inapposite name considering the nature of the traffic that thundered past it all day and a good part of the night, and beyond that was the back wall of a small plastics factory. The wall facing it was the back entry to shops fronting another busy street. Both factory and shops would presumably have closed for the day by six at the latest, so that there wouldn't be anyone to notice a stranger lurking in the shadows, or taking a short cut through the alley. On the other hand, it wasn't really intended for anything much larger than a motorbike or a handcart. More than ever was Mr. Crook convinced that the chap who had been found unconscious and dying here on Friday night hadn't got there by accident. And his death hadn't been an accident, either. Still, no one was paying Crook to do the police's job for them; he was here to find out what had happened to the little girl and get his client exonerated. In accordance with his normal habit, he liked to accumulate all the facts he could and possibly draw a number of conclusions before he came face to face with the chap whose chestnuts he was expected to pull out of the fire. Such a process also had the advantage of letting him know if the client in question was a liar or perhaps a gentle tamperer with facts. "Any parsley that's going round this dish, I can provide," he'd say.

He'd left the Superb behind for once, and he plodded on more cautiously than an onlooker would have supposed necessary. If he was being followed he liked to know it.

The same landlady opened the door. "Oh, it's you again. Well, it's not your lucky day, Miss Christie isn't back."

"You didn't warn me she was a night owl," Crook protested.

"Well, it could be the old lady's had a final stroke and passed away."

"Wouldn't she have phoned you? If she's not coming back tonight, I mean."

"It would be natural," Mrs. Brady admitted.

"Seeing I've come quite a distance on foot," Crook urged, "any objection to me waiting?"

"I can't let you into a tenant's room." Lot's wife, turned into a pillar of salt, couldn't have matched her rigidity.

"I should hope not," agreed Crook. "How about coming along to the Duck and Drake for a short one? I know they say walls have ears, but with the row going on at the bar they wouldn't be able to hear."

"What are you after, Mr. Crook?" Mrs. Brady looked skeptical.

"A little info. That's why I've made a second journey to see your lodger."

"Don't let Miss Christie hear you say that. She's a tenant, if she has only got a combined room and kitchenette, with share of bath."

"My flat!" quoted Crook.

"That's right. Well, the poor thing, she needs something besides that paralyzed old aunt."

"Occurred to me you might be able to help me," offered Mr. Crook.

"What do you think I am?" countered Mrs. Brady. "I'm not the Social Security officer."

"Wouldn't catch me within a mile of you if you were," said Crook. "Been with you long—Miss Christie, I mean? You know, not knocking your hall, very snazzy, but—more conversational at the Duck and Drake."

"Not backward at coming forward, are you?" the landlady suggested. But she took down a coat from a peg. "What's your wife going to think?"

"A chimera can't think. I'm a bachelor, none of the girls would look at me."

"If I had a pound for every man who's come here saying he was a bachelor . . ."

Crook produced a visiting card. "Name mean anything to you?"

"Lawyer, are you? Well, why on earth didn't you say? What do you want to see Miss Christie for? Someone left her a fortune? That'll be the day. I suppose you're not sweet on her yourself?" she added. "Just my joke," she apologized, seeing that for once Crook looked as grave as a tombstone.

"Haven't had the pleasure of meeting the lady yet. Just thought she might be able to help me about this little girl who's gone missing."

A hedgehog could no more have resisted a bowl of bread and milk than Mrs. Brady when she heard that. "Shocking, isn't it?" she breathed. "You don't mean Miss Christie . . ." They were walking down the road by his time. "I always thought there was something funny about her."

Crook got them settled at the Duck and Drake before he opened up. "There's a chance she saw the little girl at the supermarket on Friday night," he explained. "Didn't happen to say anything to you?"

"She never spoke about a little girl."

"Talk much about children?"

"Only to say how some of them were out of control, helped themselves to stuff at the supermarket and their parents never tried to stop them. 'If they were mine,' she'd say—but old maids are all the same. They always know more about bringing up kids than the kids' parents."

"The improving type?" hazarded Crook.

"It was like the Niagara Falls once she got going. 'It's been a hard life, Mrs. Brady,' she'll say 'Different for you, with a husband . . .' 'Maybe you haven't missed as much as you think you have,' I tell her. 'It's not always all it's cracked up to be.' "

"How long has she had this job at the supermarket?" inquired Crook.

"Seven weeks—eight— How they've kept her that long I don't know. Scatty as a kitten she is. Talking to her's like going round a maze."

"But it could be she always finds the center—leastways, that's what I've heard."

"Oh, she can be deep," the landlady agreed. "I always do mistrust the ones that play at being simple. Anyone as dotty as she likes to make herself out to be would have got herself certified before now."

"One thing," commented Crook candidly, "she clearly has something, for everyone to remember her. These old girls come a dime a dozen, and by all accounts it's not as though she ever won a beauty contest even in her youth."

"Still waters run deep, that's what I always say. Still, what's that to me? So long as my lodgers pay the rent and don't start breaking up the furniture when they've had one or two . . ."

"Like that, is it?" Crook tilted an appreciative elbow.

"Oh, not Miss Christie. Mind you, she'll buy herself a quarter bottle of brandy now and again—medical reasons, she says. Her heart. 'Just so long as you see to it your heart doesn't play you up before you go on duty,' I tell her. But honestly, Mr. Crook, I've never seen her under the influence. Can't help being sorry for her," she added kindly. "She's like a leaf that blew off a tree and hasn't anywhere to settle."

"No people of her own?"

"If she has they've got short memories. Not that she'd agree. If you could see her room, Mr. Crook—photographs everywhere, you could almost paper the walls with them. 'All yours?' I asked her once when she invited me up. 'Pity none of them come to see you, isn't it?' 'Oh,' she says, 'we're all scattered nowadays,' and she'll pick up a frame and say, 'That was Aunt Helen, a lovely woman she was.' Well, Mr. Crook, I don't have a lot of time for getting about, but even I can recognize a picture of Joan Crawford. It's being lonely, of course. No one ever comes to see her or rings her up. Sometimes I wonder if she'll be any lonelier in the grave."

Crook shivered, as though a goose had walked over his. Mrs. Brady ran cheerfully on.

"I did ask her down once to watch the telly, seeing she doesn't have one of her own, but it was jabber, jabber, jabber all the time. That chap was the spitting image of her Uncle Dan, and Dirk Bogarde reminded her of some man who was after her years and years ago, only there was this invalid mother, see? I tell you, I felt drained by the time she'd gone, drained."

She set down her empty glass firmly. Crook got the message and signaled to the barman for the same again. He had arrived expecting to find his unsentimental withers wrung for yet another of the poor Miss Lonelyhearts of the world, but he was beginning to supect that he and Miss Christie came out of the same drawer. If things don't happen of their own accord, it's up to the individual to go out and make them happen. He'd been doing it himself for more years than he cared to acknowledge. He suspected that Miss Christie was less a dotty old puss than a dark horse.

Crook and his companion hadn't got down to their first drinks when Miss Christie emerged from the subway and made her way to Rembrandt Street. She felt absolutely exhausted. As usual, Matron had asked coyly for a few minutes of her valuable time, and Elsie Christie knew what that meant.

"I really don't know how much longer we'll be able to keep Miss Christie," Matron had said. "Staff's a perpetual problem, and really, these chronic cases—she should have a private nurse."

Elsie only took on these odd jobs to have a little money to smooth things out. But even she knew the time was coming when she wouldn't be able to meet the demands. If only the old woman would die! But she seemed intent, in that closed mind to which none of them had any access, to hang on long enough to get a telegram from the Queen. "I know she must mean a lot of work," acknowledged Elsie meekly. "Still, in a way it's easier than when she was able to get about." Because while the old lady had had her senses she'd played Old Harry with everyone, accusing her fellow patients of stealing her stamps, trying to trip her on the stairs, dropping innuendos.

"What an unsympathetic girl you are, Elsie," she would say. "Grudging me the little amusement which is all I can look forward to now. You don't suppose I ever imagined I should end up in an institution like this, I, who had my own home . . ." And her glance would convey: Anyone with a heart would get me out of here and establish me somewhere where I could be free.

Month after month Elsie went down to Hurstleigh-on-Sea, hoping that in some mysterious way circumstances would have changed. She'd exaggerated slightly to Mrs. Brady—the old woman wasn't completely ga-ga, she had her moments of consciousness when she could even speak in an odd thickened voice. It would be better really, thought her niece, if she was completely comatose. As it was, there seemed no end to this pitiless road. Coming back in the train, she started to arrange the story she'd tell Mrs. Brady. 'This growing old,' she'd say, 'it's a terrible affliction.' Only if people died young it was a tragedy, or, if you were religious, you said the Lord had need of them. You really couldn't blame the Lord for not having need of an old termagant like Auntie. It would be nice to go down to Mrs. Brady this evening, she was quite kind on these occasions, though of course you had to sing for your supper. Elsie could sing like a canary, only unfortunately she was always out of tune.

When she reached Number 49 she realized with a shock that the house was in darkness, which meant that Mrs. Brady would be out. Elsie felt a sense of actual outrage. Coming back to an empty house was depressing enough at any time, but after one of her Hurstleigh days it seemed wicked—that was the word, wicked. Then she cheered up. Perhaps she's in the kitchen, she decided, making a cup of tea. She pushed her key into the lock and came into the cold hall.

"Anyone at home?" she called, but there was no answer. She stumbled down the passage toward the kitchen, which was, as often happens, the most cheerful room in the house. But not tonight, the room was empty. Besides, the house had that abandoned feeling you get when everything human has deserted it.

Poor Elsie stood in the doorway trying to summon up the strength to climb the stairs to her own room. *Perhaps she's had a phone call, perhaps she's had to go to the hospital— it must be something sudden or she'd have warned me.* All the way back in the train, which had been twenty minutes late, she had consoled herself with the thought of a friendly hour with Mrs. Brady. She had a few telling phrases on the tip of her tongue, the witty phrases that make people think what an entertaining companion you are. It should be easy to make them sound spontaneous.

She came slowly into the hall and began to climb the stairs, and then the bell rang.

She went quickly to the front door—perhaps Mrs. Brady had forgotten her key. It didn't pass through her scatterbrain mind that it's not wise for elderly women to answer doors if they find themselves alone in a house and no visitor is expected. But when she opened the door, there was nothing melodramatic about the man on the step. He was squarely built, with a pale face and a little mustache, too small for a face that size, she thought critically, but perhaps it's the best he can do.

"Does Miss Christie live here?" he inquired, and she was so startled that for a moment she couldn't reply. Then she said, "Who wants her?" and he answered quickly, "Did I scare you? I apologize. I'm a police officer." He put his hand in his pocket and drew out a little wallet. "This is a police warrant," he explained, and her spirits began to rise. She couldn't imagine what he wanted with her—her conscience was clear, goodness knew—but what a story it would be to tell Mrs. Brady when she did come back. Not that Mrs. Brady would like the idea of police at her house. "What do you want with me?" she asked.

"You are Miss Christie?"

"That's right. But I can't imagine why . . ."

"I wonder if I might come in."

She said roguishly, "Can I stop you?"

But without the glimmering of a smile on that graven image he called his face, he said, "I couldn't come in without your invitation, not unless I had a search warrant, which naturally I haven't got."

She knew a vague sense of disappointment that it hadn't been a gun he had produced, but of course in Britain the police aren't armed except on particular occasions. "You'd better come in," she said, "though I can't imagine . . ."

"I did come earlier, I'm sorry to be making such a late call, but the house was in darkness . . ."

"I've been out all day myself, and I suppose Mrs. Brady had some appointment she didn't remember to tell me, but there wouldn't be anyone else. There are two young men on the top floor but they're away for a few days. You'd better come up—Superintendent."

"Inspector Crayle," he told her. "And I'm making inquiries about a missing child."

"Well, I assure you I haven't got her stowed away," retorted Miss Christie in a gay voice. She'd often rehearsed scenes rather like this one, at least scenes in which some child or an aged person figured. *There's a child up there,* whispered the waiting crowd, gazing at the burning house. Not a chance, of course, even the fire brigade . . . Good God, who is this intrepid figure leaping through the flames. *Stand back, stand back,* chants the crowd, but the stranger vanishes into the smoke to re-emerge presently with a little unconscious bundle in her arms. Sometimes the stranger died (in her dream), sometimes she survived to perform other feats of valor. It was she who dragged the old man from under the oncoming bus, and disappeared before anyone could ask her name. She found to her surprise that she had reached the floor where her so-called "flat" was situated; she fished out another key and opened that door. The room struck her as looking a bit unkempt. She'd meant to give it a good going-over yesterday, but she'd had one of her "heads," my migraines, she called them.

"Do come in, Inspector," she called. "Doesn't it make you think of Ash Wednesday? Remember, man, from dust thou art and to dust thou shalt return. Well, we're returning to the dust all right, aren't we?"

A real screwball, he thought. Would anyone take her word for anything? The place was a clutter of ornaments and souvenirs, duty palm crosses tucked behind picture frames, innumerable ornaments of no value, picture postcards from abroad—it was surprising to find the chairs weren't occupied, except for a large stuffed pink cotton cat. "I call him Big Ben," Miss Christie explained. "He's company for me. Naturally, I'd sooner have the real thing, but you really can't have a cat in the flat, there's no outlet, and I think in these close quarters a tray is unhygienic, I don't care how often it's changed."

He remembered Mrs. Tuke's description of the woman—the orange-dyed hair, the terrible wrinkled face rouged to the eyebrows, the staccato manner, the explosive movements. Would anything she said carry any weight anywhere? he found himself wondering again. Was his visit really a waste of time? Only, when things are as serious as this you can't afford to take even remote chances.

Elsie pulled off her hat and tossed it with a cool, gaminesque gesture toward a cupboard top, but she'd misjudged the distance and it fell on the floor.

"It doesn't matter," she assured him as he stooped to pick it up. "It's only a woolen cap, a pixie hat we used to call them when I was a child."

She offered him a bright smile and he smiled dutifully back. He wondered how much she could tell him, and how much it would be safe to believe.

"It's about this little girl who's gone missing," he explained.

"I read about her in the paper—Angela Something."

"Toni."

"Oh yes. But I don't see how you expect me to help you. I mean, I didn't know her. I work at the supermarket," she added, "just the two days."

"I know. That's why I'm here."

She looked at him blankly, opening her eyes wide. She'd put on eye shadow, and like her lipstick it was put on crooked.

"There's reason to believe she was at the supermarket, possibly at your desk, on Friday night."

"I don't recall . . ."

"Try and think, Miss Christie. She was there just as you were closing, and there was a small scene. She wanted to get in out of turn. We have a witness," he added.

She commented in her silly way, "If you've got a witness, why do you want me?"

"Because corroboration's important. If you could remember . . ."

"Wait a minute. Yes, of course." Her eyes rounded, but there was no affectation now, he had her complete attention. "You mean that was *the one*?"

"We don't know, but this lady came to see us to say there was a little girl who seemed to answer to the description. She doesn't feel able to identify her absolutely—so far as she knows she'd never set eyes on her before—but she does remember there was a child, buying a bottle of sauce, she thinks."

"Not sauce," said Miss Christie. "Vinegar."

Her companion's eyes sparkled. "You're certain? I mean, why should you remember?"

"I don't know, particularly. I suppose it was rather an odd thing for a child to be buying. We don't get a lot of children on their own, not that hour, anyway, and she seemed in such a hurry."

"Did she say anything?"

"Well, not to me. I think she had tried to get in out of turn. I had a very difficult customer, the kind that argues the toss with every item—I think she was the one who spoke to the child and told her to keep in place, something like that. There was only one other customer. I remember her because she had a lot of things, and I couldn't help wondering why these women—I mean, you could see she wasn't a working girl or anything like that—had to come so late. No consideration, I told myself. I sometimes think it would be a good idea . . ."

"Would you know the little girl if you saw her again?" the man interrupted ruthlessly.

"Well—that's asking something, isn't it? She had long hair, it was very wet, and she seemed in a tremendous hurry." With a dramatic gesture she pushed at the coarse ginger-red hair over her forehead. "Of course, the young are terribly pampered these days, they expect to come first everywhere, but I did think my customer was quite unnecessarily fierce. I mean, it wasn't as if I could take the child's money and let her through, because I'd started checking up the items on the machine, and it's not like the old days when you just take an odd sum and sweep it into the till. I think I said something like you must wait a minute, dear. I do remember the other woman let her through, but I'm afraid I didn't notice her particularly, either. Oh dear, is it important?"

"Everything's important to us, Miss Christie, that might be helpful. So she waited?"

"Well, she hadn't any choice, had she? The trouble with these automatic machines is that they're not human." She wagged a finger to emphasize her point. "They're convenient, of course, and they say they can't go wrong, though I hae me doots." She laughed merrily. "I often wonder what will happen when one of these giant computers does go wrong. We'll probably all start growing backwards, and we'll be claiming children's allowances instead of the old-age pension."

"You're sure you didn't hear her say anything," he pursued. "I mean, she was alone?"

"Oh yes, she was alone, but I got the impression someone was waiting for her."

"Ah!" It was the first glimmer he'd had since the conversation began. "You don't know who? I mean, she didn't say her mother or . . ."

"No. No, I don't think so. Something about someone waiting, but then they all say that, the ones who want to get out of line. I thought it might be some little friend—a game or something."

"At seven o'clock on a pouring wet evening?" The words burst from him.

"Well, no, that doesn't sound sensible. Then perhaps her mother had sent her out in a hurry. She certainly didn't join anyone outside."

"What's that?" His head came up with a jerk. "I thought you said you didn't remember . . ."

"It's beginning to come back to me. I remember now, I saw her cross the road. I noticed particularly because as a rule these youngsters just dash into the traffic, but she was careful."

"You're sure it was the same child?"

"Oh yes. There weren't many people going about in the rain, it really was quite heavy."

"What made you watch her?"

"I wasn't watching *her*." Again that cracked laugh rang out. "I was clock-watching, isn't that dreadful? But there's a clock over the public house on the corner opposite, and I was trying to see how near seven o'clock it was. I always think they should close the IN doors of the supermarket at six forty-five, say; otherwise the clock strikes and there are still customers waiting for attention, and once they've reached the turnstiles you can't very well turn them back. That's how I happened to see her. She was standing on one of these islands in the middle of the road, waiting for the traffic to stop. Then she crossed and went down a little alley by the side of the public house."

"You're quite sure, Miss Christie?"

"Absolutely sure," she said earnestly. "I don't know why I never thought about it before. *Oh!*" Her voice ran up the scale.

He said patiently, "You've remembered something else?"

"I've only just seen the connection."

"Connection?"

"That's Hangman's Alley, and that's where they found the man they haven't yet identified, the one who was run down by a car. Why, I may even have seen the car without knowing it."

"How do you make that out, madam?" He wondered if she was playing it off the cuff, anything to make herself sound interesting. Mrs. Tuke had said nothing about a car.

"Well, he was knocked down by a car, wasn't he? And it's a very unusual place for a car to park. It was practically blocking the mouth of the alley."

"Did you notice what make of car it was?"

"I wouldn't know, I've never owned a car. But it was what I'd call a dignified sort of car, dark, solid, respectable-looking, an executive car but not a top executive. I mean, it wasn't a really posh kind like a Bentley or a Jaguar, and of course not a Rolls—I always notice them somehow, it seems so absurd they should be parked by the pavement just as if they were Minis or something like that."

"And, of course, you've no idea of the number?"

"Well, of course not."

"Did you happen to see if there was anyone in the driver's seat?"

"I shouldn't think so."

"Nobody spoke to the little girl as she came into the alley?"

"Well, I didn't really notice . . ."

"But you did see her enter the alley? Come, Miss Christie, this is very important."

"She must have gone down the alley," Elsie insisted. "There was nowhere else for her to go. She'd left the island and she wasn't in the street. When I looked a minute or two later, after my last customer had gone and I packed up for the weekend, the car had gone and there was no sign of her. And then if it was the Toni child, she lives in Derwent Street and that would be a short cut—though I don't know that I'd care to take it, not on a wet dark night. I mean, the Council won't bankrupt themselves with the amount of electricity they allow for street lighting in places like that. I've always wondered why they put a phone box there, unless it was for the convenience of the factory workers, placing bets, you know."

He reminded himself there's one born every minute. "Perhaps the driver of the car had gone to make a phone call," he suggested in his turn.

"Well, but the alley is wide enough to take a car—just—so why walk halfway down and get soaked when he could have stopped the car in front of the telephone booth? Inspector, you don't think that could have been the car that knocked that man down?"

He sighed. "Well, madam, I don't know, do I? I didn't see it."

"You didn't see it, but possibly the little girl did—and suppose she saw more than that? Suppose she saw the accident or whatever you call it, naturally they couldn't afford a witness."

"They?"

"Whoever the people were in the car." She was well away now, over the moon with excitement.

"You make it sound like a detective story," said her companion drily.

"Aren't all police cases detective stories *per se*? And there has to be some reason why she disappeared."

"You mean, the driver deliberately ran this man down, knowing the child was there?"

"Not knowing she was there, of course. I mean"—she followed up her argument with what appeared to her ruthless logic—"suppose the car had just started when she reached the mouth of the alley, the driver wouldn't know she was there. And if she saw what happened . . ."

"You're assuming deliberate murder, Miss Christie?"

She looked surprised. "Aren't you?"

"We're not so fortunate as the public, we're not allowed to presume anything so colorful."

"It could have happened that way," she insisted.

"Possibly," he agreed. "That's one of the finest things you learn in our job, never to rule out the smallest possibility. Of course, you'd need a motive—for the driver to run down an unknown man . . ." He was watching her carefully; she was the sort of witness to be treated with the utmost caution.

She stuck gamely to her guns. "We know he was run down, and we know the driver didn't stop. And he didn't report the accident. Isn't that true?"

"It's all perfectly true," he acknowledged. "But panic could be the answer."

"You mean, he might be drunk?" She could be direct enough when she pleased. "But even a drunk man must have known he'd knocked someone over. And he wasn't dead when they found him—isn't that what I read in the paper?"

"I daresay," he agreed. "The things you read in the papers sometimes surprise even us."

"And I did see a car at the time little Angela crossed the street, and nobody's seen her since. It all adds up, as they say."

"Frankly, Miss Christie," he told her, "it's simply a matter of what pattern you choose to make of the facts at our disposal. We don't yet know the dead man's identity."

"If we were in France—not that I could wish to be anything but British, naturally—he would have had to carry papers, and then you'd have known."

"I thought you were supporting a contention of murder," he said, and his voice was dry. "So perhaps A would have had the good sense to remove the papers."

"Because they might be a *clue* to his own identity? Yes, I see." Her voice sharpened as her imagination pictured the scene. "As for motive, well, one could easily supply that. Perhaps the dead man was blackmailing the other one—no, of course I don't *know* that he was . . ."

"Blackmailers don't grow on bushes," the man said tersely.

"Like blackberries, you mean. I know that, but even in this neighborhood—which the editor of our local rag describes as a cross section of the community—there have been two cases of blackmail reported in consecutive editions." He supposed that had put the idea into her head, but before he could speak she had run on. "What I mean is, if they can uncover two, how many more do you suppose are never uncovered, because the blackmailed person would rather pay up than speak? I know what you're going to tell me—that if they go to the police, whatever they say is treated in confidence, and they're only referred to as Mr. X. But you couldn't be sure something wouldn't leak out—not deliberately, of course, but—don't they say that a secret ceases to be a secret when one more person knows about it?"

She knew every cliché in the book, he thought. "Even blackmailers don't normally resort to murder," he said. "In any case, this is sheer supposition."

"But you have to start from somewhere," she urged him. "And great oaks from little acorns grow. I've always wondered," she went off at a tangent, "how blackmailers start their careers. I mean, in most professions you need either capital or a patron, though I don't think there can be many patrons left, with taxation what it is . . ."

He recalled what Mrs. Tuke had said about her. She didn't tell me the half, he decided. Mad as a hatter, but mad hatters can do a lot of harm. "You must be careful how you throw accusations around," he warned her. "You've built up a splendid case against a man unknown, but you must appreciate you've no facts."

"We've got a body," she insisted stubbornly, "and we've got a missing child."

For the first time in about forty years she found herself absorbed in a dramatic situation without seeing herself as the central figure.

"You need capital to be a blackmailer," he told her.

"That's my point. Where do they get it from? Oh, I know it's not money, it's secrets, and money is the objective. What I wonder is how they find these things out. Of course, in a sense you could say we're all liable to blackmail. I'm sure that matron at Aunt Ellen's home blackmails me, always threatening in a sidelong sort of way to turn poor Auntie out because she's become increasingly helpless and takes up more than her share of the staff's attention. She's raised her fees three times, and I'm always sending her boxes of chocolates from Harrod's—they keep a special Italian kind that she likes, fearfully expensive—and I always take down some plants for her garden when I go to see Aunt Ellen. It is a sort of blackmail, isn't it?"

He felt the time had come to put an end to the conversation. "Thank you, Miss Christie. You've helped us a good deal, that is, you've given us some facts which weren't in our possession . . ."

"You mean, the car? Oh dear, I wish I could tell you the

number, though I suppose they'd have changed it by now. They always do, don't they?"

"It depends if they know the police are looking for it."

"I read once," said Elsie, "that mostly it isn't the police who trace a murderer, the man betrays himself, and what the police have to do is keep watch and wait."

He was surprised at that, the old girl wasn't nearly so dotty as she looked or sounded. But he had something else to say. "Miss Christie, I don't want to alarm you, but I think I should warn you not to talk about this to anyone. Have you mentioned your suspicions . . . ?"

"I didn't know I had any till you pointed them out," she said, naïvely. "No, I haven't talked to anyone. Why, you don't think I might be in *danger*?"

"Anyone's in danger who might prove to be in a criminal's way. If it got around that you had seen the car—I'm sure you know how people exaggerate—in forty-eight hours you'd have told us the color, possibly even the number. Twenty-four hours later gossips would be telling each other that you'd seen the driver . . ."

"But I didn't."

He wouldn't put it past her, though, to feel certain she had caught a glimpse of him—her own remark about oaks springing up from acorns passed through his mind.

"Don't you want a signed statement?" she asked, suddenly feeling she was going to be deprived of any of the limelight. "Even if I were seen coming into the police station, I might only be going to report a lost cat."

"Tomorrow will be soon enough," he said. "I'd send a police car . . ."

But she vetoed that instantly. "Oh no. Mrs. Brady wouldn't like that. People don't, you know—like the police coming to the house. It gives the neighbors ideas. No, I'll come down just as if I'd lost a ring or something—the insurance company always makes you report it to the police even if you've lost it out-of-doors in Kensington Gardens, say . . ."

"You do that," he said. "I'm afraid I've exhausted you, Miss Christie, on top of a long day."

"I am a little tired," she confessed. "When Aunt Ellen had her senses I used to take her out whenever I went down, and sometimes I'd find myself thinking how restful it would be if she were suddenly struck dumb or something, but now that she's the way she is it seems more exhausting than ever. I mean, when she was being the curse of the nursing home, in a way she was enjoying herself, so I didn't have to be sorry for her, only for the other inmates. Now . . ."

"I expect you're longing for a nice cup of tea."

"As a matter of fact, I *am*. As a rule I have one with Mrs. Brady when I come back, but when she does go out in the evening it's usually to the pictures or a late bingo session—I expect that's where she is tonight, so I think I won't wait for her. Could I—dare I offer *you* one, Inspector? I know you're not allowed to accept spirits when you're on duty, and in any case I don't have any, only a little brandy that I keep for medicinal purposes— Oh dear, Mrs. Brady will be excited when she hears what she's missed."

He opened his hands in a gesture of despair. "You see what I mean?"

"Not even tell her? But she wouldn't—oh well, if you may not. It won't take me a minute to put the kettle on, it's one of those lightning boilers, I won it in a competition . . ."

She was through the door into the kitchenette before she'd finished speaking, and he heard the rush of water, the clatter of cups. He stayed where he was, piecing together the scraps of information she had given him. Even shorn of the parsley of speculation, the information could be valuable to the police. It was the first time anyone had mentioned a car at the mouth of Hangman's Alley. Miss Christie came back more rapidly than he'd anticipated.

"That really must be a lightning kettle," he congratulated her, taking the tray from her shaking hands. She'd really gone to town on the tea—silver pot, silver milk jug and basin. He set the tray down. She poured the tea into the two cups.

"I'm sure you take sugar," she said, tongs poised elegantly over the neat little lumps. "I always do myself. They say it makes for energy. Two or three?"

He detested sugar in his tea, but he was going to take it this evening and like it. But when she had handed him his cup he looked at it in a little embarrassment.

Miss Christie stared at him anxiously. "What is it? Oh dear, no spoon? Silly me, I quite thought I'd put out two, I must have dropped one on the way. Shan't be a jiff." And back she ran to the kitchenette.

She'd probably been running all her life, he thought, from

one job to another, from one crisis to another, and now she was running full tilt into danger—she was the sort that's so anxious to make her point, she'll walk off the edge of a cliff without noticing till it's too late. She came back, breathing rather heavily.

"You're admiring my photographs?" she said.

"Are they relations or friends? You must have a very large family."

"Oh, they're mostly relations. Mind you, I didn't know them all, but I came across a lot when I was clearing out Aunt Maudie's things—that was Aunt Ellen's elder sister, she was crippled for a time and I used to go over and help—and nobody seemed to want them, so I put them up there because—well, Inspector, I like to think I belong somewhere, and not like Topsy, just growed. I mean, that I have a place in the scheme of things. Most of them are dead now, except a nephew in New Zealand, and he might as well be dead so far as I'm concerned, but I keep them there because they make me feel real. Sometimes, you know"—she drained her tea and looked anxiously to see if he were ready for another cup, but he'd hardly touched his—"it's as though I had no roots at all, just floated in the air, blown about by every wind, as St. James says in his Epistle—I might be blown out of the window into another country or even out of this world. It's a very odd feeling. It's no wonder people liked burying their dear ones under those immense Victorian tombstones—that way you'd be quite sure they'd stay put, and of course it was a companionable idea . . ."

He returned to his first impression of her, nutty as a fruit cake, and yet she had her lucid moments, had been quite a help to him.

"You make a very good cup of tea," he congratulated her, passing his cup to be refilled, and she startled him again by flashing back, "I can boil a very good egg, too. Goodness knows, I've had practice enough."

"I'm not going to detain you any longer," he told her, swallowing the tea rather in the manner of Crook swallowing beer. "I'm sure you could do with a good sleep."

"And I'll come along tomorrow. I won't forget. Oh, and I won't breathe a word, not even to Mrs. Brady. That's a promise."

"I'm sure you won't," he said.

After he had gone the room felt curiously cold and empty.
She was quite worn out—well, it was natural when you were
no longer in your first youth, and Matron had worn her
sly air. She must remember to go to Harrod's tomorrow and
order the chocolates. She carried the tray into the kitchen
and washed the cups and teapot, put the sugar lumps back in
their packet, believing it doesn't do silver any good to leave
sugar in the bowl, decided she'd earned a little nip, and anyway she needed something to wash down the pills she took
at night, nothing a bit dangerous, of course, but they were
usually efficacious, though Mrs. Brady used to tell her it was
sheer superstition: You think they're going to make you
sleep, so they do. Although she felt so exhausted, her mind was
wide awake, she needed something to calm her, and whether
it was superstition or not, the fact remained that long before
Mrs. Brady came back she had passed out completely.

 **8**

"MISS CHRISTIE'S BACK NOW," said Mrs. Brady with a note
of relief in her voice, as she and Crook turned the corner
into Rembrandt Street. "Probably a bit put out that I wasn't
at home. She does like a bit of a natter after she's been to
see her auntie."

She had stayed longer at the Duck and Drake than she'd
intended; she had a vague feeling that she had told Crook
more than she had meant to. He had a beguiling way of
drawing a story out of you, which was funny considering his
appearance, and, stranger still, he really seemed interested in
the poor old moo.

"I'd better just prepare her," she added, fitting the key into
the lock and pushing open the door onto an area of darkness.
"I wonder what made her put out the hall light, we always
leave it on, gives the idea that there's someone at home."

Standing at the foot of the staircase she called up, "That you, dear? I've got a surprise for you."

Nobody answered, and Crook said, "Not gone to bed already, has she?"

"It's not like her. If I'm out she usually waits up till I come in. Says it makes you feel so unprotected being alone in a house if you're in bed. Mind you, I know what she means."

"Yes," agreed Crook dutifully.

"Perhaps she's just dropped off, these days take a lot out of her," Mrs. Brady offered, and telling Crook to wait just a jiffy, she hurried up the stairs. Crook looked about him, but there was nothing particular to hold his attention. Place as neat and inexpressive as a grave, and not nearly so dusty. Then he heard Mrs. Brady's voice.

"Mr. Crook! Mr. Crook!"

He came up the stairs at a pace you wouldn't have thought possible for a man of his figure.

"What's up?" He peered past her into the big shapeless room.

"She's asleep."

"Well, maybe Auntie wore her out," suggested Crook sensibly.

"She wouldn't go to sleep, not with the house empty, and her not in her own bed."

"Well, she's dropped off."

"I don't think it's that."

Mrs. Brady hadn't given him the impression of being a nervous woman, so he came quickly past her to stand beside the sagging armchair. Poor Elsie Christie was no beauty even when she was done up to the nines; caught on the left foot, so to speak, she aroused only disgust or compassion, according to your temperament. Her head was slumped against the cushion, her body lolled, her hands were open as though she had relinquished her hold on all things human. Seen like that, she reminded Crook of those caricatures children pull about on makeshift wooden carts on Guy Fawkes night.

"She doesn't look good, does she?" whispered Mrs. Brady. "Do you think I should get the doctor?"

Crook was looking at a small empty glass bottle that stood on the table edge. On it was the printed address of a chemist, and Miss Christie's own name in sloping letters of faded blue ink. One or two tablets to be taken as required, it said.

"Know what these were?" Crook asked.

"They were some stuff she took when she couldn't sleep. An aspirin compound she said."

She put out her hand, but Crook caught her arm. "Don't touch it," he warned. "Not till we know what's happened." He never claimed to be gifted with second sight, but there are some coincidences that even an optimist finds it hard to accept. And the unexpected death—because he hadn't any doubts, whatever Mrs. Brady might believe—of a witness in a murder case that's baffling authority was one of them.

Mrs. Brady leaned down to that dreadful inexpressive face. Crook found himself thinking that as in other cases that had come his way, she not only looked dead, she looked as though she could never have been alive—all personality wiped away, so that even pity was numbed.

Mrs. Brady had caught the sagging hands. "It's Nora, dear," she was saying. "Now, wakey, wakey, it's Nora. Don't you want to tell me all about your auntie, dear?"

But if Miss Christie was going to report on her visit to Hurstleigh, it wasn't going to be to her landlady, and the Recording Angel might be forgiven for not wanting to know.

At last Mrs. Brady straightened. "Do you think I should get a doctor?" Her gaze came back to the empty bottle. "Poor Elsie! Perhaps she took a double dose, not thinking. I I told you she was as scatty as a kitten." She had been such a lively, almost a frisky little woman at the Duck and Drake; now all the sap seemed to have drained out of her. Even her complexion had paled.

"You do that," Crook agreed. "After all, he's the professional. Let him pass the verdict."

"Verdict! You mean, you think—no, I don't believe it. I won't. She never would."

"Come, sugar," Crook adjured her, "let's not play any games. You and me don't reach the time of life we are without knowing a corpse when we see one." He put out a hand, surprisingly gentle considering its size, and touched her shoulder. "Look on the bright side," he urged her. "Whatever troubles she may have had, they're over. And ours," he added grimly, "are about to begin."

He'd seldom spoken a truer word.

"I'll get the doctor, shall I? Though if you're so certain . . ."

"Ah, but I ain't a professional, and nothing annoys the professionals so much as amateurs muscling in. Do you know who she went to?"

"She had Dr. West. I go to Dr. Graham myself . . ."

"Know the number?"

"She used to keep a list of phone numbers by the bed." She moved like someone sleepwalking, toward the double-purpose divan in the corner. "Yes, it's here," she said. "He won't like being called out so late."

"Then he should have taken a white collar job, shouldn't he? If he undertakes to serve humanity he can't expect to work with one eye on the clock. He'll be able to tell you what was in that bottle."

"I told you, Mr. Crook. Some kind of sleeping tablets, but she didn't take them regularly, didn't want to become an addict, she said . . ."

"Sure she used that word?"

"Oh yes. But you don't have to attach any special importance to it. She liked dressing things up a bit to make them look—well, not better, I suppose, but somehow more interesting. But I shouldn't think any doctor with his wits about him would give her anything dangerous. I don't mean she had a tendency that way, but she was forgetful. And when she thought she wouldn't sleep she used to take two tablets; she told me about it. Lying awake was dangerous, she said— yes, that was another word she used. You only kept on retracing your steps, going back and back and always ending up in a cul-de-sac. She made it sound quite dramatic, but really I think she'd had rather an uninteresting life."

"It's too bad I never met her," Crook exploded. "Her and me would have talked the same language."

Mrs. Brady looked doubtful, and no wonder. "Well, I really don't know, Mr. Crook. I mean, sometimes she talked so like someone in a book, she really began to think of herself as that person. I mean, look at all those photographs. She must have known most of them weren't relations, but she'd adopted them, so that there were times when she could believe every word she said about them was true."

Crook nodded. It seemed to him a wholly human reaction. Then he said, "How about getting the doctor, sugar? I'll hold the fort." He'd noticed the coin telephone box she'd had installed downstairs for the benefit of her roomers. When she had gone he looked keenly about him, following his own dictum of touching nothing. He wasn't what you'd call a social gadfly, didn't often go to the films or even watch the television set some persuasive salesman had once contrived to unload in his flat, still, even he recognized some of the photographs on the mantelshelf—stars of the period between the wars; there was even one that was either Kaiser Bill or his twin brother.

He heard the click as the telephone receiver was replaced and Mrs. Brady came hurrying into the room.

"He's coming," she reported. "Mind you, he started to say something about National Health patients attending his surgery. I said, 'You'd have a fit, Doctor, if this one walked in.' That shook him a bit, I can tell you." But the satisfaction died out of her voice an instant later. "Poor Elsie! I wonder what really happened. Perhaps she felt a heart attack coming on, though she always boasted her family had hearts of teak. Not always good luck, she'd say. 'If her heart wasn't so strong Auntie might have gone to her rest before this.'"

All the while she spoke her restless eyes were searching the room.

"Something missing?" inquired Mr. Crook gently.

The glance she threw him had a guilty quality. "No. No, of course not. I was just thinking . . ."

"There's no note, if that's what you were looking for."

"I wasn't," she denied with the speed of someone who feels she may have been caught out. "I mean, she never would. Oh, I know she'd say, 'If it was me I'd put an end to myself,' or, 'One of these days you'll come up, Nora, and have the shock of your life and don't say I didn't warn you.' But she never *meant* any of those things. It was just—just . . ."

"Parsley round the dish?" suggested Mr. Crook, who wasn't averse to parsley himself.

"And what's more, she knew I knew she didn't mean it," Mrs. Brady labored on.

"She may not have meant it yesterday, but yesterday ain't today," Mr. Crook pointed out rationally. "Say something happened . . ."

"What could happen when she was visiting Auntie at Hurstleigh? I mean, she couldn't threaten, 'Take me out of here or I'll cut you out of my will'—Elsie said she was past all that. Of course, that matron—I never did like the sound of her, a proper snake in the grass, all take and no give, except for venom—she might have told Elsie she couldn't keep the old lady any longer. Elsie was paying to the hilt, I do know that. That would really upset her."

"Well, but you don't come back and take an overdose just because your auntie's got to change her address," Mr. Crook objected. "She had the whole National Health service behind her . . ."

"Auntie wouldn't have liked finding herself in an institution . . ."

"If Auntie was as far gone as Miss Christie said, the odds are she wouldn't have noticed the difference. Now listen, sugar, you're going to be asked about this. Can you think of any other reason why . . ."

"She should take her own life? I've told you, Mr. Crook, she never would, and if she did, it wouldn't be here. She'd know it wasn't right. I always treated her fair and square, and she'd know as well as me that nobody wants a room where someone else has just died by her own hand."

Miss Christie wasn't the only dramatic member of the household, Crook discerned.

"And if she did have it in mind," Mrs. Brady pursued—she was like the charge of the Light Brigade, nothing could stop her—"she wouldn't go off without a word, a hint. I mean, the last thing she ever did, I mean, it would be such a waste if nobody knew."

Crook realized exactly what his companion meant. To die, said that egoist of all time, Peter Pan, will be an awfully big adventure, and an adventure loses half its point if it's, so to speak, executed in the dark. Besides, whatever her troubles, the old girl didn't sound the sort to put an end to things. You could imagine her manning the barricades and being trampled under foot by a policeman's horse, so that she'd enter the next world in a sort of hazy glory, but to lie back here and quietly snuff it with a bottle of phenobarbitone or whatever— no one who liked her dish as decorated with parsley as Elsie Christie had done would take that way out.

They were still discussing possibilities when they were roused by the noisy clangor of the bell, and then the sound of the knocker being energetically thumped.

ANTHONY GILBERT

"Cheeky monkey!" said Mrs. Brady in outraged tones. "That'll be the doctor, I suppose. Must need advertisement to make all that row."

"Probably interrupted his favorite TV program," Crook suggested. Everything he'd heard to date seemed to add up to the conclusion that had first occurred to him—it was like that childish game think of a number, and he didn't like the answer one little bit.

Dr. West was short and dark and terse. He marched into the room, cast an indifferent glance at Mr. Crook, then briefly examined the patient. "When did this happen?" he asked.

Mrs. Brady answered him. "We don't know exactly. Mr. Crook and me haven't been back above ten minutes or so—well, say a quarter of an hour—and she was like this when we came in."

"She was all right when you left?"

"Well, she wasn't back." She explained about Auntie Ellen. "I supposed she'd missed her train . . ."

"Stoppage on the line," contributed the doctor, terse as before. "Train 'ud be late."

"Why didn't we think of that?" Mrs. Brady marveled. "I mean, it's happening all the time."

Mr. Crook thought he might as well take a hand. Playing dummy had never appealed to him. "Not a medical man," he admitted, "but those tablets you gave her—would they do the job in the time?"

Dr. West saw the phial and picked it up. "Wouldn't do it in a month of Sundays," he said. "These are a weak aspirin compound; she could buy something more deadly for half-a-crown in any chemist's in the land. I don't give dangerous drugs to emotional old ladies, but if you get something on prescription it's more likely to work because you expect it to."

"Power of suggestion," contributed Mr. Crook intelligently.

From the glance the doctor sent him, you could see Mr. Crook would never be his favorite man. "You a relation?"

"You mean, it might have been a heart attack?" Mrs. Brady interposed eagerly. Heart attacks are respectable. Even Royalty can have them.

"We're all going to die of heart failure in due course," was the unsympathetic reply. "Only sometimes the process is assisted. Was she in any special trouble that you know?"

98

"Well, she did worry over Auntie."

"If everybody who worried over their aunties died of shock, you'd need a computer to make out the death certificates. And this isn't a death from shock. I'd have staked my davy this one would live to be ninety unless she fell under a bus or something, like those old trees that don't flower any more but go on living. It wasn't just that she was physically fit, she had a hold on life like the grip of a canary on a perch. Don't ask me why." He was bending over the dead woman, pulling down the eyelids, professional to the nth degree, cold as an ice-lolly, but competent—oh yes, competence was written all over him.

"Did she ever consult another doctor?" he inquired.

Mrs. Brady looked shocked. "Why, she was on your list."

"Nothing to stop her going to another medical man privately. What I'm getting at is, did she have any prescriptions in addition to those she got from me? Or wouldn't you know?"

"Well, if she did she kept it to herself, and that's not like her. Like I was telling Mr. Cook here, she was like Niagara once she got started. Anyway, private prescriptions cost money and I don't think she had much to bless herself with."

"Any family?" the doctor said.

"Only what you see on the mantelpiece."

"The great human family," supplemented Crook.

"Where do you come in?" inquired the doctor bluntly.

"Legal beagle. Hoping for some information."

"She expecting you?"

"Probably never even heard my name."

"So that can't be the reason. Calling a bit late, aren't you?"

"I came earlier, but Mrs. Brady told me she wouldn't be back before night."

"Urgent?"

"Anything to do with clients is urgent."

The doctor shrugged. The chap seemed to him a bit of a screwball, but no skin off his nose. He turned back to Mrs. Brady. "You realize I can't give a death certificate. There'll have to be an inquest."

"Oh, she wouldn't like that," the landlady exclaimed.

"She should have thought of that before. I'd say she died of an overdose of barbiturates, and wherever she got them from, it wasn't from me. Why, I didn't even give her these aspirin pills often—it's months since she came to see me."

"Could she have got them from a chemist?"

"Only on prescription, unless she could pay under-the-counter prices and knew some back-street boy who'd supply them. Or some friend to whom she told the tale."

"She hadn't got any friends," said Mrs. Brady bleakly. "I don't believe myself she had any relations except this old aunt. Oh, she used to talk about a nephew in New Zealand, I think it was, but he never wrote, not so much as a card at Christmas. If you ask me I don't think he existed. I know she let out once that she was a one-only. So you do see, don't you?"

"See what?" The doctor looked obtuse.

"Well, that there's no point in an inquest. Only upset everyone, and seeing she's got no family she might as well be buried decently. She can stay here till the funeral, my young men won't be back till the end of the week, and if they were here they wouldn't mind. I don't want her stowed in a drawer in the morgue and no flowers on the coffin. I've seen these bare coffins, like paupers' burials they are. I may not be a relative but I'm the nearest thing to family she's got, and I'd like to see her put away nice and respectable. Poor Elsie!"

The doctor sent his first glance of camaraderie at Crook, but Crook wasn't playing ball. He was remembering a quotation his Mum, the late Mrs. George Crook, used to quote to him, something about the unknown good who sleep in God's still memory folded deep. It seemed to him Mrs. Brady might well qualify.

"Have you notified the police?" the doctor demanded.

"Ask a silly question!" Crook exclaimed. "Well, of course we haven't. We were not to know she'd died of—what did you call it?—barbiturate poisoning. And they might think it funny we should be so sure. The police have very suspicious minds, in case you didn't know."

The doctor shrugged. "I suppose you've got a telephone?" he suggested to Mrs. Brady.

"It's in the hall. It's sixpence in the slot. You can't always trust your roomers to put the money in the box . . ."

"You'd better wait," the doctor told Crook, marching out of the room.

Mrs. Brady moved forward shamelessly and opened the

door after he'd disappeared. Dr. West's voice came smokily up the dark stairway.

"There'll have to be an inquest, of course," he was saying. "I'll notify the coroner, if you like, but seeing she doesn't appear to have any family, only the landlady and some chap called Crook who says he's a lawyer . . . Mind you, they can do it with a bottle of aspirin if they like, only they don't normally swallow the bottle too . . ."

Mrs. Brady closed the door. "It's downright wicked," she fumed. "Putting ideas into their heads. As if she ever would."

The doctor came in on the tail of that. "Ever would what?"

"Take her own life. That's what you've got in mind, isn't it?"

"Well, if she didn't take the stuff, someone gave it to her. Any idea who that might be?"

"That'll be for the police to find out, won't it?" suggested Mr. Crook, and now it was the doctor's turn to look blank.

The police came belting up the stairs. "Trust this Crook to make trouble," one said. "You know what they say about him—where there's Crook there's crime. And we've got enough on our plates without this."

They came into the room where they were waiting for them—three living and one dead. They listened to the evidence and asked the inevitable question.

"No note?"

"Only if she wrote with invisible ink on invisible paper."

"I suppose she might have posted it."

"Post from here goes out at seven," Mrs. Brady reminded them. "Besides, why should she?"

The police kept to themselves the notion that a woman in Mrs. Brady's position, her living depending on her roomers, might have destroyed a note and hoped for a verdict of natural death. Not likely, of course, but you hadn't been long in the force before you realized there was no idiocy of which the public isn't capable.

"Have any letters?" They looked around as if they expected to see envelopes fluttering down from the ceiling.

"She never had any letters, only the sort you address to yourself, answering ads for holiday brochures and that. I should know, I take the post in. And if you're going to ask about family, so far as I know she didn't have any of those either, barring this old aunt . . ." Once more she explained about Aunt Ellen.

"She might have had a phone call," suggested the other police officer.

"Not while I was in the house."

"Well, but you said you were out when she came back."

"And knowing she was going to get a phone call from some anonymous person she had the stuff all ready in her handbag?" That was Crook.

"Perhaps you know what happened," said the officer sarcastically.

"I could make a good guess," said Crook. "And my guess 'ud be murder."

If either of the others had said it the police mightn't have paid much attention, but this was Arthur Crook, and though he was an extravagant sort of chap he didn't often make statements of this gravity without some good sense to back them.

"You could supply a motive, sir?"

The atmosphere had stiffened—no other word would describe it. Mrs. Brady's mouth had dropped open; the doctor, who'd been on tenterhooks to get back to his TV, promptly forgot all about it, as Crook had known he would. Real life can beat fiction any day of the week.

"I had the idea she might be able to supply the missing link in a case in which I'm interested—the disappearance of this little girl Angela Toni. There was a suggestion that she was at the supermarket where Miss Christie worked on a Friday, and Miss Christie might have seen something that would help."

"You're declaring an interest?" one of the officers said.

"I'm representing that chap you've got your beady eyes on, Ben Hersey."

"No charge against Hersey has been made, Mr. Crook."

"But you've got him under surveillance, don't tell me different. And it wouldn't surprise me to know you've impounded his passport. No, no charge has been brought because you don't know the nature of the charge. You can't charge him with murder till you've a body, and so far you haven't even got evidence that the child's dead."

"If Miss Christie had any useful information, surely she'd have given it to the police."

102

"Yes," chimed in Mrs. Brady, "she would. She was ever so conscientious. I mean, if she occupied a chair in the park and no one came for the sixpence, she'd leave the money on the seat."

"Maybe she didn't know she had evidence," said Crook patiently. "That's what I was coming to find out. After all, I daresay to her one little kid looked like another. But when she started to think, she might remember something . . ."

"If you gave her sufficient time she'd remember the little girl gave her her name and address," cut in the doctor brutally.

The police made no reply to this, but continued to address themselves to Crook. "So you don't know she could have been of any assistance?"

"I didn't before I got here, but I do now. Well, if she couldn't have helped me, why is she the late Miss Christie? Someone who knew I was on my way cut me out." He spoke with barely concealed bitterness. He had only once lost a client, and this was one of the few times that he'd lost a witness, and though he wouldn't give the police any satisfaction, he didn't attempt to shrug off his own sense of his personal responsibility. He should have thought that his movements were being tailed and been on his guard.

Mrs. Brady, however, refused to be quenched. "If you mean someone came here, no, she wouldn't let anyone in at night."

"No stranger, you mean?"

"I told you, she didn't have any friends."

"But she'd open the door, surely?"

"Well—if she thought it was someone for me she might. But she'd never ask anyone up, and you don't tell me some-one crams your mouth full of sleeping pills the minute you open the door."

"Lady's got something there," murmured Crook.

"Why should anyone come?" the doctor demanded. "You open all the doors, you said," he added to Mrs. Brady.

"Ah, but I was out. He might have waited and seen me go."

"As for why he came, could be the reason was the same as mine, only in reverse as it were. I wanted her to speak, he wanted to make sure she didn't. And she won't," he added.

Mrs. Brady suddenly unfastened a scarf she was wearing around her throat and laid it over the dead woman's face. "I never did like the idea of people looking at you when you were asleep," she explained. "It seems like taking an unfair advantage. And, children apart, no one looks their best when they're sleeping. And if you still think she might have done it herself," she went on, "I can tell you she didn't. She'd asked me to go to this film at the Essoldo with her on Thursday, she said she'd collect her pension the day before. And then there was that skirt she had—Country Wear or something she called it— She'd been losing weight, poor thing, and no wonder with all this trouble about auntie, and I know she used to get very confused at the supermarket, if it hadn't been for auntie she could have lived out her last days in peace— And she took it to Alcock's to be cleaned and altered— twenty-six shillings she paid for it, she told me—Well, she wouldn't do that if she was planning to take an overdose, would she?"

"One of these days," murmured Crook to the doctor, who'd moved closer during this conversation, "some chap will endow a Chair of Logical Deduction, and you mark my words, it'll be a woman who'll occupy it. They have us standing at the post."

One of the policemen made another point. "Where's the glass?" he demanded. "She wouldn't be able to swallow all those tablets without water or something."

"Maybe she took them in the kitchen—well, she likes to call it a kitchen, though really it's only a sort of alcove with a sink and a little electric oven . . ."

"You're slipping, sugar," murmured Crook reprovingly. "You don't suggest she'd meekly take a handful of death pills and walk into the kitchen to get a glass of water."

"Someone could have fetched it for her and taken it back."

"And then gone back and washed the glass?"

But Mrs. Brady was paying no attention to them. She had run past them into the so-called kitchenette, and an instant later her cry brought them all at the double. "There was someone here tonight," she declared triumphantly. "And it must have been someone she knew, because of that."

She indicated a large old-fashioned silver teapot standing on a narrow shelf, its lid open. It was a fat comfortable pot, chastely engraved, with a silver rosebud acting as handle on the lid itself. "That belonged to her Auntie Mabel," Mrs. Brady said. "She was this other auntie's sister, crippled with arthritis she was, and Elsie—Miss Christie—used to go and visit her. She often told me. Mind you, I think she rather expected Aunt Mabel to leave her something, ever so good to her she'd been, but all she got was this teapot on the understanding even if she was starving she'd never sell it."

"She sounds a right nit," said Crook heartily. "I mean, you can't eat a silver teapot."

Mrs. Brady turned to him in dignified reproach. "That's the mistake a lot of people made about Elsie, thinking she was a fool. 'I promised I wouldn't sell it,' she told me, but there was nothing said about pawning it and you get a good price for a nice thing like that. 'That teapot,' she'd say, 'it's a bigger traveler than ever I've been.'"

More than ever did Crook regret he'd never had the opportunity to meet his lost witness in the flesh. "What makes you think it was used tonight?" he said.

"Well, but if it wasn't, it wouldn't be standing there with the lid open. She kept it in a special place—my heirloom she called it—and when she was just making tea for herself she had a little earthenware job. You'll find it in the cupboard there, I expect. You said not to touch anything, so I won't show you, but I daresay you don't count. But when she had company," she ran on like Tennyson's brook and no one attempted to stop her, "she gave them the works. Teapot, milk jug, sugar bowl big enough to drink soup out of. I know. She asked me up to tea once or twice. And when she'd washed the teapot she used to leave it standing there overnight, with the lid open. She said that was the proper way to dry it, and you had to be careful the tannin didn't stain the sides."

The simplicity of this argument took them all aback. One of the policemen began to say it wasn't proof, but Crook jumped in, declaring, "It's as near proof as you're likely to get. Some things you have to take on trust, like the law of gravity."

"So if you're right, she did let someone in," brooded one of the officers. "You say she hadn't any friends, she wouldn't invite a stranger up that hour of the night, let alone make tea for him, so it must have been someone she knew."

"Someone she met at her job perhaps," put in the doctor, who'd stayed silent long enough.

"Well, she hadn't been at the supermarket long and I don't

105

think she had any friends there. Of course, there were these little jobs she used to get, answering advertisements, but they never came to much. I know at one time she was walking three little dogs in the park because their owner was too lazy, I suppose, or perhaps she was having a baby, but she lost that job because one day when one of them was in season —they were all little ladies, you understand—there was a misunderstanding with a poodle and Miss Christie was held to blame."

"Nothing like bypassing nature," Crook agreed.

"And I know once or twice she took luggage to main stations and left it in the Left Luggage office. She quite liked that, because she got a taxi ride and she enjoyed sitting in the cafeteria afterwards and chatting to anyone at her table. It's a funny thing, you'd think she hadn't much to live for, just that old auntie, and she doesn't sound as though she enjoyed herself much as a girl, but she really did like being alive."

"Had the sense to buy herself an umbrella young," approved Mr. Crook. "Well, you know what they say—into each life some rain must fall. Nothing wrong with rain so long as you've got your brolley, and try doing without it—rain, I mean. You'll have the whole farming community at your throat. One thing, whoever came, came with a purpose. I mean, you might lose your wool and hit out with a poker or a brass candlestick, but you don't generally pay a social call with a fatal dose in your pocket. Not without your name's Borgia."

"Then it couldn't have been the vicar," Mrs. Brady decided. "I only thought of him because they do come at all hours. Not that Miss Christie went to church, but that doesn't make any difference if they want a subscription out of you. And naturally she'd want a Christian burial. Whether there's any hereafter or not, the one concerned" (the one in the coffin, she meant) "wouldn't like to think no one paid them the respect of a church service and a decent-looking wreath."

Dr. West lurched gently against Crook. "What price your Chair of Logical Deduction?" he inquired.

Mrs. Brady bridled again when the police said they'd have to seal off the room pro tem and they'd be sending for the body. "You're not going to shut her up in a refrigerated drawer," she insisted.

"Even you, Mrs. Brady, can't imagine they can hold an inquest here."

"No one's explained why she asked a stranger up for a cup of tea," the doctor insisted.

"Perhaps he was only a stranger in the sense that they hadn't met. If it was someone who told her he thought she could help him—she believed everyone should help their neighbor, it's a pity really she couldn't have married the Good Samaritan. Why, Mr. Crook, she may even have thought he was *you*."

It was one of the few times Crook found himself caught off balance. But he made the best recovery he could. "You may have something there," he agreed. "Only thing is—she'd never heard of me. And if we should meet in the sweet by-and-by I wouldn't blame her if she cut me dead for all eternity."

"She wasn't one to nurse a grievance," Mrs. Brady assured him. "And if he said he was acting for this young man the police have their eye on and she could help, oh, that would be right up her street. And if he said his name was Crook—well"—she turned to the stupefied doctor—"you've told me your name's West, but I didn't ask for your identity card, did I? And she'd be ever so thrilled to think she was assisting the cause of justice. It just goes to show, doesn't it, you can't be too careful."

"Yes," agreed Mr. Crook hollowly, "it just goes to show."

9

THE POLICE WERE PLAYING the affair very close to their chests. True, there was mention of a landlady in the morning editions, but she was a Mrs. Erskine, who thought she might be able to identify the mystery man of Hangman's Alley. She had been away for three or four days, she explained, visiting a friend in Amsterdam, and she hadn't seen any English papers.

When she came back and heard of the atrocity she immediately wondered if the victim could be a lodger who'd walked out of her house on Friday morning and not returned.

"Mind you, I did wonder at first if he could be in trouble with the police," she confessed. "There was something very unreliable about him, and if I hadn't had so much on my mind at the time (a little over three weeks ago) I'd not have taken him in. But he explained he was expecting to go north about a job—and that 'ud have been the first job he'd done for a long time, if you ask my opinion. Hands," she ran on fluently—the police were getting it both barrels just now —"he'd not done any manual work for a long time."

No, she didn't know what sort of a job, did it matter? She had thought he might be a foreigner because of the bracelet he wore. Of course, with all these beatniks and flower people and pop-art types, you got accustomed to anything, but it had made her wonder, seeing he wasn't all that young, wouldn't see thirty again in her opinion, if he might have been one of those you-know-whats.

"Homosexuals?" hazarded the exhausted sergeant.

Mrs. Erskine looked shocked. "No need to be rude," she observed daintily. He'd given his name as Burton, Edward Burton, but it did seem a bit funny to her—didn't the sergeant agree?—that his wallet should carry the initials C. H. Of course, he could have bought it second-hand or inherited it from his mother's uncle, and no business of hers anyway, so long as he behaved himself. He'd paid his rent all right, but she had thought it a bit queer when he didn't use the house telephone, but waited his turn for one of the kiosks by the town hall.

"Perhaps he had something private to say," the sergeant suggested.

"You see?" She looked delighted. "I do like people to be open. Well, it seemed to me queer that he hadn't even packed his things. Not that he had much, but it's not everyone who can afford to let shoes go, for instance, and they were good shoes, my husband was in the trade, I know a nice bit of leather when I see it, to leave them behind. Then I started looking through the papers—I always have them left the same as usual, then I can have a good read when I get back and see what trouble I've missed or can expect in the next few days—and I saw this piece about a man run down in Hangman's Alley, and I thought, Well, it could be him."

Sheer lack of breath silenced her at last. It was ungrateful of the sergeant to scowl the way he did, since there didn't seem much doubt that the mystery man was her missing lodger. She had a watchful eye, could describe his clothes pretty accurately. "He kept late hours," she added, "though I will say for him he never came back the worse for drink."

It was the mention of the bracelet that clinched the case. The murderer—because that was how the police, in private at all events, thought of the driver of the car—couldn't remove that, because it had apparently been soldered on. It was a queer thing for a man to wear, but then Mrs. Erskine could be right in all her surmises—a foreigner and one of the you-know-whats. His hands, which had remained uninjured, had caught the attention of a superior officer. "With those hands," he'd observed, "he should be a cardsharper. They're wasted on an honest man." Or, of course, a safe-breaker, another job in which you needed the delicate touch.

They let Mrs. Erskine go—many thanks, much obliged, they quite understood why she hadn't been able to come before. The body 'ud be buried at public expense since it hadn't been claimed—in the condition the head was in it wouldn't be reasonable to expect anyone to identify the features. But they weren't really much further forward. The fact still remained they hadn't got his dabs on record, though that wasn't to say he'd never been through their hands. Drawing a bow at a venture, the odds were he'd made himself unpopular with his gang, got greedy, uttered threats, or turned out to be the sort that couldn't take it at a pinch and might sell the lot of them down the river. He might or might not be concerned in the break-in at the jeweler's—there'd been a safe there very neatly picked. Not likely that Burton was his real name. It was like walking through a thorny wood. You extricated yourself from a bramble patch and found yourself waist-high in nettles.

Murder read the report but it did not bother him much, though he could have told the police what C. H. stood for. There was no mention of an old trot withering on the virgin thorn who'd been found dead from an overdose in her bedsitter in Rembrandt Street. It could be that no one had found her yet, but if they did the odds were they'd think she'd come to the end of the road and dived off into the dark. These old girls came a dime a dozen, slipping through the Welfare State net, each as much like the last as one of a box of tin soldiers.

That's what he thought.

Crook also tore his newspapers apart for a mention of Miss Christie's name, but with the same result. It was one of the rare nights when he hadn't been able to sleep. He felt he'd let the poor old moo down. Somewhere along the line there must have been a clue and he'd missed it. It's trifles like these that are indicators toward a man's retiring date.

He had to take the Superb to the garage to be decarbonized, and from there he rang his office. Bill assured him there was nothing in that couldn't either be coped with or held over, so he said he wouldn't be in that morning but would ring later. It was one of those green and gold days that transform London —not that Mr. Crook wanted it transformed, he thought it was just dandy the way it was—and he walked through the London parks all among the late spring blossoms. On the grass young men lay about in deck chairs, enjoying the sunshine. Crook didn't think, as more worthy citizens might, Unproductive so-and-sos. Living on the unemployment benefit or what was now called Social Security and in his youth had been known as the Relief. He was genuinely sorry for them, having no work to go to. Lying around was for old men and invalids. Somewhere two middle-aged chaps, foreigners no doubt, thought Mr. Crook charitably, had set up a chessboard on a little granite milestone that marked some sort of boundary, he assumed, and, stripped to the waist, were oblivious to all but their game. He stopped a minute, fascinated by the chessmen they were using, which were shaped like animals. It particularly pleased him that the bishops should take the form of hunting dogs. When he passed on he realized that neither of them had been aware of his existence.

Pretty soon, he knew, he'd have to face Mumma again, and he didn't relish the prospect, knowing himself to be the equivalent of the mourner in the hymn—nothing in my hand I bring. He reckoned he could handle Hersey better. Young Ben might be having a moldy time, but they couldn't slap a murder charge on him, not without a body, or a lot more proof than they had at present that he knew where the body was stashed. He came back over and over again to the conclusion of the night before. Somewhere along the road he'd missed his path, and the only thing to do was to go back and find out where he'd gone wrong. He spared a thought for Mrs. Tuke, too. She might be the next on X's list. She'd been the one to get him interested in Miss Christie. Ergo, X knew about her, though she wasn't the danger to him Elsie had been. Only, suppose she talked, suppose she said Miss Christie knew something, saw something, must have done—because no one commits murder for fun unless he's a raging maniac. Good Lord Almighty, thought Crook, he might be with her at this minute, passing himself off as a Hoover salesman or something. He found a telephone kiosk near a refreshment café and looked up the number, but when he got through, it was a man's voice that answered him.

"Mrs. Tuke's not at home," it said.

Crook thought if that was his normal tone and he, Crook, was Mrs. Tuke, he wouldn't often be home either.

"Who are you anyway?" the disagreeable voice demanded.

"It's Ted," offered Mr. Crook.

"Ted? Ted Who?"

"Ted Wilson. Didn't Flora tell you?"

"Who the hell's Flora?"

"Pardon me for breathing," said Crook. "I had some idea she was your wife."

"My wife's name's May if it's of any interest to you."

"You have been going it, haven't you?" said Mr. Crook. "Flora's the one I want. How was I to know she wasn't your wife? Forty Egerton Place—oh no, don't tell me I've got onto the wrong Tuke."

The receiver was slammed furiously back on its rest.

Mr. Crook found a seat and sat down. A little Scottie bitch was amusing herself with a red rubber ball half her own size, nuzzling it across the grass, chasing it, fondling it, pushing it forward again. But always, Mr. Crook noticed, returning to the point of departure. Same like me, Mr. Crook reflected. It wasn't often he found himself vis-à-vis with a dog. And a lady dog at that.

It might be all right for the little dog, who seemed to

enjoy going around in circles, but the only effect that sort of thing had on Arthur Crook was to make him feel dizzy.

And at about the same time as Crook was thinking about Mrs. Tuke, May was thinking about him.

Mrs. Tuke's neighbor in Chelsea was a woman called Anne Craig, who had a passion for gardens and an ambitious husband who refused to commute on the ground that the daily journey from a Green Belt area would probably shorten his life. By the time he was prepared to give up the rat race, Anne imagined she'd probably be past gardening. In the meantime, she did the best she could. They were very ambitious about their gardens in that part of London, and Anne had trained a clematis, a delicate white and mauve waxen wonder, in an enclosed area by her front door not much bigger than a teacup. She tended it as other women tend their Pekingese dogs. Her next-door neighbor did things the easy way, had a garden expert to replant the little front patch and the windowboxes in due season. Poor woman, thought Anne, missing so much pleasure. But then she and her Charlie were true Londoners, loved the feeling of bricks and mortar and would have been as much out of place in a real garden as a sheep in Piccadilly. On that particular golden morning she was hard at work when May Tuke came back from her expensive hairdresser, carrying her expensive hat in her hand. She brushed past with scarcely a word. The Tukes weren't what you might call matey. If they had lived in the country they'd have expected a manor house surrounded by railings and KEEP OUT THIS MEANS YOU on the gate. A minute or so later the front door opened again. A voice she didn't recognize said, "Mrs. Craig." And at its urgency she looked up to see May Tuke, shaken out of her normal aplomb, holding her front door in one hand and a bit of paper in the other.

Anne Craig scrambled to her feet. "What is it, Mrs. Tuke? Are you feeling ill?"

May managed a ghastly smile. "I was wondering—how long have you been out in the front there?"

Anne considered. "About half an hour."

"You didn't see anyone leave a letter in my box?"

"If you mean the postman," said Anne directly, "he passed both our houses."

112

"No, it didn't come by post," May said. "There wasn't anyone delivering advertisements?"

"Not while I was here. I did go in once for a telephone call, and as our instrument's at the back of the house, I suppose someone could have come without me hearing. But no one's left an advertisement at this address," she added.

"No. No, I don't suppose they did. No one left an advertisement here either."

Even Anne Craig, whose husband described her as a dreamer, couldn't miss the import of that. "You mean—you've had a letter?"

"You could call it that."

Anne didn't ask what sort of letter, there was no need. Only one kind puts that sort of look on a woman's face. "You've had a shock," she said kindly. "Would you like me to make you a cup of tea or something? Though probably brandy would be more to the point."

"No. No. Thank you." May seemed to be pulling herself together. "I just thought I'd ask you."

"If it's an anonymous letter," said Anne bravely, "couldn't you take it to the police?"

May shook her head quickly. "Oh no, I couldn't do that. Charlie would never forgive me. He's a top-ranking executive," she explained. "Any suggestion of scandal . . ."

Anne might be unworldly, but she knew what that implied. A lover—and now trying to cash in. Plenty of people in her world took lovers, and really, husbands like Charlie and her own Basil only had themselves to thank if it happened to them to be asked to wear the horns—all their major efforts expended on their careers and their individual fortunes, with wives coming a not particularly good second.

"I don't know what to suggest," said Anne. "I don't suppose you'd consider telling your husband."

Mrs. Tuke didn't appear to have heard the suggestion. "It doesn't even make sense," she burst out. "I mean, he—or she—suggests a threat, but nothing definite."

"You mean, you've no idea who sent it?"

"Of course I've no idea. If the writer had wanted me to know, there'd be a signature, wouldn't there?"

"But anonymous letters don't come out of the blue." Another thought occurred to her. "Perhaps it wasn't meant for you."

113

"With my name on the envelope? What would you do in my shoes, Mrs. Craig?"

Anne started to say she'd tell her husband. And stopped dead. Because she could imagine Basil's reaction. He'd probably roar with laughter. The notion that his wife could be embroiled in anything that resulted in anonymous letters would strike him as a joke. "No," she discovered in surprise. "Unless, of course, I knew what lay behind it." She tried to imagine herself the recipient of an anonymous letter. "Nothing so exciting would ever happen to me," she discovered.

"Exciting?" May looked as if she thought her neighbor had taken leave of her senses.

"Perhaps that's not the right word," Anne amended. "But it does mean you have an existence outside your own home, you're in touch . . ." She stopped in confusion. "I don't know what made me say that. And anyway, Basil wouldn't believe it, he'd say, 'Someone's pulling your leg, darling. Tell them to try the other one, it's got bells on.'"

May Tuke's expression changed. "If this is someone's idea of a joke— I'm sorry to have troubled you, Mrs. Craig." She laughed a little. "I'm just thinking of Charlie's face if I told him. He'd probably take the same viewpoint as your husband. The truth is, husbands don't really take their wives seriously, do they? If you had had the letter, Charlie would be full of good advice—but then you're someone else's wife." She spoke as if she were discovering fresh things about her husband every minute.

"Oh, Basil would be serious enough if it was you," Anne Craig agreed. "What—what does your correspondence threaten?"

"Just a sort of silence is golden and it won't pay you to forget it. I suppose if you were playing a practical joke on someone—not that it seems funny to me—that's the sort of thing you would say. Nothing definite like I know where you were last Tuesday night. Not a blackmail note," she added quickly. "There's no mention of money."

"Blackmail doesn't always involve money. Not that I can imagine you . . ." Her voice died away. She had discovered suddenly that if someone told her May Tuke was being blackmailed, she wouldn't be convinced there was nothing in it. And if her first suspicion was the correct one and a lover was involved, mightn't the lover also be the writer of the note?

She looked away and her gaze fell on the clematis. How simple and true were flowers, how uncomplicated. If Mrs. Tuke had been stepping out of line and got herself in a jam, it was up to her to extricate herself. She didn't give the impression of being the helpless kind.

No one had ever accused May of being hypersensitive, but she realized instantly that she had lost her neighbor's sympathy. "What a lovely plant that is!" she said. "Isn't it called Old Man's Beard?"

"I didn't expect to hear you call it that. It's the countryman's name for it. I'm very proud of it. I long for the day when it stretches right across the lintel of the door and under the bedroom window."

May thought, If you had to choose between that silly plant being killed and me, you wouldn't hesitate. And she added aloud, "That was quite an idea you gave me—about the letter being a joke, I mean. It might sound silly to you, but it's precisely the sort of thing Charlie might do, if he thought he was being neglected or something. Not that I can recall neglecting him, but—oh well, he always says I haven't got a sense of humor. He plays practical jokes on our visitors sometimes. Of course, at the time they laugh and pretend they're very funny, but that's on the surface. 'You want to be careful,' I tell him. 'One of these days a weight might drop on your head or something, and no one will be more surprised than you.' But of course he doesn't take any of it seriously. 'You're coming along, old girl,' he says. 'You'll develop a sense of humor one of these days, after all.' "

She seemed to be talking for talking's sake, her original fear (and that had seemed genuine enough) banked down by a lot of inconsequent chatter.

"So just forget I asked you," May went on. "I should feel such a fool if it got about and it was Charlie, after all."

"And if it isn't?" Anne was surprised to hear herself say the words.

"I don't see that I've got anything to fear," May argued. "I can't forget something I never knew—or talk about it either."

She laughed again, only the laugh sounded a bit stagey. "I might try turning the tables, I mean, ring Charlie and say something in an assumed voice. Only, if he did recognize it or it it came out, his sense of humor wouldn't carry him very far. He'd be more likely to hit me over the head with a hatchet. Oh well, you can't win, can you?"

She turned back toward her own door. Anne Craig felt very uncomfortable. Her notion that Mrs. Tuke might have stopped somewhere on her way up from the hairdresser and had a couple didn't seem very sound. And the woman had appeared not just afraid but terrified. If she'd been putting on an act—what sense in that? What's more, she doesn't believe her husband wrote it, decided Anne, shrewdly. She said in a quick voice, "Your lawyer—couldn't he . . . ?"

"Lawyers like facts to go on. An anonymous letter isn't a fact. It's like these maniacs who ring up from call boxes and start an obscene conversation—we all know about them. This maniac may have been dropping letters through a dozen letter-boxes, tomorrow it might be you."

But it wouldn't, of course, and May knew it. And it wasn't a practical joke. It was a very definite threat. And of course Charlie hadn't written it.

> *And if you should remember*
> *'Twere wiser to forget.*

And underneath, in the same scraggly disguised handwriting:
Be warned by Christie's fate.

"I won't say anything about this to anyone else," Anne was promising earnestly.

"I'm sure you won't," May agreed in absent tones. The message might have been more alarming still if it had been signed with a skull and crossbones. "I'll ring my husband," she said decidedly. "And if he makes light of it, I'll be waiting for him with the coal hammer on his return."

She went into her own house and spread the piece of paper on the table. The envelope, addressed in the same hand that assumed virtual illiteracy, lay beside it. She picked up the receiver and dialed her husband's office. His secretary, a high-nosed young woman who looked as if she'd stepped off the wall of the National Gallery, said in mincing tones that Mr. Tuke wasn't available, and could she take a message.

"It doesn't matter," said May. "I'll be seeing him tonight. And don't bother to tell him I phoned."

"Is that Mrs. Tuke?" inquired the refined voice.

May assumed a more earthy tone. "Who else did you think he would be meeting tonight?"

"Pardon me for breathing," the voice said, and the receiver was jammed down with unnecessary force. One thing, thought May, if I did think Charlie was having fun on the side, it certainly wouldn't be with that woman. By the time she thawed out he'd have lost his appetite.

She sat awhile longer looking at the paper. Then she took up the receiver again and dialed Mr. Crook.

Crook, tiring of watching the little dog chase its ball, going from nowhere to nowhere, walked out of the park and into a café across the road that boasted it served hot meals all day. He discovered too late that it didn't have a license, but the bangers and mash were okay, and if the plum duff had been intended by the cook for interring her worst enemy, at all events it provided a good stomach lining, and his was still a bit queasy when he thought about Elsie. She shouldn't have died, he kept telling himself, still wondering where he'd put a foot wrong. He didn't like this sense of confusion, it reminded him of a day when as a little shaver he'd got lost in the Hampton Court maze. All the other kids had found the center, whence it was simplicity itself to return to the entrance, but he was absolutely foxed. "That ugly boy with the red hair was there last time we went by," he heard one girl whisper to her companion. At last the fellow in charge had had to mount his steps and shout through his megaphone to guide him out—it was closing time, anyway. He'd been a surly chap. "Why don't you use your loaf?" he'd said.

Which was a perfectly reasonable comment, only that must have been one of the days when the baker didn't call. He felt much the same way now. When he left the café he dived into the Sailor's Return for a pint to settle the plum duff, and then he rang his office.

"Client waiting," Bill said. "Been here quite a while."

It proved to be May Tuke, apparently as permanent as the Rock of Gibraltar though less composed.

"Say I'll be right along," Crook promised.

There were taxis cruising hopefully in the sunlight, but Crook's suspicions had been aroused. On his day he could be as imaginative as the Faerie Queene. And if They could get Elsie Christie, They might have a go at Arthur Crook. There's safety in numbers, declares the old saw, so Crook, like the cautious old mole he saw himself to be, followed the chaps who were diving underground. At least, he reflected while waiting in line for his ticket, they hadn't got May Tuke yet.

 **10**

MRS. TUKE ROSE from one of the most uncomfortable chairs in London when Crook flung open the door, and she said, "Well, anyhow you're all right. Mr. Crook, what's this about Miss Christie?"

"Take it easy, sugar," said Mr. Crook. "Who told you anything had happened to her?"

"So something has," said his visitor acutely. "As to my source of information, he—or she—preferred to remain anonymous."

She opened her big handsome crocodile bag and laid the sheet of paper in its envelope on Crook's desk.

"How come?" asked Crook, when he'd digested the contents.

"It was in my letterbox when I came back from the hairdresser's. Whoever wrote it must have seen me go, and chosen the time carefully, because my neighbor, Mrs. Craig, was gardening in the front a lot of the time, but she says she did go indoors to answer the telephone once, and he must have taken his opportunity."

"Friend of yours, this Mrs. Craig?"

"I told you—a neighbor. No, we don't really know them, she's one of these Flower women with a capital F. You see them at the meetings of the Royal Horticultural Society. 'I'd give my soul if I'd invented the camellia,' I heard one of them say once."

"Tell her what was in it?" asked Mr. Crook curiously.

"I suppose you think it was silly of me to confide in her, but it was such a shock. Anyhow, I passed it off as a sort of joke, I said it was the kind of thing Charlie would think a scream—and in point of fact he might, only I don't think he wrote this."

"No," agreed Crook. "I don't either."

"To say nothing of the fact that he wouldn't have the chance. He went off more or less at crack of dawn to make a bit more money for us, I suppose. Not that you need worry about the Craig woman," she added reassuringly. "She doesn't speak to anything but flowers."

"Might be a good thing you did tell her," said Mr. Crook in thoughtful tones. "No indication of what you're supposed to forget, I note."

"That's what makes it so tricky. How can I forget something I don't even know?"

"It's not so much a question of you not knowin' it as not knowin' you know it," Crook pointed out. "Now, the way it looks to me, this Miss Christie she saw something and knew she'd seen it, and it was something X couldn't let her pass on."

"You haven't told me yet what happened to her."

"Oh," said Crook, "she died. Last night."

Mrs. Tuke clutched at the table edge. "You said died."

"That's right."

"Did you mean died or was killed?"

"You catch on fast," said Crook. "Well, they haven't had the inquest yet, but according to the doctor it was an overdose of barbiturates."

"You mean, she took them? Did she say why?"

"Or was given them."

"But that would be murder."

"That's right, sugar."

"*Be warned by Christie's fate.* But, Mr. Crook, I don't know anything. If I did I'd have told the police already, whatever Charlie might say. I mean, it would be my duty."

"It isn't everyone that's special strook on duty," Crook reminded her.

"And anyway," May followed up her own train of thought, "she was as crazy as a coot."

"Even coots can be dangerous to someone."

"It wasn't me put whoever did it on her track," Mrs. Tuke assured him. "Why, I didn't even know her name."

"Ever hear of me before this?" Crook inquired.

119

"Well, no," May acknowledged. "But . . ."

"But a lot of chaps have, and if it gets around that I'm all set to interview a lady called Christie in connection with the Toni case, well, you do see, don't you?"

"How would anyone know—about you, I mean?" inquired single-minded Mrs. Tuke.

"You knew, didn't you? And then X might wonder why I was so keen to see the lady. I mean, she ain't the sort you'd date to take to Prince Charming's ball—not from all accounts. And say she might supply the missing link where the little girl's concerned . . ."

"Do you think there's any chance she's still alive—Angela, I mean?"

"I ain't paid to speculate," Mr. Crook pointed out. "Now, put your thinking cap on and do a bit of arithmetic. Start from the supposition that X knows I'm working for this Hersey boy. So I'm under observation. You come to see me, and he's going to wonder why."

"Why should he tie me up with that particular case?"

"Well, you didn't come just to have a cup of tea, did you? And just after your visit I go round to Miss Christie's land-lady. And like I said, there has to be a reason. And the easiest way to find out the reason is to go to the fountain-head."

"You mean, call on Christie on chance?"

"This ain't just the disappearance of a little girl," Crook reminded her. "The police are tying it up with that chap who was found dead in Hangman's Alley. They don't think that was an accident either, and though me and the police don't always see eye to eye, on this occasion we're like the two hearts that beat as one. Now, say there were any witnesses . . ."

"Like the child?"

"That alley's a short cut to Derwent Street, as you know."

"I didn't," May confessed. "I don't believe I've ever been down it."

"Now, say Elsie Christie saw the child turn into the mouth of the alley—she could do that from the supermarket, couldn't she?"

May Tuke considered. "Most likely she could. But she didn't go to the police."

"She may not have been too quick on the uptake. One kid looks very like another, particularly at seven o'clock on Friday night when the rain's teeming down and you've got to get back somehow. The report about the girl going missing would be in Saturday's paper, but she works at the supermarket, and maybe doesn't see the story till that night. And even then she might not tie it up. And there's always the chance she wouldn't go right away, even so. It isn't everyone wants to get tangled with the police, and most likely she couldn't swear to the kid—no one had suggested that Angel was in the supermarket that night. Then Monday she goes down to Brighton to see her old auntie."

"Hurstleigh," murmured May.

"That's right. But it's all the same area. And before she can do anything, if she has a mind to, that is, X steps in and shuts her mouth. Now, he must have known she could tell a story that could prove dangerous to him—well, we know she had a visitor that night and she got friendly enough to make him a cup of tea."

"She must have been cuckoo," said May simply. "Asking a stranger up . . ."

"Well, but he could have represented himself as having a legitimate interest."

"You mean, he could have said he was the police? Wouldn't he be wearing a uniform?"

"Not if he was C.I.D. And they're the boys who handle murder."

"In her place I'd have asked to see a warrant," May told him.

"Ah, but you've got your head screwed on tight. From all accounts hers wobbled more than somewhat."

"And he persuaded her to tell him about anything she might have seen? And she did see something . . ." May was like a hound dog on the trail. "And he knew he couldn't afford to let her talk. Suppose she hadn't offered him any tea?"

"You know all the answers, don't you? I daresay he had some other ideas in mind. You see, like we used to say, you can't hang twice, and though nowadays you can't even hang once, a life stretch ain't a very attractive prospect."

"And you think he was the one who ran down that man. Didn't I read they'd found out who he was—the victim, I mean?"

"I wouldn't go that far," said Mr. Cautious Crook. "They know what he was calling himself and where he'd been staying for the past few weeks. It's a start, but no more. It don't tell you precisely why he had to be—what's the word?—eliminated."

"I suppose because he knew too much."

"About what? You see? And say the little girl saw too much?"

May shivered. "It's all horrible. All the same . . ."

"Yes?"

"He was taking a fearful chance, wasn't he? I suppose you have to take risks in his shoes."

"What special risk did you have in mind? Beyond the fact that murder's always a risk?"

"He couldn't know the house was going to be empty."

"He could have known I'd called there earlier in the day, and why should I do that if it wasn't to see Elsie Christie? So, in his shoes, I'd hang around, waiting for her to come back."

"So he'd see you both going off? But you might come back at any minute."

"Like you said, some risks you have to take. And if Mrs. Brady had stopped at her post, well, X has only got to tackle Miss Christie before she gets inside . . ."

"How would he know who she was?"

"If he saw her making for the gate he could stop her and ask her name. Tell her a tale. Mrs. Brady's had an accident, been knocked down, in hospital, no relatives who can be traced, but seeing she lives in the house—oh, he could have persuaded her it was urgent. Might say Mrs. B. was asking for her, on the danger list. Well, I don't know exactly what he'd have said—do I?—but that's the way I'd have played it, and it's always safer to assume the opposition has the same amount of brains as Providence dished out on your plate. And if I've got the lady's number right, she'd have beetled along, only I don't think she'd ever have reached the hospital. Not that it matters," he added, "since it didn't work out that way. Then Miss Christie told him something—what it was we'll never know—and he reckoned—it's like what we used to say in the First War—the only good German's a dead German."

"And then he sends me this note."

"To warn you to keep your trap shut. Well, he don't know you couldn't incriminate him, and maybe you could."

She shook her head. "I don't understand."

122

"Let's go over it," said Crook. "Here you are round about seven P.M. standin' at the checkpoint, facing the alley."

"But I wasn't watching the alley. I was simply concerned with getting back before Charlie did."

"If you'd looked through the window, though, you could have seen a car stationed there."

"Was there a car there?"

"We don't know for certain, of course, but it seems likely."

"Waiting for this man?"

"He wasn't killed by accident," Crook reminded her.

"And your idea is that Angela Toni took a short cut—you did say it was a sort cut?—and saw what happened?"

"I've taken a look at the location myself. I don't think anyone from the supermarket could have seen the crash, but they could have seen the child go into the alley, could have seen a car. Well, Miss Christie must have seen something or she'd still be with us."

"I feel so useless," May burst out, "not able to help you more. But, as I say, my chief concern was to get back. I had these parcels, and when I came out I hung about a minute or two just on the chance an empty taxi did loom up, though it wasn't very likely. The little girl had left the supermarket before I did, so whichever way she went I wouldn't see her. Then, when I realized I was simply wasting my time, I crossed the road and went down to the bus stop. Fortunately, not many people were traveling in that direction, so I got a bus quite easily. I didn't give the child a second thought, not till there was all this fuss in the paper. Then I began to wonder . . ."

"And you told Charlie?"

"And Charlie said don't go to the police, but I was still worried. I had a little girl myself once, but we lost her. And I found out about you acting for this boy, Hersey, so I thought I'd compromise. In fact, it seemed to me rather a good idea. The police thought they'd got the person responsible, you were looking for someone else . . ."

"You did quite right, sugar. All the same"—he drummed his big fingers on the desk—"the only way we can get young Hersey's name cleared is to find the chap or chaps really responsible. All we've got is a lot of speculation."

"But what more can we do?"

"I'm coming to that." He was silent for a minute or so, as if he were collecting his thoughts. "Remember what you told me just now about taking risks?"

"Yes."

"Prepared to take a risk that won't do you any good, but might help us to clear things up?"

"I'm not a heroine," May confessed. "What sort of a risk?"

"You can't pretend you're in any very favorable position the way it is," Mr. Crook pointed out reasonably. "You're like the chaps in the Good Book, you stand in jeopardy every hour. Well, whoever wrote this"—he slapped his big hand down on the anonymous note that still lay on the desk in front of him—"didn't do it just to pass the time. He had some plan in mind."

"You think *I* might be the next victim?" She stared at him, like some child threatened by an unbelievable punishment.

"How does it seem to you, sugar?"

"But—no one tried to stop me coming to you."

"I noticed that."

May thought. "You could be in danger too," she discovered.

Crook beamed. "Kill two birds with one stone. Even if you were out of the way, now I know about this"—once again he indicated the anonymous message—"I could make plenty trouble for them. Besides, it could be they—he—don't know what you're going to tell me."

"But I can't tell you anything," protested May. "I mean, I don't know anything."

"Maybe Miss Christie thought she didn't know anything either, and you see where it got her."

"Doesn't that prove that she did—know something, I mean?"

"It could be you know something, too."

"But I didn't even see where the little girl went."

"That don't help, sugar, if X thinks you did. Anyway, he's in it up to his neck. What's one chance more or less to him?"

"What do you want me to do?" asked May abruptly.

"Help me to spot X," returned Mr. Crook, equally simply.

"You mean, you have a plan?"

"I thought of taking a leaf out of the Frenchies' book. Mind you, it's a bit different there. When they think they've nailed a chap but haven't the proof, they set up a dummy of the crime and take him along, the idea being that when he sees the place and the show's on, he'll give himself away."

"Does it work?" asked May.

"I daresay," said Crook carelessly. "They're an emotional lot, the frogs."

"But—you're not expecting X to attend your rehearsal?" May sounded puzzled.

"If he's really on your trail he'll want to know what you're up to."

"You think he'll be there? Won't that be a bit obvious?"

"Depends on the setup. Anyway, it's the only bit of cheese left in my larder to bait my trap."

"Drawing a bow at a venture," suggested May, but Crook said that was the only way he knew to draw a bow. "You're not just trying to make my flesh creep?" May asked rather suspiciously.

"If it ain't creeping already, you've got more asbestos in your composition than I have," Crook assured her candidly.

"I still think it's a pretty wild throw."

"Wilder throws have brought down a wicket. Besides, it's going to have X guessing. You know and I know we're still fumbling around in the dark, but X don't know that, and when you know a thing yourself it's often hard to believe other chaps don't know it. But assuming he is following you, if he ain't it's sweet Fanny Adams so far as tonight's concerned. Yes, I thought tonight, the sooner the better—then he'll be curious, to put it no stronger, and that's brought more chaps down on their kissers than I've had hot dinners. And he won't be able to forget that Crook mostly gets his man, even if it takes time, so . . ."

"You really are walking into trouble, aren't you?" May said.

"Man is born to trouble as the sparks fly upward, and we'll have quiet and to spare in the grave. Besides, there's young Hersey, they haven't pulled him in yet, but they've still got an eye on him, and even if they never make a move in his direction, there are the neighbors. They're going to wonder how much he knows and how did he get away with it. An albatross round your neck would be no more than a string of beads compared with that. And he's a young chap, and then, of course, he is my client," Crook wound up simply.

"Mr. Crook." May hesitated. "You don't think it's possible that he . . ."

"No," said Crook, "I don't. And you don't either, sugar. Now, are you on?"

His voice was still optimistic, but she suspected the ruthless-ness of purpose behind it. "What do you want me to do?"

"Just what you did on Friday night. Go to the super-market . . ."

"It'll be closed."

"Then we'll have to get it re-opened. Anyway, we don't want the populace milling around. I'll attend to all that. All you have to do is go through the same motions as you did on Friday night, only this time I want you to watch the street, the way Elsie Christie must have, and see if you could have distin-guished a car—provided one was parked in the mouth of Hangman's Alley—or anything else out of the ordinary."

"I couldn't have seen the man run down, not from where I was standing. It was by the telephone kiosk, wasn't it? And that's round a sort of curve."

"Well, there ain't much mystery about him. But you might have seen the little girl."

"She won't be there, though." Mrs. Tuke sounded dazed.

"Her understudy will. Now, sugar, you've been on the boards, you told me so, this should be child's play to you. Specially as you've got your words all written, while the rest of us have to ham 'em. Now, I don't say this is goin' to get us anywhere—X may bypass it altogether—but that's the chance you take. Same like X, writing you that letter."

"I shouldn't have thought you could have told much from that. Assumed writing, left by hand . . ."

"Someone might have noticed, someone passing, someone lookin' out of a window, what I call the invisible witness. If you want to escape takin' risks, you should be a stillborn child, it's the only remedy I know."

"You said X. Do you think there's only one person in-volved?"

"What do you think, sugar? Assuming we're barking up the right tree—someone had to drive the car, someone had to nip out and empty the chap's pockets, and be ready to make a lightning getaway if a third party came whistling down the alley to use the blower. And then there was the little girl. I don't think one chap could have handled all that. Anyway, seeing the police are tying this up with the jewel robbery—and I daresay they have their reasons—they believe three people were involved in that."

"And you think this man—what was his name, Burton—was the third?" May discovered.

"This chat about honor among thieves—well, in my opinion it's more often honored in the breach than in the observance. My guess 'ud be that Burton, if that's his real name, got a bit greedy, wanted a bigger share, or thought he was being done down. When you're on the wrong side of the law it's always a mistake to fall foul of your partners, because you can't invoke the police. Maxims of Arthur Crook," he wound up rapidly, not wishing to antagonize her.

"You do get a lot of fun out of all this, don't you?" May said, and Crook said if that was true he was the only one. He didn't suppose she was enjoying it much, and he knew Mumma wasn't, or the Hersey crowd, and he didn't even think X himself was having a ball. "So he set up a trap—wouldn't Barton, Burton, have been suspicious? It's a lonely sort of place on a night like Friday turned out to be."

"All to the good. Burton wouldn't want to be seen, and X wouldn't want anyone to rumble him. That alley is cobbled, you'd hear footsteps—well, not a little girl perhaps, but you or me, we'd give a bit more warning of our approach. Matter of fact, we know no one did go through the alley that evening because it was some hours before the body was reported—by a rozzer. And if someone else had found it who didn't want to tangle with the police, there was nothing to stop him giving a warning call from the kiosk."

"It was taking a risk all the same. Suppose the man hadn't been killed."

"That's one of the risks X didn't take. If it had been your Charlie, you might have thought twice before identifying him. And I don't think X will bring up his reinforcements, and in any case there'll be four of us, you and me and Mumma, and, of course, Bill."

"Is he the one I saw when I came in?"

"That's the one. He'll be driving the car. The Superb's at the garage anyway, she's a bit too noticeable for the occasion."

"It's all very well," May burst forth, "but aren't you rather counting your chickens? If he knows I've been to see you he might try and prevent me keeping tonight's appointment."

"That don't make sense, sugar. He might have tried to stop you coming here . . ."

"I came in a taxi. It wouldn't be so easy."

"But seeing you've spilt the beans, he'll know puttin' out your light won't do him much good, not so long as I'm in the land of the living. Besides, he'll want to know what I have in mind. Now, you turn up—six-thirty say—I'll have a word with this fellow Butts. He's bound to be a good citizen, otherwise he wouldn't be manager of a high-class supermarket—anyway, he wouldn't let us on the premises without him being there. How about Charlie? Can you tell him some tale—unless you've changed your mind and feel like telling him the facts. I daresay we could do with an extra man."

But she shivered and said oh no, he'd wonder what she was doing in that part of London. "You may think it funny, Mr. Crook, but he's as jealous as a tomcat." And probably not without reason, Crook thought. He wasn't too keen on her tale of going to a cinema with a girl friend. He hardly thought girl friends were in her line. And anyway, May went on, he wouldn't be in tonight, because he had this conference at Leicester. In a way you could say it was providential.

Crook went through the gesture of doffing a nonexistent hat. "Always dips me lid to Providence," he explained. "It does ease things a bit. Now, let's have Bill in and we'll work out a plan of campaign. And it might be a good idea for him to drive you back."

"So that all the neighbors can report that I was out with a strange man when Charlie was away? No, thank you, Mr. Crook, I'll have a taxi, and I'll have another taxi up to the supermarket tonight."

She didn't suggest a way of going home when the play was over, because neither she nor Crook could be dead sure where home was going to be. When she asked him about his own plans and how he meant to play out the charade, he said quite seriously, "By guess and by God. If nothing comes of tonight, will our faces be red! But it's a comfort to remember there are a lot of corpses who'd be glad to change their faces for ours."

He really is as mad as a hatter, May reflected, walking down the stairs and entering the taxi Bill had called for her. She didn't suppose he'd outlined the whole plot, was aware that before midnight anything could happen, and no one, but no one, would care to take a bet on the consequences.

11

ANGELA HAD BEEN MISSING since Friday night, a period of less than four complete days, but to Mumma it was as if time had stopped altogether. She found herself jammed against a great block of it, like the end of a cul-de-sac. Push as much as you like but you can't stir the granite mass. You can't go forward, and if you look back you find yourself in the position of the character in the nightmare, who, desirous of retreat, discovered that the road had closed up behind him. For the last two mornings she hadn't been to the hospital, hadn't been around the shops. A neighbor slipped in and put food on the table, hurrying out again as if she thought Mumma might throw the dish at her. Her other jobs missed her, too. In fact, it was astounding what a gap her absence left in the district.

At the hospital, nurses began to get irritable, they were asked so often, *Is there any news?* No need to inquire news of what?

"I hope this creature, whoever he may be, appreciates what he's done to us, quite apart from the child," one of the older nurses observed to a colleague. "We're going to have a wardful of neurotics if something isn't discovered soon." And she snapped off the head of a junior who came up asking a perfectly reasonable question.

In the wards Mumma's name could be heard at every bedside. "It's queer," remarked Miss X to Mrs. Y. "I never took much notice of her before, but now the best news I could hear would be that that little girl has been found, safe and well."

Mrs. Y, who had been unduly depressed at the prospect of an operation the doctors had assured her was simply child's play, was ashamed of her obsession with her own troubles. They all knew Angela, who would come slipping into the ward at the start of visiting time in the evening, often bringing small commissions that Mumma had executed for them.

"The fact is," declared Miss X, "Mumma is a person,

whereas so many people are simply types." They didn't mean that doctors and nurses weren't persons, too, but these were, so to speak, tarred with the brush of being part of the hospital routine. They could actually visualize Mumma sitting in her empty room waiting for a knock on the door, the sound of feet on the stairs. Even the unromantic among them were moved.

When Crook came thundering on the door of Mumma's room nothing happened for a moment, then when he knocked again she came heavy-footed across the floor. She had had a chain fixed to the door so that no one could push his way in. Crook surmised, accurately, that this wasn't to protect her from evildoers but from the ardent gentlemen of the press. When she recognized her visitor she withdrew the chain and Crook breezed in.

"You have news of my Angel?" She put out her hands and folded them around his wrist.

"Not as of now, but we may have something definite by this time tomorrow. I fancy we may be moving in the right direction."

"How you find the direction?" demanded Mumma suspiciously.

"I'm taking a leaf out of the Frenchies' book."

Mumma let him understand succinctly her opinion of the French.

"I thought you'd like to be in on it," Crook continued. He stopped there, because Mumma made a sudden gesture that made him think perhaps she'd been a tigress in a previous existence.

"You think maybe I interested?" she mimicked him. "This is my Angel, my daughter, and you think perhaps I will be interested. Yes, Mr. Crook, I am very interested, and you want to know why—because this is my Angel, not a little dog or a doll . . ."

"Calm down, Mumma," implored Crook carefully, keeping the table between himself and the outraged parent. "The point I'm trying to make is that it could be dangerous."

"Dangerous!"

Crook felt as if he'd strayed into the snake house in the zoo. "Well, as dangerous as taking a pin out of a hand grenade, say."

"That," announced Mumma, "depend on who hold the grenade."

"At the moment I don't think we hold it," Crook allowed. "Point is—we could be there when it goes off, and that ain't exactly a healthy situation."

Mumma made an expressive gesture with her hands, throwing them up as though she scattered the dust of years on the unappreciative air. "They go with us."

"Well, yes, but it won't be much consolation to me in the tomb. What I want you to understand, Mumma, is that it ain't going to help your Angel much if she comes back in one piece and finds you in six, even if everyone else is in about sixteen."

Mumma sent him a smoldering look. "You are not a mother," she assured him scornfully.

"Can't blame me for that," Crook protested.

"If my Angel need me, I am there. That is why mothers in the first place." Emotion was playing havoc with her command of the English tongue, but if she hadn't spoken at all, her expression and gestures would have made her situation clear. Crook was wont to say it took a lot to get him embarrassed, but then he didn't often find himself face to face with naked feeling, as he did now. He felt about as comfortable as a man in the full glare of a television arc lamp. Any minute he expected to smell scorching flesh.

Persuading Mumma to sit down ("And just sheathe that battleaxe," he implored, "it makes me nervous"), he outlined the scheme he had agreed to with May Tuke.

Mumma appreciated the situation much more quickly than May had appeared to do. "You think he follow, you think he find out, you think he attack. How that help my Angel?"

"Once he sees we're on his track, my guess is he'll make straight for home, wherever home may be."

"And you think my Angel . . ." Mumma couldn't finish the sentence.

"I'll be frank with you," said Mr. Crook, and he looked as though the words gave him actual grief to utter, "this is my best throw. If she ain't there, then we're back to Square One. But one word of warning—just remember, seeing your little girl's the object of the exercise, you must stick to the plan. I've only got two hands and I'm going to need them both, so don't start any continental jigs. We're out on a limb and it's anyone's guess how long that limb will hold up."

"You think, Mr. Crook, maybe your guess come right?"

Crook was no stranger to trouble. Fate hadn't cast him for

a novelist or poet, but he had imagination enough to picture her sitting, helpless and raging, in her flat, doing the waiting part, which is always the hardest. Like being an idiot in a library of masterpieces—the truth was there, somewhere, and she couldn't read a word of it. He wasn't sure he read much of it himself. He was taking a mighty chance, and if it didn't come off, there might be a mass burial.

"Now," he adjured her, "you've got faith, I've got hope. That's two thirds of the great trilogy." They must hope Providence would be on hand to supply the charity. He knew, none better, the risk they ran, but he counted on X's curiosity, realizing that Crook was like the man in the poem. *Bats are flying in his belfry, In his bonnet hums a bee.* And he reminded himself valiantly that men have died of bee-stings. For once it was a comforting thought. And he knew, if the others didn't, that from now on he was going to be X's chief target.

As May had surmised, Mr. Butts didn't at first take at all kindly to Crook's proposal that they should make use of his supermarket as a setting for the plot. He said his manager wouldn't approve. Crook asked how his manager would know. Mr. Butts said primly that one owed a duty to one's employers. Crook said one also owed a duty to the helpless—meaning Angel.

"Of course, if you'd rather, we can turn it all over to the police," Crook offered. "And my bet is you'd prefer my company to the rozzers, and your boss likewise. Unfair, I daresay, but whoever said life had to be fair?"

The supermarket was due to close at six, and by six-fifteen the place was like a deserted fairground. Employees dashed for their scarfs and umbrellas, and were off to make the most of their brief hours of liberty. Mr. Butts always stayed to see the last of them off the premises. All the counter-checkers had instructions to leave their tills wide open so that a curious Peeping Tom could realize they were empty—arguing, sensibly enough, that only a real nutter is going to risk a prison sentence for a few loads of tinned goods and frozen merchandise. The cleaners came in early in the morning, and before they were due to depart, Mr. Butts would be there, making certain that one of them, sillier than the rest, hadn't nicked a jar of instant coffee or some meat from the refrigerated section. In any case, a cunning arrangement of alarms kept most of the stock inviolate. These alarms were constantly changed around, so no one knew precisely where they were set.

When the last member of the staff had vanished, Mr. Butts locked the street door and switched off the lights, the same as he did six evenings a week. The weather, from Crook's point of view, was being most co-operative. A heavy sleety rain had started to fall, which threw up cascades of dirty water in the gutters, enraging pedestrians and drivers alike. When the members of the cast arrived they were admitted by a private door, and the play began. Mr. Butts switched on some of the lights— in such weather no one was going to stop and wonder why they should be burning at this hour; probably an official check, they'd think, if they thought at all—and took his place where Elsie Christie had been on Friday night. Crook, who was representing the unknown customer, came across and went into a splendid mime of watching goods being taken out of a basket and checked up. Behind him stood May with a trolleyful of groceries; and behind her, Mumma flourished a bottle of vinegar.

Crook went into his act with a will. This item was too dear, that surely was underweight. There was a cut-price shop in Walham Green where a packet of soap flakes was being offered for threepence less.

Mr. Butts, forgetting for a moment the gravity of the situation, entered into the spirit of the thing. "It 'ud cost you more than threepence to get to Walham Green," he said.

"That's what you count on, of course," snapped Crook, putting an invisible parcel into a make-believe shopper. "How'm I going, sugar?" This was to May Tuke.

"The perfect housewife," May agreed. "I'll believe in reincarnation after this." But there was no humor in her voice. The situation was too tense for humor.

Crook prepared to depart, and then Mumma broke in, "Please, you let me through. I have only this." And she waved the bottle.

Crook picked up his cue. "That's the modern kid all over, always pushing and expecting to get the advantage over its elders. When I was your age . . ."

Mumma put in a line on her own account. "I don' remember," she said. "We don' do no ancient history at our school."

Mr. Butts gave an involuntary yelp of laughter. Crook huffed and puffed and moved out of the way.

133

"All right, dear, you go through," May said good-naturedly, moving her cart aside.

Mumma put down the exact money for her vinegar and May took her place.

"Now," prompted Crook, "what can you see through the window?"

"Just rain and umbrellas and traffic, just what I saw on Friday last. I didn't know I was looking for anything special, you see."

"I can see more than that," exulted Mr. Butts. "There's the clock and—isn't that a car standing under the lee of the Horse and Cart?"

"You've got good eyesight," Crook prompted him. "How was Miss Christie's, by the way?"

"I remember her saying once that she could see the number of a bus when it turned the corner."

"Did she wear glasses?"

Mr. Butts hesitated. "I wouldn't be absolutely sure. She was only temporary staff, Mr. Crook, and so far as I was concerned she couldn't be too temporary. I'd say she probably did wear them. I know she gave the impression of being held together by safety pins."

"She did wear them," Mrs. Tuke recalled suddenly. "I remember they were this flyaway pattern, a bright red that clashed with her hair. Mr. Crook, is there really a car there?"

"There was a car there Friday night," Crook reminded her. "At least, there was a car somewhere, and my guess is it was there, and Miss C. saw it, because if not, why was she first home in the Churchyard Stakes?"

"You didn't say." Mrs. Tuke sounded troubled. "I mean—why—you're not going to run anyone down?"

"Not the way you mean it, but if X should surface, a car could be useful. Now"—he turned back to Mr. Butts—"you're Miss Christie, you've had about as much as you can take, you look at the street, just by way of a refresher, say."

"That's very neat of you, Mr. Crook. I was constantly having to remind her that she wasn't hired to be a lookout man but to take the customer's cash."

"Very nicely put," approved Crook. "Mind you, I don't suppose she did any arithmetic, and it probably wouldn't seem odd to her that a car should be parked in the lee of the Horse and Cart, especially having regard to Friday's weather."

"It hasn't got any rear lights showing," Mr. Butts pointed out acutely.

"There could be a reason for that."

"Wouldn't someone notice?"

"He might, but—ask yourself what you'd do. You've just shut up shop, it's teeming cats and dogs, and you've got a home to go to. It's no skin off your nose if some chap's forgotten to switch on his lights, so—you exercise the Englishman's prerogative of minding his own business. And for your information, no one drew the landlord's attention to a parked car without lights Friday evening, because I inquired. He said if he'd thought it belonged to one of his customers, he'd have asked if the car belonged to any of them—well, you wouldn't want one of your regulars picked up just for a mistake."

"Why was it there?" asked May.

Mumma moved impatiently. Talk, talk, talk, and all the time Angel was waiting.

"I fancy it was waiting for Mr. Burton to take up his stand by the phone box."

"Why they wait?" Mumma intervened. "They not know my Angel coming."

"I'm afraid, Mumma, the fact is they couldn't care less about your Angel. Not that they had anything against her. It could have been you or me. It's just her bad luck she got pushed into the wrong picture. And once she was there . . ." She had to be obliterated, he meant, self-preservation being the first law, but he tied it up a bit more neatly. "Now, sugar," he turned back to May Tuke, "you've got your gear, you're moving out. You didn't see the little girl hanging around?"

"I didn't see anyone. I waited a minute in case there was a miracle and a taxi appeared, but of course it didn't. But she could have gone down the alley out of sight."

"But Miss Christie could have seen her," Mr. Butts chimed in. "She could have given evidence if she'd been asked."

"She said—the child, I mean—something about meeting an uncle," May Tuke recalled.

Mumma threw up her head. "Maybe you not hear so good."

"It's what she said," May insisted. "And Miss Christie might have heard it, too. So if she saw someone approach the little girl, there's no reason why she should have been suspicious. That would explain her not going to the police. X wouldn't know— It seems to get more complicated with every step."

"And if someone came to call, thinking—I mean, she might think he came from the police . . ."

"I'd have expected her to show more sense all the same," Mr. Butts declared. "Alone in the house . . ."

"She was in a spot," Crook reminded them. "A fellow that don't draw the line at running down one of his mates and abducting a little girl, he ain't going to be too delicate about removing an old pussy like Miss Christie. And there's no reason why she shouldn't have believed him," he added. "Probably saw herself as Lady Molly of Scotland Yard—the poor old moo!"

Over the road the rear lights of a practically invisible car flashed out and were dark again.

"Action stations," said Crook. "Now, Mrs. Tuke, you're taking Angel's part— Yes, we had all that out, Mumma, I want you with Bill. I don't say it's a safe position, but it's safer than the rest. Wait here, sugar, till I'm in position. Then you come out and snake along the wall, the way a kid would on a night like that, not running, but not creeping either. My guess is the car had started before Angel went into the alley. They couldn't have risked a witness, and kids are diabolical once you get 'em in a box. No, the way I read it, the car moved on, not knowing of her existence. She came through the short cut and saw or heard something that made her a danger. She didn't have to see the thing, only the consequence. She could have cried out. Anyway, X plus accomplice knew she was there, and knew he couldn't let her go on and tell her story. Now, say X is lurking—we don't want you laid out, Mumma . . ."

"I suppose I don't count," said May pettishly.

"Forewarned is forearmed," Crook reminded her. "Where'd I put that zipper bag I was carrying?"

"What zipper bag?" asked May.

"It's in my office," said Mr. Butts.

"Props," explained Crook.

"I hope he knows what he's doing," said Mrs. Tuke uneasily. Now that they were on the spot she seemed to be experiencing doubts.

"Come on, Mumma," shouted Crook from Mr. Butts' private office. An instant later they could be seen standing on the curb, looking this way and that. Mumma was no sylph, but Crook looked simply enormous.

Mr. Butts, who seemed to have taken over the job of stage manager, was looking at the second hand on his wristwatch. "Now it's your turn," he told May. He switched off all the lights and went into his own office, from whose narrow window he still had a pretty good view of the circus Crook was laying on. May walked over the road, and as she reached the opposite pavement, the black car moved out of the shadow of the Horse and Cart and started to go slowly down the alley. Crook was around the bulge and so out of Mr. Butts' sight.

When Crook reached the telephone kiosk he found it in darkness, some joker having removed or smashed the bulb, but, undaunted, he hauled a sizable torch from his pocket and waited. He could hear Bill's car, a little black Vidor, coming steadily toward him, and he switched on the torch to indicate his whereabouts. The second car, coming up behind him and going the wrong way of the street, caught him off guard. He only heard it and recognized its purpose in time to switch off the torch and leap back against the kiosk. The driver came straight at him, crashing against the glass-paned door, so that the heavy splinters flew in all directions. Crook, who had contrived to fasten himself inside, pressed against the back of his involuntary prison, but the great car made mincemeat of the woodwork. Crook lost his balance, falling across the door of the kiosk. The driver moved forward as far as the wall, then deliberately put his car into reverse. At that instant Bill's car came blazing round the bulge in the lane.

The driver of the attacking car did a lightning change. An instant later the car leaped forward, almost crushing the Vidor against the opposite wall. Only Bill's foresight in stamping on the accelerator and putting his vehicle just beyond his enemy's reach saved the two of them from being plastered on the brickwork. The big car shot around the corner and out of sight. Bill flung open the door of the Vidor and rushed to Crook's side. Crook had never laid any claim to being an Adonis, and any pretensions he might have had had gone now. The torch, which had fallen from his hand, had magically sustained no damage beyond a cracked glass. Bill snatched it up and played the beam over Crook's face, now liberally bedaubed with blood. Lots of chaps *in extremis* might have been grateful for that, thought Bill.

Mumma, who had extricated herself from the car, now crossed and flopped down beside Crook like a miniature elephant. She caught the unconscious man's arm and shook it, not gently but with an urgency that made Bill wince. "You wake up," she adjured Crook. "You not die till you find my Angel." Opening her huge shabby handbag, she rootled among the contents and brought up a roll of lint and a packet of elastoplast. She snatched a clean handkerchief from Crook's pocket and began to mop at the blood. To Bill's relief he saw that it came from an ugly gash in the forehead, but there was no sign of deeper damage. "You take the smelling salts," commanded Mumma, pushing her bag toward Bill.

Bill felt in it and found the little phial. "You ought to give this to the British Museum," he said as he unscrewed it. "I didn't know you could buy such things any more."

"A lot you don't know," rejoined Mumma ungraciously. Her voice might be unsympathetic but her handling of the invalid was masterly. Bill supposed she'd picked up hints in the hospital. She had Crook's head propped against her knee, and as she unfastened his coat she uttered a sharp cry. His unnatural size was now explained. Apparently anticipating some kind of attack, Crook had buttoned two solid cushions inside his coat.

"Old school trick," murmured Bill, "only they're usually worn elsewhere. Good for him, though, they're as useful as a Mae West."

This was gibberish to Mumma, and she treated it with the disdain she considered it deserved. Then fresh steps sounded in the alley and Mumma threw up her head. "A policeman? No, of course not." Her voice classed policemen with husbands as a pretty useless lot.

Mr. Butts hove into sight. "What happened?" he demanded. "I saw the car— He's not . . ."

"No," retorted Mumma scornfully, "he is not. He is not made of china. When I was with Signor Toni he strike me many times, more hard than that, with a bottle, with a spade, and do I die? I ask you, do I die?"

"You'll outlive the lot of us," said Bill placatingly. "But don't worry. Crook 'ull run you a good second."

"I think he's coming round," opined Mr. Butts.

Crook opened his eyes. He didn't put any of the fool questions so beloved by dramatists and fiction hounds— Where am I? What happened? He saw almost at once where he was, and after a minute he could remember, more or less—more rather than less—what had happened. His gaze passed from Bill to Mumma and settled on Mr. Butts. "Did you get it?" he asked.

"Yes, Mr. Crook. I wrote it down." Mr. Butts produced a slip of paper and read out some letters and figures. "That's a Barnwell car number," he added. "When they gave Barnwell county status they had to invent a new code, and this is it."

"Get into the phone box," said Crook, "unless they've put that out of action, too." (They hadn't.) "And ring the police. Give them the number of the car, tell them what's happened. Okay, Bill, not to worry, Mr. Butts can do it as well as you or me." Mr. Butts looked correspondingly grateful. He looked as pleased as a boy scout who had conducted a successful rescue operation. "And tell them if they sight the car, not to stop it, just follow—thump that into their thick heads. My guess is that X is streaking for home, and it's a case of where your treasure is, there shall your heart be also."

He frowned as he spoke; the analogy didn't sound as clear as usual. Even a lump of teak, which was his own way of describing his cranium, can't meet a hammer blow without sustaining some kind of damage.

"You think—my Angel?"

What Crook had really meant was—assuming the police hadn't been on the wrong track from the start, if and when they ran X to earth they'd find part at least of the missing jewelry stashed away.

"That's what you and Bill are going to find out," he told Mumma. "Okay, Bill, Mr. Butts will wet-nurse me till the police arrive— Did they sound interested?"

"When they heard it was you— Here they are now, aren't they?"

"Get away," said Crook to Bill. "At the double, and take Mumma with you. We can't stop them doing their job, it's what we pay them for, but that's no reason why they should muscle in on ours."

If Bill moved pretty fast, Mumma was his equal, and before the police car had joined the group around the telephone kiosk the Vidor was out of sight.

"Who did this, Mr. Crook?" Authority asked.

"I give you three guesses," offered Crook. "Mine would be

that it's the same chap who did it before. They can't resist repeating their triumphs, and you have to admit it's been a triumph to date—and this time it was more or less an inside job."

Mr. Butts had a sudden thought. "Mrs. Tuke," he said. "Good Heavens! I noticed there were two people in the car, but I didn't think. Do you mean X has abducted her, too?"

"You aren't thinking," Crook chided him. "I've been in the legal racket for longer than I care to remember, but I've yet to learn that it's a crime to abduct your own wife."

"It's a pity, Mr. Crook, you didn't see fit to take us into your confidence."

The speaker was a superintendent, no less, and they were now all at the police station, including Mr. Butts, who constituted a material witness and had no intention of having his nose jammed in the door.

"I thought you wanted to catch the chap," said Crook. "It's a compliment to you, really. Our precious pair thought they could pull the wool over my eyes, but even they couldn't expect to bamboozle the whole of the force."

A message had been received that the car had been sighted on Bamford Bridge, heading east. It was being discreetly tailed.

"I hope your chaps know how to spell the word," remarked Crook ungratefully. "I wouldn't put it past Tuke to be armed. Well, we used to say in the old days that you can't hang twice. He's already got Burton to his score, and we don't know about the little girl. I suppose you could call his attack on me grievous bodily harm . . . and of course," he added carelessly, "there's the matter of the break-in at the jeweler's."

Mr. Butts, who'd had no previous experience of the police and couldn't, therefore, be expected to understand their laws of etiquette, here broke in eagerly, "Mr. Crook, when did you first suspect that Mrs. Tuke was part of the plot?"

"A very good question," said Crook. "At first, though it pains me to admit it, she flummoxed me completely. You know, that woman must have been quite a good actress in her time. Easy to say, 'Well, if you really want to help you'll go to the police,' but suppose Charlie really had been in trouble, you couldn't blame him for not wanting to stick his neck out again. And then the police had their eye on young Hersey. She told it very nice," he added frankly. "Especially the bit about the little girl mentioning her uncle. That was poetic license, if the phrase ain't out of place. I'll eat my titfer if Angela ever mentioned the word. She might have said my mother, only if anyone had seen her going off with a man, Mrs. T.'s evidence would come in very handy. I made a bloomer there, I let her see I was interested in poor Elsie Christie, and of course she couldn't be sure how much Miss C. had seen. Not too difficult for her to find out that the poor lady had gone to Hurstleigh for the day. And that's another mistake she made—when I said Brighton, she corrected me right away, but seeing at that time there hadn't been anything about Miss C. in the press, how come she knew?"

"How did she know?" inquired Mr. Butts.

"Shouldn't be too difficult to get her address and ring up Mrs. Brady, hear she was out for the day. Mrs. B. didn't happen to mention it, it's true—but if she reported faithfully to Charlie, he might drop round, ask a neighbor—anyway, he'd be waiting for her return. And that's another thing—how did Mrs. T. know me and the landlady had gone out for a snort if she or her accomplice hadn't been on the lookout? All the same, I mightn't have tumbled if she hadn't—like so many dames or criminals of either sex, come to that—tried to gild the lily. Mind you, she was in a bit of a spot. She'd broken through once, established a connection, given herself an excuse for trying to find out what I was after, but with Miss Christie's death she could only bow out, because on the face of it that was no concern of hers. Therefore—the anonymous letter."

"You didn't mention that to us, Mr. Crook," said the superintendent.

"She turned up, on the morning after Miss Christie had been poisoned, with a piece of paper and an envelope—the kind you always hear about, cheap quality, can be bought anywhere—with a message anyone could have written, *provided they knew the facts*. Be warned by Miss Christie, it said, or words to that effect. But—how did she know anything had happened to Miss Christie? At that time there hadn't been a whisper of it in the press—the only people who knew she was dead, and that the doctor had refused to sign a certificate, were the police, Mrs. Brady, the doctor, of course, West his name was, and myself. It all came out later, of course, but *not before this mysterious letter appeared in Mrs. Tuke's letterbox.* I'm like the White Queen," acknowledged Mr. Crook frankly, "who could believe six impossible things before breakfast, but even I gibe at the idea that a letter can be put in a slot of a house halfway down a row, and nobody, but nobody, notice it. Her neighbor was gardening in the front a good part of the morning, and she didn't see anyone. It's true she said she went to answer the phone once, but she was only away for a minute or so and that wouldn't have been time for someone to have turned into the street, walked as far as Number 42, opened the gate, delivered the letter, shut the gate and vanished. Besides, there are always the other people who don't get allowed for. Someone lets a dog out or runs to the pillar-box, or just looks out of the window, watering the geraniums, say, or expects a guest and comes to the gate. Or a taxi comes oiling along— And then how could this invisible man know how long the coast was going to be clear? No, I'll stake my day Mrs. T. wrote that letter herself; it was to be a sort of Open Sesame to Part Two of the Burton-Toni mystery. *I'm in danger, Mr. Crook, what can I do? And don't say go to the police, because I can't. There's Charlie* . . . I don't say my final plan was the most brilliant I've ever evolved," Crook added handsomely, "but it was the best I could think of, if the Tukes weren't to get right off the hook. So far no one's been able to connect them with Burton, if that's his name, living or dead; no one's had a smell of the missing jewelry; no one knows where the little girl is. I didn't happen to mention to Mrs. Tuke that Mr. Butts would be acting as lookout. He switched off the lights and locked the door and round the corner he went. Mrs. T. didn't think that tides can ebb as well as flow . . ."

"Mr. Crook said a mystery car might put in an appearance. Whatever it did he and Mr. Parsons would deal with it, but come hell or high water, I'd got to get the number."

"A rather highly colored plan, Mr. Crook," the superintendent suggested.

"The only proof of a plan's success or otherwise is if it brings home the bacon," retorted Crook, who never minded mixing his metaphors. "And in this case you must admit it did. We know the number of the car; your chaps are on the trail. The police might have thought up something a bit more classy, only the police were looking the other way, in young Hersey's direction."

Bill would have realized that Crook was still suffering from the effects of the evening's activities. In point of fact, he was feeling more than a bit woozy. The superintendent observed coolly that it was always a help if citizens would confide in the authorities, to which Crook said that wasn't much use unless the police were going to take what they were told at face value. Fortunately, at that moment, before the authorities could think of an adequate reply, the telephone rang.

The superintendent listened for a moment, then his roar of "What's that?" sounded like the lions' enclosure at feeding time. "Yes. Naturally. And call back right away."

"Lost the quarry?" inquired Mr. Crook, correctly interpreting the superintendent's wrath.

"Got held up at a light by a lorry with a trailer of new cars," the superintendent said. "Lorry wanted to go left and there was some confusion—but they'll pick up the trail again."

"And if they don't," said Crook, "there's always Bill."

"Mr. Parsons?"

"That's the one."

The superintendent goggled, while Crook recalled that during his days on the wrong side of the law no one had ever picked up Bill, and since he joined the side of the angels— to wit, came to work with Arthur Crook—no villain had so much as dented him.

"I'll tell you something else," Crook continued. "If any harm has come to that little girl and your chaps lay hands on the one responsible, don't bother to call out your strong-arm men. Just leave him alone with Mumma. She'll chew him to bits with her own teeth, and very nice teeth they are," he added approvingly. "No credit to National Health dentistry there."

Mr. Butts surprised them all, including himself, by saying, "I'd like to give her a hand—or rather a jaw. I wear my own teeth, too."

The superintendent thought desperately, You can't win.

143

The unofficial judges of society do a lot more harm to the criminal than all the old gentlemen in their silly wigs and robes of office, and he wished he could be the one to tell them so.

 **12**

THE HOUSE CALLED WAVERLEY COTTAGE, situated just off the Worpledurham Road, had been built by an egocentric misogynist who named it for himself. It might quite as well have been called Hermit's Retreat. The villagers of that time had sometimes wondered what the old fellow lived on, since he was never seen in the village or even passing by the doors of the pub. And in fact he had been dead more than a fortnight before anyone knew about it. The coroner had proved unsympathetic. "If human beings deliberately cut themselves off from their kind, they have only themselves to blame if no one is aware of their passing," he had pontificated.

The house's next purchaser changed the name to The Cottage, and had a signpost put up indicating its whereabouts. It was a longish low house erected behind a dense shrubbery, whose front door was approached up a narrow lane regimented by tall dusty privets. This signpost was for the benefit of the postman if he brought any parcels. For the rest, a wooden box was nailed to the gate, with a piece of piping for newspapers. Having made these concessions to society the new owner remained almost as invisible as the old. In the village they said he held orgies there—cars sometimes stopped by the house after dark—but when he died in due course, there was nothing on the premises to support such a contention. In 1966 the house was bought by a Mrs. Haggard, reputed to be a widow, and as much of a recluse as her predecessors. She left a plastic bottle container at the gate for the milkman and she didn't take a newspaper. She might have had children, but if so, she never spoke of them, but she did have occasional friends to stay. Although she lived in the village she was never of it. Her friends were referred to as townees, who arrived with hampers from Fortnum and Mason and brought their own drinks. She didn't attend the church or take part in any local activities, but if she did chance to see a neighbor she would mutter good morning or good afternoon and duck hurriedly past. She ran a car, a biscuit-colored Prideaux, which made some say she was a foreigner. Miss Mapes at the telephone exchange reported that she sometimes made London calls and sometimes received them, and that was all anyone knew about her. The cottage had the vague reputation of being haunted, but not in any blood-curdling or chummy way. If the ghost of Old Man Waverley did walk there, you could be certain he'd met his match. And since the house had no immediate neighbors, it really attracted no local attention.

Once or twice passers-by thought they heard a piano being played, but there was no television aerial, and no tradesman ever called.

It was to this remote dwelling, virtually removed from civilization, that the child, Angela Toni, had been brought in a drugged condition on the fatal Friday evening, when the rain was so malevolent that even the habitués of the Crickers' Arms mostly favored an evening at home round the telly. If anyone had seen the car arrive he or she wasn't talking, and in fact it had probably gone completely unnoticed. The room in which she had existed for four days and nights was an attic with sloping ceiling and one sloping wall. It was sparely furnished with a bed, a chair and a small round table. There was a primitive sort of bathroom opening off it, the bath itself chipped and rusty, and when the creaking taps were turned, the water that came out was rusty too. How she had arrived here, the child herself did not know. After she'd been hustled into the car she remembered making a wild protest, and a man's voice saying, "For God's sake, shut her mouth," and presumably someone had obeyed him, because the next thing she was here, lying on the bed, and a tall fair woman who told her to call her Aunt Lily had brought her a tray. "Eat up and don't ask questions," she had said, "and then you'll be all right."

"Where is Mumma?" she had demanded, disobeying the first order.

"You do as you're told and you'll soon see her again," Aunt Lily retorted, and had marched out, banging the door after her. Angel had thrust the tray aside and run across the room, but though she tugged and thumped and shouted the door remained obstinately closed. She stamped furiously, but she might have been alone in the house for all the effect it had. No one even came out of a downstairs room to tell her to stop that blasted row. She ran to the windows that were shuttered, but these had either been padlocked or were nailed up; she went into the makeshift bathroom, but here there was no window at all, it was no more than a sort of cupboard or cell off the main room. So, she reflected, she was a prisoner. Being a child, she could accept a bizarre situation more easily than an adult would have done. When Aunt Lily returned to fetch the tray, always keeping carefully between the captive and the door of the room, Angel said, "Why did they bring me here? Is it because of the man in the alley?"

"I don't know what you're talking about," Aunt Lily said in a flat tone. "Have you had a bad dream?"

"It was the one in the supermarket," Angel said. "The one who let me go through."

"There's no supermarket here," the woman told her. "I told you it was a dream."

"It wasn't here, it was in London." She paused. "Where is this?"

"I told you not to ask a lot of questions."

"It's because of the man, isn't it?" She had had time to collect her thoughts; memory was going great guns. "It was in Hangman's Alley. Is he dead? Why did they want to kill him? Was he a bad man? Why didn't they tell the police?"

The questions poured out, jerky and spasmodic, like the rusty water creaking from the tap.

Aunt Lily came over and caught her arm. "I've warned you once. If you won't be told, you'll have yourself to thank, whatever happens. Just don't ask a lot of questions."

"But if I don't ask questions, how am I ever to know? Aunt Lily, who was the man?"

"I don't know anything about any man."

"He wore a raincoat. I could see that in the light from the telephone kiosk. She wouldn't let me go any nearer."

"She?"

"The one from the supermarket. She said I must come in

the car and we would tell the police there had been an accident. But it wasn't an accident. He drove over him, I saw it." At that acute recollection she instinctively flung her arm over her eyes. "Does Mumma know where I am?"

But that was a silly question, if you liked. If Mumma knew where her darling was she'd be hammering on the doorstep, all the locks of the Kingdom of Heaven wouldn't keep her out.

"If you behave yourself you'll soon be back with Mumma," Aunt Lily declared. "Just keep quiet and do what you're told."

She went away and Angel ran over to the windows. The extraordinary quiet of the house was alarming to one brought up in the noisy friendliness of a town society. Listen though she might she could hear no sound of motorcars braking, revving up, coming to a standstill, no voice pierced the silence, even the birds scarcely cheeped. And inside, the silence was as unnerving. No radio played—and what kind of a house was it that didn't even possess a radio? Once she heard a door slam and knew that someone had gone out. The fear assailed her that she might now be alone in the house, of set purpose. She hadn't liked Aunt Lily, but the house's emptiness was more alarming still. She ran back to the door and shouted till she was hoarse, but no one replied. She stayed there, rigid, for what seemed an endless time, until she heard a door close again and that was Aunt Lily coming back. She realized that she must be in the country; when planes went over they went very high, so that the noise they made was no more than the cry of a bird. She never heard another voice—the sound of a child crying or a dog barking.

"We are at the back of the world," she said aloud, and her own voice seemed a desecration of the silence. Once she heard a faint shrilling of a bell and she knew that was a telephone. There was only a thin mat on the floor, and by thrusting this aside and leaning her ear against the crack, she could make out the sound of a voice but never distinguish any words.

"Why don't you try and rest a bit?" Aunt Lily would inquire, coming in with the tray. She brought three trays a day and a glass of milk at night. She never threatened, there was no question of violence.

"Why don't you let me go?" the child asked.

"It doesn't rest with me," Aunt Lily said.

147

"I should like something to read."

"I'll try and find out a book." Later she brought some cheap women's magazines. Angel leafed listlessly through them; there was nothing there to interest her. They were what Mumma called trash.

"You've taken my ball-point," she said on another occasion. "It was in my bag, it isn't there now."

"You must have dropped it. Anyway, why do you want a pen? You can't write any letters."

"I could draw a picture."

"What do you want to draw?"

"I could draw the man in the alley."

They always came back to that.

"That's silly." Mrs. Haggard was momentarily caught off guard. "He wasn't anyone you knew."

The child sent her a sharp glance. This was the first time Aunt Lily had acknowledged the man's existence. "He was standing on the curb, waiting for the car," she explained.

"What car?"

"The car that ran over him. Mumma always said not to go by the alley, because bad things happened there, but I thought not when it was raining and so dark, and it was late. Mumma always comes back tired on Fridays; I like to have the fire lighted and the fish in the oven and the table laid. Then afterwards if it's fine we sometimes go to the cinema, just the one big picture."

She forgot her audience, remembering that dear and familiar way of life. Friday night the cinema, Saturday (when Mumma didn't go to the hospital) the Portobello Market, where Mumma carried a big straw fish-basket and she took the yellow plastic bag. It was a treat to watch Mumma shop. No one yet had ever sold Mumma a bruised tomato or yesterday's vegetables. And Mumma didn't care what people thought. She poked and prodded, and if the stall-holders objected, she would demand, "What you got to hide you not want me to see?" But there was a respect for Mumma in the market that even a child could recognize.

Saturday morning was the highlight of the week. They would arrive so early that sometimes the Walrus Café on the corner wouldn't be open. A great paper sack of rolls, plastic bags of chips ready for frying, and a note stuck against the glass—sixteen quarts, sometimes twenty quarts. On the way back they stopped here for coffee for Mumma and an ice-cream soda for the child. Then they would loiter past the china stalls and curiosity shops. Mumma had worked once for an antique dealer. She knew a good bit of china when she saw it. That's a piece of Meissen, she might say, indicating two entrancing dancing figures. They looked at the old silver, too—silver, Mumma said, was often better than money—money was paper, money was nickel, but silver remained unchanged.

Her thought returned to Friday night. She had been a long time crossing the road, the traffic seemed endless. Other, more daring, souls slipped through the line of vans and cars and rushing buses, but she found herself isolated on the island in the middle of the road, the pitiless rain soaking through the thin wrapping on the fish. It would be not only cold but soggy by the time she returned. She got through at last and decided to take the short cut through the alley. She had done her best to protect herself and the food from the storm, wondering why Mrs. Hersey hadn't allowed Mary to lend her a mackintosh. There had been a car at the mouth of the alley that she hadn't noticed until it began to move. She let it slip past, then emerged from the black shadows of the walls and started to run. She reached the curve in the road when she saw the man waiting on the pavement, waiting, she supposed, for the car. The car accelerated. She thought, How mean, they're not going to stop. Then it came straight for him. For a minute she couldn't see him, because of the bulk of the car, then it moved slowly on and she saw the dark mass on the pavement. The whole thing had occupied a manner of seconds. Before she could find her voice the car began to reverse, coming back to complete its task. And at that she screamed. "No! No! You can't!"

There had been a jarring sound and the car had ground to a halt. A moment later the passenger door opened and someone got out and hurried toward her. A strong arm was slipped around her shoulders and she was twisted about. "Don't look, dear," said a voice. "What a shocking thing! He must have slipped, what with the pavement being so wet."

"He was going to drive over him," she whispered, and the woman said briskly, "Nonsense, my dear, you mustn't say things like that, you mustn't even think them. My husband was coming back to see what had happened, what he could do. Come to that, who are you and what are you doing by yourself in a place like this at this hour of night?"

"I was going back to Mumma." And then she had recognized the woman. "Why, you're the one in the supermarket," she had discovered. "You let me through, because Mumma will worry." She tried to twist herself out of that firm grip but she was helpless.

The husband, who had been examining the prone figure, came up. "What is all this?"

"She's frightened, naturally. She saw him slip, it was a horrible experience for a child."

"I don't know what he was after," the man said. "A lift perhaps, or begging. Anyway, he mistimed the distance . . ."

"Is he dead?"

"He's pretty badly hurt. We'll have to get a doctor."

"You could telephone."

"I don't know any local doctors. We'll get on to the police, they'll get an ambulance here quicker than we could hope to do. You'd better come with us," he added to Angel. "They'll want to talk to anyone who was nearby. It's a queer thing"— he turned back to his wife—"he doesn't seem to have any evidence of identity on him."

Angela asked wonderingly, "You don't know who he is?"

"That's what I'm saying."

"Then why did you want to kill him?"

The man looked across at his wife. "What's the kid talking about?"

"She saw you reverse the car, she thought you were going to run him down."

"That's a pretty daft idea. I wanted to see what we could do. But he's beyond our help. And to crown everything, some joker's put the telephone out of action. Well, we'd best be getting along."

"You mean, leave him?" whispered the child, appalled.

"He's not conscious. Anyway, the police will have an ambulance here in five minutes."

"I . . ."

"No, dear," interposed May firmly. "We're not going to leave a little girl of your age hanging about alone at this time of night. We'll see about him."

Willy-nilly, Angela was hustled into the car. She sat in

the back with May while Charlie drove. The rain seemed to be increasing in fury. The wind flung it in handfuls against the windows.

"We're going the wrong way for the station," Angela discovered in a few minutes.

"I know the way we're going," retorted Charlie grimly. "You leave things to your elders."

But Angela was not to be so easily silenced. "He's dead, isn't he?" she cried. "And you killed him. You were coming back . . ." She doubled her fists and thudded them against the glass. "I saw, I'll tell them . . ." She snatched furiously at the car handle, but being unused to cars she caught the window lever instead.

"You're not going to tell them anything," promised Charlie savagely. "May, for God's sake, shut that kid's mouth."

Angela felt her shoulders caught in an iron grip. She was pulled back, a rug or something enveloped her head, and as she struggled to free herself she felt an arm firmly grasped, there was a prick like a safety pin, she felt dazed and suffocated. Through the gathering darkness she thought she heard the woman say, "That should put her out for a while," but the words made no sense. When she once more became conscious of herself as a person she was in this room, and the woman she called Aunt Lily was with her. Aunt Lily was like the famous trilogy of monkeys who saw nothing, heard nothing and spoke nothing. In her own impersonal way she was kind, fetching drinks of water, finding an additional blanket for the bed, but never asking questions, never wanting confidences.

"Have the police come, Aunt Lily?"

"The police? Why on earth should they come here?"

"Because of the man in the alley."

"There's no alley anywhere near here."

"You didn't tell me where I was."

"You're having a little change in the country."

"I don't want to stay in the country. Mumma says the country is for cows and machines, not for people. Haven't you got a telephone?"

"I thought you said your mother wasn't on the telephone."

"I could ring up Mary—or Father Jackman—at least he could tell Mumma, if he knew where I was."

Once she had seen a dormouse in a revolving cage. Round and round it went, and never advanced a step. She felt like that dormouse now.

In one corner the paint was peeling from the wainscot. The room had an old-fashioned gas bracket but illumination was by a weak electric lightbulb high in the ceiling. Even if she stood on the chair she couldn't reach it. It gave the room the only light it knew, and was controlled from outside the room. When it came on after darkness she knew it was morning; when it was extinguished, then it was night. Each morning as it came on she would desperately chip a bit of paint from the wainscot. In this way she could calculate the number of days of her incarceration. Her great fear, that she dared not confide even to Aunt Lily, was that some disaster had befallen Mumma, for how was it possible that she—the undefeatable, the indomitable Mumma Toni—should not have broken into the house, come storming up the stairs and smashed down the door? She had been careful to give no hint of her address, but they could find out where Mumma lived, everyone in the neighborhood where she lived, knew Mumma. She stood by the shuttered windows, recalling a world where movement was free and voices sounded. No voices sounded here, not even tinned voices over the air. Around her neck she wore a medal on a fine silver chain. Mumma had given it to her to commemorate her First Communion. The medal was dedicated to the Mother of Compassion, and on the back was her name and a text— Feed My Lambs.

"Holy Mary," she pleaded, "keep Mumma safe, and send her here."

It might have shocked her to realize that though her devotion was offered single-mindedly to the Blessed Virgin, all her faith centered in Mumma.

According to her calculations it must be Tuesday, although the days had ceased to have any particular meaning. Downstairs she heard a bell ring—that would be the telephone. Outside the rain battered at the windows, you could hear it even through the shutters. She lay on the floor, her ear to the crack, but all she could distinguish was Aunt Lily speaking on a higher note than usual, sounding excited. A minute or so later steps sounded on the stairs, and she only just had time to pull herself erect before the key grated in the lock and Aunt Lily came in. Her usual cool, not to say indifferent, manner seemed to have vanished. Now she was resolved, snapping out orders. "Get ready quickly, Angela," she said. "We are going out."

She looked at the woman unbelievingly. "Tonight? In this rain?" It was too like last Friday for comfort.

"That's what I said. Now, don't argue, we've got our orders."

"Where are we going?"

"You'll see. For goodness sake, child, hurry. I'm doing you a favor if you only knew it, possibly the last I'll ever do anyone, but I never bargained for a child being dragged into this."

Most of this passed over Angela's head. She didn't see this opportunity as a possible answer to prayer; her suspicions were still too near the surface.

"I've brought you a cardigan," Aunt Lily continued. "It'll be too big for you, I daresay, but you can wrap it around you. And I've got a plastic mac—well, you'll need to wear something white."

She pushed the child's arms into the cardigan, which was of a cheap quality and mass-produced. It was going to take the Big Five all working in concert to identify that as the property of a woman called Lily Haggard.

"I must go to the bathroom," said Angela in a stifled voice.

"I suppose so." Mrs. Haggard sounded grudging. "But be quick, there isn't much time." I must be mad, she confided to herself, waiting for the sound of the cistern to flush, and it may not be any good either. The cistern flushed and Angela reappeared, clutching the cardigan about her throat. She pushed her arms into the mackintosh, which was the type that had a hood attached.

"Now don't start creating," said Lily in a hectoring voice. She pulled the hood smartly over the child's eyes. "You can push it back once we're away from the house. Hang on to me and you won't come to any harm."

Dazed and blinded, Angel blundered onto the landing. "Stairs here," a voice said, and after a moment, "Now turn," and they went down another flight. The house was low, only two stories. Now they were moving along a paved hall—she heard her companion's feet click—then they were on a rug, then they had reached the door.

"As soon as we're out of earshot you can take off that blinder," the woman promised. "You're wearing it for your own sake as much as for mine."

They went down a narrow path, with branches stretching out to catch and hold you, then a gate clicked. A minute later the woman said, "You can breathe now if you want to," and she pushed back the hood. All about Angela lay a black, a lightless world. To a child accustomed to a big city, where the streets are almost as bright by night as they are by day, the darkness was terrifying. It was a moment before she could become accustomed to it; then she saw a light-colored car and Aunt Lily opened one of the rear doors. "Sit in the back," she said. "Don't lean forward. The fewer people see you, the better." The child stumbled in, and Aunt Lily got into the driver's seat. Leaning over she locked both the back doors. "Don't try anything silly," she warned Angela. "If you knew the risk I'm taking on your account you'd want to co-operate every step of the way."

"Where are we going?" Angela whispered.

"If I put you down near a railway station, do you think you can find your way back to London? I'll look after the money side of it."

"Where are we now?"

"A long way from London, but you know what they say, all roads lead . . ." She swerved abruptly. "A hedgehog," she explained. "The stupid things, they will come out at night and behave like the worst sort of pedestrian. Sometimes in the morning you'll see half a dozen that have got themselves run down."

"We stayed in the country once," the child said. "The lady had a pet hedgehog, it used to come onto the lawn for bread and milk. She said she kept it to keep the black beetles down."

The car seemed to turn a number of corners with suspicious frequency. So far the pair of them might have been occupants of an otherwise unpopulated world. Once a car went by in the other direction, but the road was so treacherous that the driver had no attention to spare for fellow travelers. Then the light car turned again.

Angela's head began to spin. Suddenly a church clock

started to chime, and her voice brightened. "It's playing a hymn tune," she discovered. Her voice sounded pleased.

"Oh yes?" Lily was only listening with half an ear. The rain's violence never let up for an instant. She was driving fast, against the clock she might have said, it took her all the skill she possessed to keep the car on the road.

"There's a church on the river," Angela explained. "Mumma took me there once, that had a church bell that played a tune."

"Whatever it is it sounds pretty doleful," said Lily briefly.

"It's 'Nearer My God to Thee,' " Angela told her in reproachful tones.

"I wouldn't call that exactly a lively idea. Sit back," she went on in the same voice, "we're coming to a village. You don't want to be stopped now, you might never get back."

Angela shrank into a corner of the car, so much impressed by her companion's tone that she could actually feel herself shrinking, pressing against the upholstery as if she could melt into it. Peeping through the rain-sodden windows she saw lights as they flashed by. Here were houses, once or twice she heard the sound of a television set being played, lights streamed from a doorway as someone pushed open the door of a local, a full-throated laugh rang through the darkness. The car swerved again. A blasted dog, Aunt Lily told her.

"You didn't hurt it, though."

"We haven't any time to waste reporting an accident to a dog," said Aunt Lily briefly. "Why can't folk keep the wretched things under control?"

At a street corner a bevy of youths in mackintosh capes, oblivious to the rain, argued furiously. One of them had a motorbike that was pouring out a jet of smoke. As the car came into view they half-turned as if to demand assistance, but Lily Haggard went by at the speed of light.

"Don't keep him waiting, will you?" one of the youths shouted after her.

"Oafs!" Lily muttered.

A great lighted monster came thundering toward them from the opposite direction; it was the local bus, more than half full. It seemed by contrast so safe and honest that the child turned to stare through the car's back window. But it was going a ripe pace and soon the rear lights had disappeared. They must have left the village behind, for now there was nothing to be seen but the gaunt shapes of trees that had a frighteningly human look, arrayed along the road, watching the flight. Then came some open country, and a black object loomed up, a little darker than the night. It opened its mouth and uttered a melancholy sound.

"It was a horse," Angela said. "Do they have to stay out in the rain? I thought horses lived in stables."

"This is a working-class horse," said Aunt Lily, with a sudden abrupt laugh that ceased as unexpectedly as it had begun. "It's like the rest of us, it has to take what's handed out to it and like it."

The echo of that sobbing cry seemed to follow them as they plunged into a valley. Now Angela was straining her eyes, looking for possible signposts, but even if there had been any and she had been able to distinguish them, the car would have swept by before she had a chance to read their message. Once she thought, Perhaps it's not true, perhaps we aren't going to London at all, and a knowledge of her helplessness swept over her afresh. The thought that Mumma might never know what had happened was almost too much for her control. "Where are we?" she asked.

"It doesn't matter. Now, listen. Quite soon I'm going to stop the car. I have to go back. I shall put you down at a crossroads; you'll have to walk about half a mile to a station. From the station you'll be able to get a train. I'll give you a pound, and when you get to the other end one of the station staff will help you. Don't ask any difficult questions, what you don't know can't hurt you. I met a judge once," she went on in a wondering sort of voice, as if it still surprised her that she had once hobnobbed with anyone so mighty, "he told me there's one infallible defense. Do you know what infallible is?"

"The Pope's infallible," Angela said.

"I wouldn't know about that. Still, I suppose it means you understand. If anyone accuses you of something, just say I don't know, I wasn't there, everything went black. You're going to be asked a lot of questions, Angela. Remember what I say. It's best to know nothing."

"I don't know very much," Angela agreed. "I know I was in a house, I don't know where it was, and I know the lady from the supermarket brought me there. She had a man— I didn't really see him."

"If you've got all your buttons," the woman said puzzlingly, "you won't remember where you met her either. Not that you'll have much chance, I daresay," she added resignedly, "all those voices throwing questions at you—What happened next? Do you remember? Yaketty-yak."

"I'll tell them you were kind," Angela promised.

The woman laughed in the same odd way as before. "That would be a nice epitaph," she said, but Angela, confused, exhausted, and clinging to self-control by an eyelash, didn't know what she meant.

The car stopped at last under the shade of a great holm oak, where the wind and rain rustled through the leaves as though someone watched from the branches.

"You'd better take this," said Mrs. Haggard. She opened her purse and put a pound into the girl's hand. "Walk straight up that hill, it's not as far as it looks, then it's about a quarter of an hour to the station. I can't take you any nearer, I've got to get back. I'm sorry this had to happen to you," she added, "but try and remember I did my best."

While Angela climbed out of the car she was wondering about the mackintosh, if she'd have to give it back, but Aunt Lily said, "Oh, they come a dime a dozen that kind, and anyway you should wear something white, it's not fair to drivers." The last words were spoken over her shoulder as she turned the car.

Angela knew a passionate desire to cry out, beg her not to go, leaving her in an immense lightless world where even nature seemed inimical. But the sound of the receding car became quickly fainter, then the rear lights vanished around a corner and Angela was left, clutching her bag and facing the dark uphill climb. The world here was quiet and empty, but as she came near the top of the hill she saw houses on one side of the road. The golden lights gleamed like hope. She wished she dared push open a gate, be received into a normal world, sit beside a fire, tell her story. She wanted someone else to take over, she'd been on her own too long. But these past days had done their work. Now and for a long while to come she would be wary of the human race, seek the underlying motive and find it malicious and cruel. In one house a window opened and the sound of a pop program floated out. She thought how often she and Mumma had sat confidingly by their fire while Mumma sewed and she read bits out of the paper—Mumma didn't read so good, in her own phraseology. "What for I want to read?" she would demand. "Nobody pay me to read."

Suddenly the tears that had been accumulating through the dark days and nights spilled over. Angela leaned against a hedge—the houses had given way to hedgerows again—and her grief was more drowning than the rain. She couldn't have said why she cried—she had escaped, she was on the way back to Mumma, the Blessed Virgin had heard her prayers, after all, but her body shook, her legs wouldn't move. Behind her a car climbed the hill, slowing as it approached. She shrank back instantly, her arm over her eyes. The car stopped, a window was lowered. She stood still as death. Then a voice said, "What are you doing there on a night like this? You should be in bed."

She said, in a choked and foreign voice, "I'm going back. I missed the bus." It was the best excuse she could think of on the spur of the moment.

"The bus doesn't come down this road. Here, hop in, I'll take you wherever you want to go. You can't hang about here by yourself."

Terror overwhelmed her. "No, no. I'm too wet, I'm nearly home, I only have a little way to go."

"How far?" inquired the voice suspiciously.

"Near—near the station."

"That's the better part of a mile. You'd better get in. I'll drop you off at the end of the road if you don't want them to see you drive up."

"No," she cried, "I'm not coming and you can't make me." She moved her legs, trying to make them run, wondering if this car would follow the example of the one she'd seen in Hangman's Alley and come darting after her. There was no way out.

"Please yourself," said the woman in indifferent tones. The car window was wound up and the car shot away.

13

SHE HAD JUST TOPPED THE HILL when the second car approached. This came from the opposite direction and the lights suddenly flashed on, half-blinding her. Instinctively she shrank back. A door opened and a voice called, "You all right, luv? It's a nasty night."

Without daring to lift her eyes she whispered, "Yes. Yes, I'm quite all right. I haven't far to go."

"The lady said the station. Come on, that's quite a step."

She looked up imploringly to find a young man in a familiar blue uniform coming toward her. Behind him the big car shone white in the rain. A blue illuminated notice read POLICE.

She gasped. "The lady?"

"That's right. Said she offered you a lift, but you weren't playing. Still, you won't mind coming with us."

She remembered what Mumma said. "The police, they think they God, do this, do that, give orders like a wartime general." And with one of her inimitable gestures she had clapped a hand to her breast as though slapping on a medal. "But in trouble you trust the police. Remember what I say, Angel. They paid to take care of us."

"I didn't know," she stammered. "I thought—Mumma always said . . ."

"Does she know you're out? Here, what's your name?"

So she told him.

A long whistle split the dark. The other policeman leaned out to inquire if they supposed they were ducks. When he heard the name of their passenger he ejaculated, "Well, get her in quick before she does another vanishing act."

"Sit in the front between us, luv," the first invited. "It's warmer. You look as if you could do with a hot drink. Who were you going to see?"

159

"The lady gave me a pound. She said I could go to London."

"Well, you've missed the last train, unless you want to go all round the county and you'd only arrive with the milk then. Still, not to worry. We'll find you a shakedown." And he said casually, "What lady was that?"

"Aunt Lily. I don't know her other name. She said she was doing me a favor."

"By turning you out in the rain?"

"Yes. She couldn't stop. Someone telephoned. I could hear but not what they said."

The policeman who wasn't driving put a large warm hand over hers. "Hold your fire, luv," he said. "You'll have to tell this all over again to the sergeant. Don't want to wear yourself out saying it twice."

But the other man wondered, "You don't know the address, I suppose?"

"How daft can you get?" snapped his companion. "You don't suppose they'd have sent her out . . ." He stopped abruptly. "Nothing for you to worry about," he assured Angela. "We'll do that from now on."

"Will Mumma come?" Her hands were ice-cold in his.

"If there's a train. Anyway, we'll give her the good news. You'll soon be seeing her again."

She said in an agitated voice, "There's—there's nothing wrong?"

"See what you are, Bert? Now you've got the young lady all worked up. No, of course there isn't anything wrong. If you want to know, your mother's got the police force of about three counties on their toes till they don't know if they're coming or going. Wouldn't surprise me to know she was out hunting for you at this minute."

"They might hurt her." The voice was muted and strained.

"She wouldn't be allowed out on her own. Anyway, they'll get a message through quite soon."

When they entered the station, the child drooping between her companions, the constable on the desk said, "Running out of ammo, aren't you, if that's the biggest criminal you can find?"

"I don't know where they pick 'em these days," retorted Bert. "This is Angela Toni . . ."

"What? The little girl . . ."

Another door opened and a dark man came in. "Forbes

and Ross," he began, and then, "Hullo, what have we got here?"

So they told him. After that everything seemed to happen by magic. She found herself divested of mackintosh and wet shoes and stockings, crouched by a fire, with a cup of something hot in her hands and an alert, smiling young police-woman who said, "Call me Terry," encouraging her to take a bite from something on a plate at her side. When she had been coaxed to eat and drink a little, Terry said, "Do you feel able to answer a few questions to help the police? They wouldn't bother you but you're the only one who can do anything for us."

"About Aunt Lily?"

"Who was she?"

"She was in the house. But she was kind. And she gave me a pound. If I don't need it for the train I ought to give it back."

"She can have it back any time she likes to call for it," the inspector said. His name was Lloyd, he told her, and he'd be grateful for anything she could tell him. Where she'd been these last days, for example.

"In a house."

"Well, yes. What was it like?"

"It had two floors."

"How many rooms?"

"I don't know. I only saw the one I was in."

He tried another tack. "What was the view from the window?"

"I couldn't see. They were locked, shuttered, I mean."

"You mean, you were in the dark all day?"

"There was a light. Aunt Lily put it on in the morning, and when she turned it off I knew it was night."

"Did you see anyone there besides Aunt Lily? No? Do you know her other name? Were there any visitors? Did anyone else speak to you?"

"There was a telephone call, and then Aunt Lily came up and said I was to go, she was doing me a favor, and she gave me the pound."

"Did she tell you why you were there?"

Angela's surprise was unfeigned. "Because of the man in the alley."

"Did Aunt Lily tell you that?"

161

"She pretended not to know, but I saw the lady, she was the one in the supermarket. And they said they would go to the police because it was an accident, but they never went and it wasn't. Did he die?"

"Yes, Angela," said the inspector. "He died. And you saw it. And then they brought you to this house. Now, when you were coming away, did you notice anything special about it, was there a garden or a monkey puzzler or . . . ?"

She explained about the blinding mackintosh hood.

"Weren't taking many chances, were they?" the inspector observed ruefully. "Did you notice what the car was like?"

"It was a light color, but not so light as the police car."

"Of course you didn't notice the number?"

"The seats were red leather. I sat in the back."

He gave up the line about the car. "How about Aunt Lily? What did she look like?" He breathed heavily. "Anything special that you remember?"

Angela considered. "She had a silver brooch shaped like a cat," she recalled.

"That's the sort of thing we want. Anything else? Color of hair?"

"Sort of sandy."

"And you would know her again?"

"If she looked the same." It was obvious she was almost at the end of her tether, but the inspector didn't dare let the opportunity slip.

"Is there anything else, anything at all, that might help us to identify the house or the neighborhood? There wasn't a particular smell of some special flower . . . ?"

She said, "There was the church bell. It played a tune. 'Nearer My God to Thee.' It's a hymn. We heard it soon after we left the house."

The inspector looked at the woman policeman. "Find out if anyone recognizes the description. There can't be so many churches playing hymn tunes."

Though even if they found that out, it wasn't much to go on. A lady called Lily, a house on two floors—you could be certain the windows would be unshuttered by this time—a church with a freak bell, a cat-shaped brooch. Patiently he turned back to the child. An officer came in, a young police constable, and handed the inspector a message. It was from London and said that Mrs. Toni couldn't be traced for the

moment, she'd joined in the search. The inspector crumpled
the paper with a mutter of exasperation. Why couldn't these
mothers stay at home and leave the job to those qualified to
get on with it? He soon desisted after that; the child looked
dead beat, but he hadn't dared postpone the questioning till
morning. He was a father himself and he knew what a single
nightly interval can do to a child's recollection. Kids had
the sense to live for the day; yesterday was dead and done
with.

"You've helped us a lot," he said. "Now we'd like you to
try and get some sleep, then you'll be fresh when your mother
gets here. The lady policeman is going to take you back . . ."
("She can come to our place," Terry had told her superior.
"Since my sister got married we've got a spare room, and if
there's anyone living who can keep out the press it's my
mother.")

"We'll have to issue a statement," the inspector agreed.
"Make it snappy. The child was found this evening walking
along a dark road in Blankshire, and is being looked after by
the police until she can be reunited with her mother. And when
that's done the rest of the force better get weaving to find
the lady with a light-colored car and a brooch shaped like
a cat."

Lily Haggard had stabled her car and was listening to the
latest news flashes from the radio when she heard the noise
of a powerful vehicle coming down the road and a moment
later the familiar creak of the gate. The path really wasn't
wide enough for that great car, but clearly Charlie wouldn't
dare leave it in the open, not with everybody knowing its
number and being on the watch. She was trembling as she
went to open the door. She wasn't a particularly intelligent
woman but she knew she had never been in a more dangerous
spot in her life.

Charlie Tuke was not an abnormally large man but he
seemed to fill the little hall. He was carrying a black leather
briefcase. Behind him came May, wrapped in a big traveling
coat and carrying a large black leather handbag.

"Everything under control?" Charlie said.

Lily nodded, indicating a sandwich tin that stood on the
main table.

Charlie flicked off the lid and looked greedily at the contents. "That was quite a haul," he said. "Too bad that some of the best of the stuff's too hot to handle. Some of the rings are safe enough." Thoughtfully he picked out a diamond pendant. "That's a lovely thing," he murmured in regretful tones. "But it's not worth the risk at that. Probably be best to unmount the stones, the setting's too distinctive. Even if you got past the disposal point some Nosey Parker might remember seeing a picture in the press."

"You can take the lot," cried Lily in harsh tones. "I don't want it on my premises."

"Getting cold feet? You haven't minded taking your share of the lolly to date."

"I didn't know you were going to run a man down, did I?"

Charlie didn't turn a hair. "Burton got what was coming to him. He was holding the lot of us up to ransom, turning Queen's Evidence if we didn't double his cut. A man like that is a persistent danger. And he'd have involved you, Lil, don't forget that."

"And then the child. I never agreed to fight a child."

"You're getting quite melodramatic. By the way, where is she? What have you done about her?"

"She's—disposed of."

That caught the attention of both her visitors. "What have you done?" demanded May sharply.

"I blindfolded her and drove her about forty miles and dumped her. She's got money; she only had to walk about a mile and she could get a train to London."

Charlie was staring as if he couldn't believe his ears. "You something fool!" he ejaculated softly. "You set her down in a neighborhood where she can be identified—the police of the whole southern region are on the hunt."

"What did you expect me to do? Strangle her and put her under the floorboards? That would have suited your book very well, wouldn't it? You've nothing to fear from her. She never saw the house, she doesn't know the name of the district, it was pouring and dark—and forty miles is a long way."

"When that kid asks for a ticket someone's going to get curious." Charlie's voice was dangerously controlled.

"So what?" Lily sounded defiant. "She can't tell them a thing."

"She'd know you again, though, wouldn't she?"

"Come to that, she'd recognize May."

"May and me are catching a late flight to the continent and we won't be back for quite a while. These"——he indicated the rings and a number of beautifully articulated watches that he had selected from the sandwich tin—"will keep us going for quite a while."

Lily laughed harshly. "You think they won't be on the lookout for you?"

"They won't be looking for a couple with passports in the name of Longmore. And they'll be looking for a clean-shaved chap, not one with a beard and a bald crown. They don't have any of our prints . . ."

"Angela Toni would recognize May, though. She knew her in the alley on Friday night. The one who was in the supermarket, she said."

"By the time she gets to London we'll be gone," Charlie retorted coolly. "If you're afraid they'll turn up at the airport with the kid in tow, you can forget it."

"I might have guessed," Lily cried. "You'd leave me to carry the can, wouldn't you?"

"All you've got to do is keep your trap shut, and you'll do that for your own sake. You're in this with us, you know, and a lot of the loot will stay here with you. No, I don't think you'll go to the police, and if you're telling the truth they won't track you down here."

"I didn't know you were going to run Harry down."

"We didn't run Harry down; he slipped and fell in front of the car."

"I suppose that's why you didn't report the accident to the police. And anyway, that's not the way the child tells it."

"The child didn't see a thing."

"So why kidnap her? It's no good, Charlie, you're in a spot."

"Well, we're getting off it in just over an hour."

May said suddenly, "Why shouldn't Lily come with us? Then she couldn't give us away."

"And leave the place open for any nosey copper who fancies a bit of promotion?"

"You said yourself they wouldn't suspect her or this house. And if Angela really never saw it . . ."

"Yes," said Lily, "I think that's a very good idea. I've got a passport, and at this time of year it shouldn't be too difficult to get a place on the plane. I don't fancy being left here on my own."

There was a long silence. Then Charlie said, "You really do mean it, don't you?"

"I know you'd sell me down the river without a thought," Lily accused him bitterly.

"All right," said Charlie. "But don't blame me if there's no spare place. These night flights get pretty heavily booked, even this time of year."

"Then I shall just be someone coming to see you off. But there are nearly always last-minute cancellations."

"She doesn't trust us as far as she can see us," Charlie remarked to his wife. "But maybe it's not such a bad idea. We may as well have you under our eye."

"Don't think you can try any tricks," Lily warned him. "Where are you making for?"

"You'll see when we get to the airport."

"What am I supposed to write on my luggage labels?"

"You can't bring much luggage, in case you don't get a passage. We don't want to make more trouble for ourselves than we've got already. I still think it's a daft plan, but if you insist—I suppose in a sense one could say you hold the cards. We'll travel in your car," he added. "No one's on the lookout for that."

"And yours?" she countered sharply.

"It'll be safe in your garage for a few days. Then we can get the number changed and give her a respray. If you're coming, Lily, there's no time to lose, but you've still time to back out if you think our company's dangerous." And he laughed.

"Was that such a good idea?" May inquired when Lily had hurried out of the room.

Charlie was carefully packing the jewelry he proposed to smuggle abroad. He had a false bottom to the document case, and it was improbable that any official would want to examine that. He wouldn't let May take any, he said women's handbags were too easily suspect. Then he turned to answer his wife's question. "The woman's dangerous," he said abruptly. "She's like Burton, she can't be relied on. If the police get her and grill her she'll break, where the child's concerned. And then, don't forget, the child could identify her."

"She could identify us, at all events, me."

"We shan't be here. No, it's not safe to leave Lily. A chain's only as strong as its weakest link. Here she comes."

The door opened and Lily came in, carrying a small overnight case. "No sense hanging round," she told Charlie briskly.

"Best put this away, though, with the other gear." He tapped the sandwich tin. "I'll tell you what would make you laugh, my dear. If some thug broke in and collected the lot. We'd all be laughing then, one side of our face or the other. Now, are you sure you haven't left any clue to show that the child was here?"

"Nothing," said Lily. "No one would guess anybody had been sleeping in that room for six months."

"I'd like to be sure of that," Charlie said. "We don't all want to be tripped up on account of a dropped button or something."

They mounted the stairs, all three of them, Lily grumbling about unnecessary risks. Charlie reminded her again she didn't have to come. "Perhaps I like to have you under *my* eye," she retorted tartly, to which he replied that trust funds had touched their lowest level yet, and laughed again.

But she was right about the room. It had the unused, impersonal air of a place where nothing human had been in a dog's age. Coarse blankets were folded on the bed and covered with a counterpane.

"How about sheets?" Charlie asked.

"They're put ready for the laundry. They're the same as I use myself, nothing unusual there. And he doesn't call. I take them in a bag and collect them myself." She stood beside the bed, smoothing an imaginary fold. "Satisfied?"

Charlie's arm shot out and wreathed her neck. He jerked her head backward. Taken by surprise, her feet almost gave way under her; shock made any struggle virtually impossible. In any case, she had brittle bones and Charlie had been trained more than twenty years ago by the commandos. There was a crack as her neck broke, and when he released her she fell across the bed.

"Did you have to do that?" demanded May. "Won't there be any end?"

"She was too dangerous, you knew that as well as I. Like that stupid chattering woman from the supermarket." He walked across to the wall. "Those gas brackets," he said. "Is the gas still connected?" He tried to turn the tap, but it was stiff from disuse and resisted him.

"If she's dead, what's the sense . . . ?"

"If they should find her and smell gas, it could put them off the track."

"Not for long."

He gave a final twist and the gas rushed from the unlit burner. "Come on, May. We'll just get that plane if we hurry. Lucky, really, to get a couple of returned seats, and who's going to suspect Mr. and Mrs. Longmore of Gordon Flats of having any connection with a jewel robbery or a dead man in Hangman's Alley?"

The rain still descended in a steady inimical stream. The night seemed thicker. "Hope to goodness there won't be a fog," Charlie muttered. "Though it could hold up the police." Lily's car was in the garage. "Get a couple of cans of petrol out of ours," Charlie said. "Don't want to run short."

"Fill her up here," suggested May. "We don't want to have to stop on the road."

"The sooner we get that big car under cover the better," Charlie declared. "While I fill up this one you back ours into the road. Make sure no one's coming, but this is such a back-of-beyond place, even the birds go to bed early."

He heard his wife shut the car door and back through the gate, a tight fit, and she scraped a bit of paint off against the latch. "What does it matter?" she demanded when Charlie started to show temper. "You said yourself it would have to be resprayed."

While she retreated he backed the pale tan station wagon through the gate, and they transferred the luggage. They had agreed to leave the shutters drawn in the attic room, which would encourage any Nosey Parkers to think that the house was temporarily unoccupied. He turned the milk indicator to No Delivery. Now nothing would be suspected unless the postman called with a parcel, and even then he'd only leave a printed slip asking the householder to call for it at the local office. May drove the big car into the garage, which closed with an automatic lock. They gave a final glance to the house to make certain no lights had been left burning and then they were away.

"Let's hope Lily keeps her car in good order," Charlie said. "We don't want to miss this flight."

"Will they take off in this weather?" May wondered, but

he asked if she'd never heard of radar, and he didn't think the fog was thick enough to alter the airline's plans. When they reached the airport everything seemed very quiet. A few people sat about reading papers, or bought cigarettes from vending machines. Baggage lay in a big pile waiting to be transported. Charlie left the car in the official park. A friend would be calling for it tomorrow, he said, or possibly the next day, he could post the ticket on. He supplied the fictitious friend's name and address.

"Don't want a lot of embarrassing questions asked before we're out of the country," he explained to May. "They won't bother now for a couple of days, and luckily the police don't know anything about that car."

In the main hall an official was announcing a slight delay in the flight's departure owing to weather conditions. Fog was reported near the coast and it was thought advisable to wait until this had cleared. Meanwhile refreshments could be obtained—ample warning would be given—etc., etc.

May said, "The luck's turning, I feel it," and he said roughly that she was a fool. He led her into the refreshment room, where a good many tables seemed to be occupied by a mixed party, all with bright yellow labels attached to their hand luggage. This was a self-service buffet, and he left May in charge of their possessions while he fetched drinks and something off the hotplate.

"Who on earth are they?" May inquired as he came back. "They must have chartered more than half the plane."

"Cut-price package tour. I believe you can do the whole fortnight, hotels included, for very little more than the actual fare."

A worried-looking man stood up and said, "Ladies and gentlemen, may I have your attention, please? I'm speaking to the tour members of Cyprian Voyages. Will you please make certain that all your baggage, your hand luggage as well as your cases, carries this label?" He held up a bright yellow label with Cyprian Voyages printed on it, and a suburban address. "If there is anyone who needs more labels, will they please come and collect them now? This is your last opportunity. The company cannot be responsible for any luggage that is not officially labeled."

To May's surprise Charlie pushed himself to his feet and walked up to the worried man. He asked for two labels for himself and his wife. "Didn't realize we had to have the hand luggage labeled too," he explained.

The worried-looking man sighed. "It was all in the brochure, and labels were supplied." But he handed out two more. A few of the other tourists also asked for additional labels, which they proceeded to tie onto cameras and thermos cases.

"Stick with this crowd till we get aboard," Charlie instructed his wife. "Then destroy the label, we don't want any awkward questions. But if the authorities think we're with this lot they'll pass us through automatically."

May looked about her. For the most part the Cyprian travelers were young folk, but there were a few of what is inaccurately described as uncertain age, mostly traveling on their lonesome, all hoping to pick up some congenial companion for the length of the tour. The young people talked endlessly, the whole place buzzed with the sound of their voices. One or two turned on transistor radios, and were requested to switch them off again. Charlie bought a couple more drinks, glanced at his watch. The thought passed through both their minds that the fog on the coast might thicken rather than decrease, and they might be here more than half the night. Telephone bells rang frequently, and after each one Charlie looked around in an expectant way, but they had been there for an hour and a half before they got the welcome news that passengers might now board the aircraft, and please have tickets ready. They'd been through passport control with no difficulty. There was only this one last hurdle to jump.

The worried-looking man was assembling his troupe (as May thought of them, no doubt recalling her thespian days) and marshaling them into some kind of order. One of the elderly ladies announced with a high titter, "The animals went in two by two," and someone nearby added sotto voce, "That's what you think, darlin'."

They came out into a night that had become very cold and more than a little blustery. Charlie and May joined the tail of the Cyprians and they walked across the asphalt. The rain had almost stopped, a few stars were actually trying to struggle through. As they neared the aircraft Charlie whispered, "Look at that. This chap's got a comprehensive ticket for his lot, and the man at the steps is counting heads. Get rid of the label." His own hand crumpled up the identifying yellow slip. May did likewise, opened her bag and dropped it inside. Charlie put his in his pocket; it wouldn't be safe to drop them here, later they could be destroyed. The worried-looking man gave a final glance around and mounted the steps into the plane. For him the first hurdle had been accomplished. Charlie produced the tickets for himself and his wife as an air hostess checked through the passenger list.

"Mr. and Mrs. Longmore," she concurred.

Out of the shadows a hearty voice said, "That's the one," and an official touched Charlie's arm. "Mr. Longmore? We'd be glad if you could come along to the office for a moment. There seems to be some slight hitch . . ."

"Look here," said Charlie, blocking the gangway, "we've been hanging about for over an hour. If there were any questions, why couldn't they be asked then?"

"We're sorry to inconvenience you," said the official suavely. "If you can clear up this point satisfactorily, you could make the flight, after all." He murmured something to another uniformed man standing close by.

"What is all this in aid of?" Charlie said, and the same robust voice answered him. "Justice, mate. And if you don't know what that means, remind me to buy you a dictionary for Christmas."

As he spoke the long beam of a torch flashed out, causing Charlie to fling up a free hand and cry, "Turn that damned thing off."

Another voice said, "Oh yes, Mr. Crook, that's the lady, Mrs. Tuke she said her name was."

"That's it. Still, it's a lady's privilege to change her mind as often as she pleases. Tuke yesterday, Longmore today, and who knows what it may be by the morning. And this," he continued chattily, "is doubtless Charlie." He looked interrogatively at Mr. Butts.

"Quick-change artist if it is," said Mr. Butts rather doubtfully. "He's grown a beard in record time."

Crook put out an unexpected hand and caught the beard. Charlie let out an infuriated yell.

"Okay," said Crook. "He's wearing a hairpiece, too." For in the struggle Charlie's hat had become dislodged. "Or

171

should I say a non-hairpiece?" It was the kind of joke he enjoyed, and it won him a wince from Authority. "Wouldn't surprise me," he went on, unmoved, "if you was to recognize him when he's so to speak restored and in his right mind."

"Where does this man imagine he saw us?" Charlie inquired.

"Hangman's Alley—this afternoon." Mr. Butts' voice sounded startled even in his own ears. Could so much have happened in so short a time?

"It's a case of mistaken identity," the man insisted. "Neither my wife nor myself has ever heard of the place."

"Short memory?" Mr. Crook asked May, who hadn't so far opened her mouth. "Anyway, there's been enough about it in the paper and even on TV. Or don't you indulge?"

Authority apparently considered that this had gone far enough. A new voice, speaking with some force but quietly for all that, intervened. "If you take my advice, sir, you won't say any more at the moment. There'll be plenty of opportunity later on."

"And how!" murmured the irrepressible Crook.

"If it should prove to be a case of mistaken identity, I can promise you you'll be put on the next flight, but we have to follow up information when the situation's as serious as this."

"Serious for whom?" snapped Charlie. "You're going to be sorry for this. The next flight will be too late."

"And that," whispered Mr. Crook to his companion, keeping his voice low in deference to the Powers That Be, "is probably the first true word he's spoken since our arrival."

The small grim procession re-entered the building. Through the great glass windows they watched the propellers revolve, the plane proceed down the airstrip; slowly, a little jerkily at first, then, gathering speed, she rose into the darkness, taking the last vestige of hope with her.

"I hope you know what you're doing," Charlie exclaimed venomously, staring at Crook as if he'd gladly see him burned at the stake—and most likely he would. To be bested by this common fellow, with his absurd bandage tied around his great wooden head, a caricature of a human being, he thought, this was the unkindest cut of all. It was May who had a thought to spare for Lily Haggard. If the police had tracked them, then most likely they'd find her, too, and this wasn't going to be a case of dead men—or dead women—telling no tales.

 **14**

WHEN CROOK RECEIVED THE NEWS, via the official grapevine, that Angela Toni was safe and asking for her Mumma, who in Bill's company would be safe, too, he put on his thinking cap, found a map and started to plot the Tukes' probable movements. When he hadn't got Bill for an audience he was inclined to talk to himself, on the theory that he liked to hear a clever chap talk and a clever chap reply. The freeing of the child from wherever she had been incarcerated seemed to him to point to only one conclusion—the Tukes knew the game was up and they'd be getting out but fast. He rather doubted that their plan had included the release of the little girl. This Aunt Lily, so far unidentified, must have some humane instincts, for which, Crook grimly suspected, she'd later receive a bill. He and the police had a mutual love-hate relationship, which meant that though there was no affection lost between them, they respected one another, and even on occasion, of which this was one, worked together. When Crook had reached his conclusions, which didn't take long, he put through a call to Swanton airport, and then got into the Superb and went around to see the inspector.

"They know the game's up," he insisted. "They can't afford to travel in that car till it's been resprayed and got fresh number plates. Their one chance is to get out before we catch up with them. It don't seem likely they'd be going by sea, since Blankshire's a couple of hundred miles from the coast . . ."

"So you deduce they're going by air?"

"There's a flight leaves Swanton airport, which deals mainly with charter flights, at eleven P.M. It's often not too hard to get a passage at the eleventh hour, since charter parties don't usually want a whole plane, even if it's only one of the small offbeat ones. If they're within a fifty-mile radius of Swanton they could just make it."

"And now I suppose you're going to tell me that a mysterious couple booked at short notice? You do get around, don't you, Mr. Crook?"

"They wouldn't tell me that," objected Crook, looking scandalized. "But you're the police, they won't hold out on you, they wouldn't dare, even if they wanted to. Of course," he threw out airily, "they ain't likely to be traveling in their own name, but then a lot of classy chaps go incog—look at Royalty, at all events they used to go around as Mr. So-and-So."

"Do you know what I'm glad about?" the inspector said, lifting his telephone and summoning an under-strapper. "That you never thought of joining the force. You'd have us all shaking in our shoes, waiting for the chopper."

"I take that very handsome," said Mr. Crook, and meant it.

An officer came in, listened to what his superior had to say and beetled off to put the orders into effect.

"This Aunt Lily may be with them, of course," Crook speculated. "May have too much sense to hang around and carry the can. And she can't be under any illusions, not when you remember Burton and that poor Elsie Christie." His face sobered as he said her name. It was going to be a long time before he'd forgive himself for that death.

It wasn't long before the officer returned. "A Mr. and Mrs. Longmore booked through London this afternoon," he said. "The man paid for the tickets in cash. He asked for a plane going to Amsterdam, but there wouldn't be one for thirty-six hours, so he took what he could get. This plane's embarked for Zurich."

"Didn't strike the office as peculiar that a man who wanted to go to Amsterdam was prepared to take Zurich instead?"

"Gentleman said he had business in both cities and he'd simply have to reverse his program and take Amsterdam on the way back. Well, they wouldn't think much about it, sir. They're only there to sell tickets."

Crook hauled out his big topheavy watch. "A tight squeeze," he said. "It's all of two hours to Swanton, unless the flight's held up."

"For once the weather may be on our side," the inspector murmured. "Do I take it you propose to be there?"

"You know what they say about the old Superb. She was never yet too late to join a fight. And you know, Inspector, it wouldn't surprise me to know when I get there that the flight has been delayed."

"Or the—what did you say their name was, Longmore?—the Longmores may not have traveled on it."

"Be seeing you," said Crook hopefully.

"Mr. Crook, allow me to remind you that this is a matter for the police. Not that we're not obliged for your assistance, it's always gratifying to find the public co-operating . . ."

"Gertcha!" said Crook vigorously. "How do you think you can hold them without someone to identify them as Mr. and Mrs. T? True, I don't know him, but she's quite a confidante of mine, and even if she's wearing a disguise—and she could, you know, she might have done quite well if she'd stopped on the stage and not been too ambitious—there are things you can't hide. The way you walk, and hands—but you don't need me to tell you about hands, Inspector."

"Very considerate of you, Mr. Crook."

"And if you're afraid I may let a natural enthusiasm run away with me," continued Crook, flourishing his hideous hat and making for the door, "I'll take my witness along with me. He's one of those sober chaps in the George Washington tradition. Father, I cannot tell a lie. And he ain't got no axe to grind." He stopped. "Funny, that. Wasn't there some story about George Washington and an axe?"

No one answered him and he oiled out. "Open the window a bit," the inspector suggested. "The temperature always seems to go up about six points when Crook's in the offing."

Mr. Butts had settled down cozily in front of television with his nice sensible wife, called Winifred, but his mind wasn't on the play. He was remembering this afternoon, well, evening really, and the part he'd been called upon to play, better than anything you could see on a screen. Winifred was just going to suggest putting on a kettle while the commercials were being shown when the front doorbell rang with a vigor that might have heralded the victory over the Armada some centuries before.

"I'll go," said Mr. Butts, a considerate husband who didn't like his wife opening the door after dark, not with all the villains there were about. When he saw Crook his mouth dropped open.

"Put on your bib and tucker, there's dirty work at the crossroads," Crook said. "No questions now, we're workin' against the clock and running late as it is. You're going to help justice a bit tonight, assumin' it ain't against your conscience. Well?" He stared in genuine amazement. Mr. Butts was grinning from ear to ear.

Winifred, hearing strange voices, stuck her head out of the door. "Who is it, dear?"

"Come to abduct your husband, pro tem," said Crook rapidly. "We're co-operatin' with the police, with their knowledge and connivance. Your husband could be a material witness, invaluable, come to that."

"It's more to the point that he should remain a valuable husband," Mrs. Butts asserted in spirited tones.

Crook favored her with his alligator grin. "He'll do that all right. He wouldn't dare do anything else, leastways, I wouldn't in his shoes."

"Is he in trouble then?"

"You'd want to get the chap who took away that little girl, wouldn't you?" wheedled Crook. "Hasn't the news come through on the box yet? Well, it will. They've got her back but they're after the chap responsible. Say it was your daughter—that is, if you've got one as old as nine nearing ten?"

"Our daughter, Mr. —"

"Crook's the name, Arthur Crook."

"Our daughter, Mr. Crook, is sixteen."

"Well," said Crook frankly, "you could have fooled me."

"Put up the catch when I'm gone," commanded Mr. Butts, winding a muffler around his neck. "I'll be back as soon as possible. But Mr. Crook's right—I must say it's a relief to know no harm's come to her."

"Her mother . . ." Winifred began, but Crook said, "You thank your stars she ain't on the warpath. She's the sort that scratches your eyes out first and asks for explanations later. There's times I'm grateful no dame ever looked twice in my direction. I like to play it safe."

As Crook himself had been heard to remark, Ananias was slain for less than that.

"Hold on to your hat," Crook warned his companion as he started up the Superb, "and don't ask more questions than you can help. It's going to take me all I know to keep up to schedule, and time is of the essence."

Mr. Butts had heard the expression going like the wind, but he'd never experienced it until now. He could never have mapped out the path again, because Crook barely stopped to draw breath. Fortunately, they traveled largely through unrestricted areas, when the Superb did everything but take wings. There were some night-going lorries on the road, but Crook dodged around them, jumped between them and sped on regardless of the opinions of their drivers, which were frequently expressed in flowery language—stinking hellebore, say. The landscape changed with startling rapidity, dark silent roads merging into hamlets or market towns, but before Mr. Butts could give any of them a name they were back in open country. Up this hill, down into the valley, and out again. Crook barely spoke.

"Follow my lead," was all he said, "and remember what they taught us as kids—don't speak till you're spoken to. But remember, when you do, you may have to back up your words on the Book, and that's a sobering thought."

Mr. Butts mostly lay back, deep in thought. But it wasn't of the child he was thinking or even of the aggressors. He was remembering all the years of his working life, wherein his main excitement was the nailing of a shoplifter or the rarer occasions when he was notified of some small increment in his salary. Up till now he'd been pretty satisfied; his ultimate dream was of one of these bungalows on a new seaside estate where he could take Winnie and the younger children of a Sunday or at Bank Holiday weekends. It all seemed pretty small beer now. Who could have imagined, he was reflecting when they turned a corner and a great notice flared out *To the Airport,* that crime could be such fun? He went on thinking that till they were all standing in the airport office watching the plane depart. Then he caught sight of Crook's face and for the first time he began to surmise the strain under which he'd been laboring.

"If the bar's open," said Crook, "I could do with a swallow."

It was Charlie himself who pointed the way to The Cottage, though naturally the police were convinced they would have identified it eventually in any case. The attendant at the car park remembered a bearded man leaving a cream-colored car and saying that it would be called for on the following day or possibly the day after, and identified Charlie as the man in question. That, of course, left the situation wide open for the police. All they had to do was find out from records the name of the driver to whom this car was licensed, and, of course, it proved to be a Mrs. Lily Haggard. A carload of police went to The Cottage, rang, knocked, and walked around when there was no reply to their summons.

"Shutters are up at the back, sir," one of the men reported. "Looks as though the place might be shut up."

But they got the garage open and found the Tukes' car inside. So—either Lily had walked out on her own two feet, a pretty improbable conclusion having regard to the weather, or she'd gone with them, in which case why hadn't she ever reached the airport? Or—and this was the solution most favored by authority—she was still on the premises and either couldn't or wouldn't answer their summons.

"Front door's not bolted," one of the experts discovered. "If she's gone for good or even for a holiday it's not likely she'd leave the place more or less wide open." He meant, as he hastened to explain, that the sensible thing would be to go by the back door. When the police broke in they found her without much difficulty. The smell of gas was shocking. An officer covered his face, and guided by a flashlight, found the open gas jet hissing away like a tireless snake. But when they tried to fling open the windows they found these were bolted and padlocked.

"Never mind about them, get her out," said the chap in command, and they dragged her off the bed onto the landing. The first thing the most intelligent of them noticed was that normal discoloration due to gas inhaling was absent.

"This woman didn't die of gas poisoning," said the inspector harshly. "She died of a broken neck. But don't quote me. This is a job for the doctor. And let Mr. Murdering Tuke laugh this one off, if he can. Presumably this is where the child was imprisoned," he went on after a minute. "It answers the description. I don't want her dragged back here to identify it," he added. "If we could find any proof that she really was here."

In the teeth of all probability, the proof was forthcoming. One of the officers, looking into the cupboard-like bathroom, exclaimed so sharply that the others came with a run.

"Look at this," he said, and indicated a small silver medal hung on a fine silver chain that dangled from a nail over the bath. Inscribed on the back of the medal was Angela's name and a date, and a text *Feed My Lambs*. Prescott, one of the constables who was a Catholic, said it was the sort of thing mothers gave their kids on the occasion of a First Communion. The child would have been wearing it . . .

"And left it there as a guide? That was sharp of her to think of leaving a clue for us to find."

The inspector said very drily, "It wouldn't surprise me to know it was her mother she had in mind. I doubt whether she's got any particular faith in the police."

And that clinched the puzzle.

"It's a funny thing," said Crook. "All this playing safe—where does it get you? Charlie Tuke thought if he could rid himself of the car, he was riding high, but if he'd had the sense to ditch it somewhere and hire one to take him to the airport, he might have pulled it off, even now. Bloody, bold and resolute, that's what you need to be if you're to succeed in a criminal career. They're mostly bloody enough, but they're all out for security. All this government wet-nursing," he added unjustly, "look after you from cradle to grave, puts ideas into their heads."

When Crook returned to the police station he found Bill waiting for him. The grapevine had picked him up, and Mumma and her Angel were together again.

"In the bag?" asked Bill, who'd been put in the picture by the sergeant on the desk.

Crook nodded. "In the bag."

"If Tuke only knew, he'd be on his knees thanking heaven that he's in the hands of the police and not Mrs. Toni," Bill agreed. "Where do we go from here?"

"I have to be getting back," said Crook as though it were approaching twelve midday instead of twelve midnight. "I've got a client—remember?"

"How about Mumma?" murmured Bill. "She'll want a

lift, won't she? It's my belief she'd sooner sit on a fence till morning than admit she'd spent the night in a police station."

Inside the station a very kind welfare worker was saying to Mumma that perhaps a little holiday would be a good idea for both of them.

"Holidays are for the rich," Mumma retorted. "We working people."

"I'm really thinking of your little girl. There's been a great deal of publicity about her, she might like a little—well, period of withdrawal, don't you think?"

"She been withdrawn long enough," declared Mumma.

"After what's happened to her . . . surely, you do see."

"What count not what happen to people but what people they happen to," Mumma said, a bit of philosophy of which Crook would instantly have approved. "We belong in our own place, Angel and me. Besides, she got to have her education."

"Children are often quite cruel without meaning to be," the welfare worker insisted. "She'll be—well, not exactly pointed at . . ."

Mumma shrugged that off as the sort of rubbish you might expect from an unmarried woman. Angel was Angel, wherever she was, and where she was going was back to her own place.

"Even men coming from prison go home," she said, elaborately explanatory. "You think Angel lower than a criminal?"

"The woman's hopeless," the welfare worker declared.

"Just what she ain't," opined Crook. "She's got enough of that commodity to keep a whole band going."

Eventually he drove the couple home. The news had got around in the mysterious way news does, and when Mumma reached her home she found the neighbors had rigged up a chain of little flags, probably left over from the 1945 Armistice. There was enough food piled outside the door of her flat to keep the pair of them going for a week.

"Now, Mumma," urged Crook, who'd accompanied them upstairs, "keep your wig on and remember enough is enough, and that goes for pride as much as anything else. We agreed I had the hope and you had the faith and here's the charity, in the best meaning of the word."

Mumma opened the front door. "Come round some

other time," she told Crook flatly. "Now—my Angel needs her sleep."

"What a woman!" marveled Crook. "There's been no one to touch her since Boadicea."

When he got down he found the press clamoring like the wolf at the door. "Come round some other time," he assured them. "Angels need their sleep, and if you don't believe me, try telling Mumma different."

"It's an ill wind that blows nobody any good," said Mrs. Hersey. "We shan't hear any more of that Freda Gale, you mark my words. And Ben 'ull think twice before he offers anyone else a lift—and in someone else's car at that!"

Her husband came in, booted and spurred. "Where are you off to in your Sunday clothes?" his wife demanded.

"I must go round and see Mr. Crook, find out what we owe him."

"Owe him?" Mrs. Hersey looked scandalized. "What's he done for us?"

"Got Ben off the hook, for one thing."

"The police did most of that. And he was innocent anyway. It's ridiculous to be expected to pay when you're innocent, and I hope you'll tell him so."

"Got me off the hook, too," Mr. Hersey went on.

His wife stared. "Are you out your mind?"

"You're getting your dates mixed. I have been, now I'm back again."

He walked out, master in his own house for the first time in twenty years. He hoped Mr. Crook would agree to come and have a drink to a salubrious future. And when they'd done that, he'd nip along and suggest to the boss some raise in salary, goodness knows it had been long overdue.

To the surprise of most of the neighbors, Angel Toni walked out of the house next morning at her usual hour and turned toward the school, as though she'd never been away. A flood of press hawks rose out of the paving stones or descended from the roofs, beaks bared.

Angela pressed her back against the plate-glass window of a travel agency. "It's no use asking me anything," she declared. "I wasn't there. I don't remember. Everything went blank."

181

Mary Hersey, loitering disconsolately toward the school gate, saw her friend and rushed at her with expressions of joy. "Oh, Angie, you're back."

"We got back last night," said Angela, looking surprised.

"I know. It was in the paper. Oh, am I glad to see you! Life's got so dull at home, Mother watches me every minute, soon I won't even be allowed to go to the bathroom by myself. And Ben's a reformed character. And you've had your picture on TV, and—did they really shut you up in the Black Hole of Calcutta? That's what one of the papers said."

"There was a light," Angela assured her. "And Aunt Lily was very kind. And I got my medal back . . ."

"I don't know how you can be so calm," Mary marveled. "They said you might have been killed. Oh, Angie, you don't know how lucky you are."

At ten o'clock the door of the hospital ward was pushed open and Mumma marched in, her arms full of papers. She wore her usual black dress, her flat slippers, her familiar black shawl. There had been one or two changes during her absence—one patient was discharged, one had gone to Surgical, a third had been taken away on a covered stretcher. Mumma took it all in her stride. A pretty young woman, a stranger, was in the first bed. Mumma paused beside her.

"And what for you this morning?" she inquired with an alligator grin almost approximating Crook's own. "A nice dish of macaroni?"

She whipped a copy of the *Record* from the pile in her arms and waited for the money.

〉〉〉 If you've enjoyed this book and would like to discover more great vintage crime and thriller titles, as well as the most exciting crime and thriller authors writing today, visit: 〉〉〉

The Murder Room
Where Criminal Minds Meet

themurderroom.com